"There has to be a way for us, Quinn."

"I'll find it. After all, I found you, didn't I?" Quinn looked at Nora with wonder, as if the thought just struck him anew. "In all the city, after all this, I found you."

Nora let her head fall against his strong hand. "Find us a way, Quinn."

It was as if the topaz in his eyes ignited, as if she'd unleashed something fierce and powerful in him. Quinn took both Nora's hands in his and kissed them gallantly. "There's not a thing can stop me now. I reckon we have about a minute left." He stole a look to the door behind him. "Say my name one more time."

"You're being…"

"Fifty seconds. Say it."

"Quinn, be careful."

"Not at all. I'm done being careful. Can't you see that?"

His defiance lit fire to hers. Nora brought both his hands to her lips and kissed them tenderly. Quinn melted under her touch the way she had under his and began to pull her closer.…

Books by Allie Pleiter

Love Inspired Historical

Masked by Moonlight
Mission of Hope

Love Inspired

My So-Called Love Life
The Perfect Blend
*Bluegrass Hero
*Bluegrass Courtship
*Bluegrass Blessings
*Bluegrass Christmas
Easter Promises
*"Bluegrass Easter"

*Kentucky Corners

Steeple Hill Books

Bad Heiress Day
Queen Esther & the Second Graders of Doom

ALLIE PLEITER

Enthusiastic but slightly untidy mother of two, RITA®
Award finalist Allie Pleiter writes both fiction and
nonfiction. An avid knitter and unreformed chocoholic,
she spends her days writing books, drinking coffee
and finding new ways to avoid housework. Allie
grew up in Connecticut, holds a BS in Speech from
Northwestern University and spent fifteen years in the
field of professional fundraising. She lives with her
husband, children and a Havanese dog named Bella in
the suburbs of Chicago, Illinois.

MISSION *of* HOPE

ALLIE PLEITER

Steeple
Hill®

Published by Steeple Hill Books™

STEEPLE HILL BOOKS

Steeple
Hill®

Recycling programs
for this product may
not exist in your area.

ISBN-13: 978-0-373-82842-5

MISSION OF HOPE

www.SteepleHill.com

Printed in U.S.A.

He who began a good work in you will carry it on
to completion until the day of Christ Jesus.
—*Philippians* 1:6

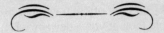

For Nora

May your future always be the best of adventures

Acknowledgments

One does not tackle the great San Francisco earthquake and fire of 1906 without backup. And while people look at you sideways when you get on an airplane with a dozen disaster books, I am grateful to all the fine texts out there that made my research complete. Thanks galore to historian and general good sport Eileen Keremitsis for enduring questions, finding obscure facts, and graciously unearthing errors. Any historical errors in this book can only be laid at my own stubborn and ignorant feet, certainly not at hers. Special thanks go to my local and national buddies from American Christian Fiction Writers for befriending me despite my many oddities. Krista Stroever continues to be the finest editor God ever gave me, and I could never have survived this cyclone of a publishing career without the careful guidance of my agent Karen Solem. And you, my dear readers; God bless you all.

Prologue

San Francisco, July 1906

The world rumbled and heaved. Screams and moans pierced the thundering roar, the staccato breaking and snapping, drowning out her own cries for help as the earth swallowed her up like a hungry beast. Nora Longstreet grasped for any hold she could reach, but everything dissolved at her touch so that nothing stopped her fall.

Something soft smothered her face, and she shot upright, clawing at the thing. "Annette!" she screamed for her cousin who'd been beside her just moments before. "Annette!" The monster was eating her, devouring her.

A hand clasped her shoulder. "Hush, Nora. Wake up, love, and be still."

Nora opened her eyes to find no beast, no rumbling, no danger. "I…"

"We're safe. We're at Aunt Julia's and we're safe. Breathe now, there's nothing to harm you." Mama pulled a handkerchief from the sleeve of her nightshift and dabbed at Nora's brow.

"Oh, Mama, she was there. Right beside me, asleep, I could hear her breathing. And then…"

Why must she live that horrible morning over and over when she closed her eyes? Nora moaned and leaned back against her pallet in the parlor of her aunt's Lafayette Park home where she'd been camped since the earthquake. She was soaked with sweat, and although it was nearly dawn, she felt as if she had not slept at all. Still, she couldn't let that stop her. Today was too important a day. Nora swung her legs over the edge of the cot and raked her fingers through her hair. "I'm going to the rally," she said to her mother. "I think Papa needs me."

Chapter One

It was her. It had to be. It was the eyes that made him certain, even from this distance.

Quinn Freeman stared harder at the young woman—not much more than twenty from the look of it—sitting uncomfortably onstage. She was trying to pay attention to the long rally speeches honoring the city's recovery, but not quite succeeding. And the speeches were surely long. Politicians fought banks who fought insurance companies and everyone nursed a grudge over how things had been handled. The most eloquent speech on God's green earth couldn't explain how one man was still alive while another's life had come to an end. The uncertainty of everything made for chaos.

Still, she was here. By some astounding act of God, she was here. And what a sight she was. Even in the gray light of this cloudy morning, she looked clean and pretty, and he hadn't seen anything clean and pretty in days.

It was the eyes, really, that captured his attention. Round and wide, framed with golden lashes. Even in the brown tint of the charred photo he'd found, he'd somehow known they were an unusual color. Something between a blue and a violet, now that he saw them. The color of the irises Ma was fond of in one of the city gardens.

Quinn fished into his pocket for the battered locket he'd found last week as he walked home from yet another insufferably long bread line. He'd seen it glint in the corner of a rubble pile just south of Nob Hill, a tiny sparkle in a pile of black and brown timber. Usually, Quinn was looking up; he was always looking up at the buildings—or parts of buildings—still standing, admiring how they'd survived with so much rubble marking where others had fallen. It wasn't as if bits of lives couldn't still be found all over the city—even months out as it was, Quinn was forever picking up one shoe or a bit of a cup or a chipped doorknob.

This was different. There was something amazing about the fact that the locket was still shut, and that despite the soot and dents, there were still two tiny photographs inside. Two young women about his own age. Sisters? Cousins? He kept the charm in his pocket, making up a dozen stories as he worked or walked or waited, because everything now took hours longer than it had before. Yes, it was dirty and dented and the chain was broken, but the faces inside had survived an earthquake and a fire. And now he knew the people had, as well. Or at least one of them. Quinn just couldn't ignore the hope in that.

Reverend Bauers never called anything a coincidence. No one was ever "lucky" to Reverend Bauers—they were "called" or "blessed." Quinn had survived the earthquake and the fire. His mother had, too. But he was beginning to wonder if he'd survive the next two months. A few months ago he'd been just another grunt down at the printing press, scratching out a living, trying to hang on to his big dreams. Then the world shook and fell over. He'd survived, but why had God kept him alive while scores of others died?

"God does not deal in luck or happenstance," Bauers always said to Quinn when something went their way or a need miraculously became met. "He directs, He provides and He is very fond of surprising His children." The saying rang in Quinn's ears when he saw the familiar face on the stage this morning. And he knew, even before he pulled the locket from his pocket and squinted as he held it up to her profile, that it was her. *Well, Lord, I'm surprised, I'll grant You that.*

When that pretty woman saw him hold up the locket, her eyes wide with amazement, he made the decision right there and then to do whatever it took to return the locket to her, to bring *one thing* home.

The man fished something out of his pocket and held it up, comparing it to the face—her face—before him.

Annette's locket. With the elongated heart shape that was so unusual, the one Annette had picked out for her birthday last year, it just *had* to be. He had Annette's locket!

It took forever for the rally to end. The moment she could, Nora swept off her chair in search of the fastest way into the crowd. He couldn't have missed her intent given how hard he seemed to be staring at her. Surely he would wait, perhaps even make his way toward the stage.

The crowd milled exasperatingly thick, and Nora began to fear the man would be lost to her forever—and that last piece of Annette with him. Nora pushed as fiercely as she dared through the clusters of people, dodging around shoulders and darting through gaps.

She could not find him. Her throat tight and one hand holding her hat to the mass of blond waves that was her unruly hair, she turned in circles, straining to see over one large man's shoulders and finding no one.

"This is you, isn't it?" came a voice from behind her, and she turned with such a start that she nearly knocked the man over. He held up the locket. Nora let out a small gasp—it was so battered now that she saw it up close. The delicate gold heart was dented on one side, black soot scars still clinging to the fancy engraving and the broken chain.

Soot. A fire seemed such a terrible, awful way to die. Nora clutched at the locket with both hands, her grief not allowing any thought for manners. The two halves of the dented heart had already been opened, revealing the remains of a pair of tiny photographs—one of her, the other of Annette. Nora put her finger to the image of Annette and thought she would cry. "Yes," she said unsteadily, "that's me, and that's my cousin, Annette. However did you get this?"

The man pushed back his hat, and a shock of straw-colored hair splashed across his forehead. "I found it last week. I've been looking for either one of you since then, but I didn't really think I'd find you. I just about fell over when you walked onto the stage this morning, Miss... Longstreet, was it? The postmaster's daughter?"

Nora suddenly remembered her manners. "Nora Longstreet. I'm so very pleased to meet you. And so very pleased to have this back...although it isn't...actually mine." She felt her throat tighten up, and paused for a moment. "It's Annette's, and she isn't...she's isn't here. Anymore." She pulled in a shaky breath. "She died...in it."

"I'm sorry. Seems like everybody lost someone, doesn't it?" He tipped the corner of his hat. "Quinn Freeman."

"Thank you for finding this, Mr. Freeman. It means a great deal to me."

Quinn tucked his hands in his pockets. He wore a simple white shirt, brown pants that had seen considerable wear and scuffed shoes, but someone had taken care to make sure they were all still clean and in the best repair possible given the circumstances. "I'm sure she would have wanted you to have it, seeing as it's you in there and all."

"I'm sure my father would be happy to give you some kind of reward for returning it. Come meet him, why don't you?"

Quinn smiled—a slanted, humble grin that confirmed the charm his eyes conveyed—and shrugged. "I couldn't take anything for it. I'm just glad it found its way home. Too many people lost too much not to see something back where it belongs."

Nora ran her thumb across the scratched surface of the locket. "Surely I can give you some reward for your kindness."

He stared at her again. The gaze was unnerving from up on the stage, but it was tenfold more standing mere feet from him. "You just did. It's nice to see someone so happy. A pretty smile is a fine thing to take home." He stared for a long moment more before tipping his hat. "G'mornin', Miss Longstreet. It's been a pleasure."

"Thank you, Mr. Freeman. Thank you again." Nora

clutched the locket to her chest and dashed off to find her father.

She found him near the stage, talking with a cluster of men in dark coats and serious expressions. "Papa!" She caught his elbow as he pulled himself from the conversation. "The most extraordinary thing has happened!"

"Where have you been? You shouldn't have dashed off like that."

"Oh, Papa, I've survived an earthquake and a fire. What could possibly happen to me now?"

"A great deal more than I'd care to consider." He scowled at her, but there was a glint of teasing in his eye. She was glad to see it—he hadn't had much humor about him lately.

She held up the battered charm. "Look! Can you believe it? I thought it lost forever."

Her father took the locket from Nora's hand and held it up, turning it to examine it. "Is this Annette's locket? That's astounding! However did you find it?"

"A man gave it to me, just now. He said he recognized me from the photo inside. The photographs hadn't fully burned. Can you imagine? I knew there was a reason I needed to come with you this morning. I knew I should be beside you up there. Now I know why!" Right now that dented piece of gold was just about the most precious thing in all the world. The moment she fixed the broken chain, she'd never take it off ever again.

"Well, where is this man?" Her father looked over her shoulder. "I'd say we owe him a debt of thanks."

"I tried to get him to come over and meet you—he knew who I was and who you were—but he said he didn't need any thanks." She left out the bit about her smile. *Oh, thank You, Lord,* Nora prayed as she took the locket back from her father. *Thank You so much!*

"Did you at least get his name?"

"Freeman," Nora said, thinking about the bold stare he'd given her at first, "Quinn Freeman."

Chapter Two

The mail had always been mundane to Nora. A perfunctory business. Hardly the stuff of heroes and lifesaving deeds. Papa had told her stories of how they'd soaked mailbags in water and beaten back the fire to save the post office. And now, the mail had become just that—lifesaving. Thanks to Papa's promise to deliver all kinds of mail—postage or no postage—mail had become the one constant. The only thing that still worked the way it had worked before. It was amazing how people clung to that.

No one, however, could have foreseen what "all kinds of mail" would be: sticks, wood, shirt cuffs and collars, tiles and margins of salvaged books or newspaper had been pressed into service as writing paper. Each morning Papa would take her to the edge of an "official" refugee camp—for several questionable "unofficial" camps had sprung up—and they would take in the mail. Standing on an older mail cart now pressed into heavy service, Nora took in heart-wrenching messages such as "We're alive" or "Eddie is gone" or "Send anything" and piled them into bags headed back to the post office.

Nora—and any other female—could only *accept* mail, for mail delivery had become a dangerous task. Arriving mail consisted of packages of food or clothes or whatever supplies could be sent quickly, and that made it highly desirable. The massive logistics of distributing such things had necessitated army escorts in order to keep the peace. Even after months of relief, so much was still missing, so much was still needed, and San Francisco was discovering just how impossible it was to sprout a city from scratch. The nearly three months of continual scrounging, loss and pain turned civil people angry, and there had even been a few close scrapes for Nora in the simple act of accepting mail. Those incidents usually made her father nervous, but today they made Nora all the more determined to help. Someone had delivered something precious to her, and she would do the same. It was not her fault the postmaster had not been blessed with a son who could better face the danger. If God had given Postmaster Longstreet a daughter, then God would have to work through a daughter. Father had always said, "We do what we can with what we have." What better time or place to put that belief into practice?

"Please," a young boy pleaded as he pressed a strip of cloth into Nora's hand. Its author had scrawled a message and rolled up a shirtsleeve like a scroll, tied with what looked like the remnants of a shoelace. "Martin Lovejoy, Applewood, Wisconsin" was printed on the outside. "All we got is the clothes we're wearing," the lad said, "but Uncle Martin can send more."

"Is your tent number on the scroll? Your uncle Martin needs to know where to send the clothes."

"Don't know," the boy said, turning the scroll over

in his hands. He held it up to Nora again. "I don't read. Is it?"

The scroll held none of its sender's information. "What's your tent number?"

The tiny lip trembled. "It's over there."

The boy pointed across the street to the very large "unofficial" encampment that had taken over Dolores Park. Nora bent down and took the boy's hand. "Which…" she hesitated to even use the word in front of him, "…shack is yours?"

He pointed to a line of slapped-together shelters just across the street. "There."

The shack stood near the edge of the camp, but still, he was so small to be here by himself. Nora looked around for someone to send back with him—the unofficial camp was not a safe place to go—but everyone was engrossed in their own tasks. The little boy looked completely helpless and more than a little desperate. It was by the edge, not forty feet away, and perhaps it wasn't as dangerous as Papa made it out to be. Taking a deep breath, Nora made a decision and hopped down off the wagon. Five minutes to help one little boy couldn't possibly put her in any danger, and her father looked too busy to even notice her absence. Nora held out her hand. "Let's walk back together and we'll sort it out. We can ask your mama to help us."

The little boy looked away and swiped his eye bravely with the back of his other hand. "Mama's gone," he said in an unsteady voice. "My daddy wrote it."

Nora gripped the little hand tighter. "All the more reason that note should get through. We'll do what it takes to reach your uncle. It'll be all right, I promise. What's your name?"

"Sam." The boy headed into a small alleyway of sorts between two of the shelters.

The official refugee camps were surprisingly orderly. Straight rows of identical tents, laid out with military precision in specific parts of the city. Pairs of white muslin boxes faced each other like tiny grassy streets.

The sights and sounds of another world rose up, though, as Nora crossed the street into the unofficial camp. An older man to her left coughed violently into a scrap of bandage he held to his mouth in place of a handkerchief. The thin material was already red-brown with blood. He looked up at her clean clothes with a weary glare. Even though the blouse she wore was three days old and the hem of her skirt was caked with dirt, she looked nothing like the people she passed. The scents—so full of smoke and char everywhere else— were also different here. Intensely, almost violently human smells: food, filth, sweat. A hundred other odors came at her with such force that she wondered how she had not smelled them from the other side of the street. She realized, with a clarity that was almost a physical shock, that her concept of how bad things were paled in comparison to *how bad things actually were*. Nora felt a powerful urge to run. To retreat back to the official, orderly camp and its neat rows of tents before the depth of the unofficial squalor overtook her like the beast in her nightmares. This felt too close to the awful hours of that first morning.

It wasn't as if Nora didn't understand the scope of the catastrophe before. She did. But she'd somehow never grasped the sheer quantity of lives destroyed. Walking down this "alley," the real-life details pushed her into awareness. The air seemed to choke her. Her clothes felt hot and tight.

The lad pointed to what passed for his front door, saying, "It's just there."

Nora's brain shook itself to attention just enough to notice a small crowd had gathered at her appearance. It was not a friendly-feeling crowd—it had an air that made the hairs on the back of her neck stand on end— and she understood all too clearly why her father had not allowed her to venture off the cart before.

A young man to her right fitted scraps of cardboard into the holed soles of his shoes. Sam rattled off a list as he pointed to the surrounding shelters. "Elliot went for bread, Mrs. Watkins for bandages, Papa for water and me for mail." It seemed an awful lot to manage at his young age, but he spoke the list with such an everyday dryness that Nora's heart twisted to hear it.

"Papa!" Sam ducked into the shack, calling for his father. It left Nora standing in the aisle alone, listening to the shuffle of feet come to a stop behind her. "Papa!" Sam cried again from inside the shack, but no one answered.

A man came out from the next shelter. "He went back for more water, Sam." He eyed Nora, his expression confirming how out of place she already felt. His eyes fell to the scroll in her hand.

"I need Sam's tent number so I can add it to his father's letter."

"Who're you? The postmaster?" It was more a hollow joke than any kind of inquiry. The man took a step closer while two more even shadier characters came out from between two battered structures on the other side of the alley.

"My father's office is doing everything they can." She had to work to keep a calm voice.

"He is, is he? And how about *you?*" A skinny, greasy-looking young man smiled as he wandered closer. "You doin' all you can?"

"Of course," Nora answered, until the glint in his eyes turned the question into something she didn't want to answer. The wind picked up and made a shiver chase down her neck.

The man twisted a piece of string around his fingers in a fidgety gesture. "Really?" He stretched out the word in a most unsavory way. "You sure?"

"I am," came a deep voice from behind Nora. She spun around to see Quinn Freeman step solidly between her and the leering man. He hoisted a large piece of steel in one hand with a defensive air. "I'm really sure, Ollie. Want to find out how sure I am?"

"Charity's a virtue, Freeman." Ollie grinned, but it was more of a sneer.

"Just make sure it's virtue you got in mind. Miss Longstreet was just helping out, I imagine, and I'll make sure she gets back to the mail wagon safe and sound, don't you worry." Quinn nodded at Nora, taking the scroll from her as if to personally see to its security.

"You do that." Ollie kicked a stone in his path and started walking back down the alley. "You just go ahead and do that."

With Ollie's retreat, Nora felt the rest of the gathered crowd sink back to wherever they had come from. She let out the breath she had been holding. "It seems I owe you yet another debt, Mr. Freeman."

He put down the piece of steel and handed her back Sam's scroll. "I'm not so sure it was a smart idea for you to wander over here like that. Even to help Sam. Things can get a little…rough around here if you're not careful."

"My father would agree heartily. He'll probably be rather sore at me for trying. I hadn't realized…thank you again. First the locket, and now this. Surely there's some way to thank you."

He smiled the engaging grin he'd shown her back at the rally. His eyes were a light brown, an almost golden color that picked up the straw shades of his hair. He had a strong, square jaw that framed his easy grin—the sort of face at home with a frequent smile. "Like I said, Miss Longstreet, I was happy to see *something* find its way home." The sadness in the edge of his voice— the sadness that caught the edge of so many voices all around her—undercut the cheer of his words. "But there is something I'd like to show you. Something you ought to see before you leave with Ollie's version of how things are in here."

"Do you live nearby?" She realized what a ludicrous question that was, as if he had a house just up the street instead of a shack somewhere in this makeshift camp.

He tucked his hands into his pockets and nodded over his left shoulder. "Two rows down. The charming cottage on the left." When Nora blushed, feeling like an insensitive clod for asking such a useless question, he merely chuckled. "It's okay, really. I've seen worse. My uncle Mike says we might get back into a house next month. Just come see this and I'll walk you back across the street before your papa begins to worry."

He led Nora through one more row of shacks to where a cluster of children gathered. The gaggle of tots surged toward Quinn when they saw him, parting the crowd to reveal a rough-hewn teeter-totter pieced together out of scrap and an old barrel. She knew, instantly, that the makeshift toy had been Quinn's doing.

"Mister Kin, Mister Kin!" a chubby blond-haired girl greeted. Nora guessed it to be her approximation of Mr. Freeman's given name. "It works!"

Quinn hunched down and tenderly touched the tot's nose. "Told you it would." Nora smiled. How long had it been since she had heard children's laughter?

The girl giggled. "You're smart."

"Only just. Go ahead and take another turn, then. It'll be time to get on back to your ma soon, anyway."

Nora stood awed for a moment. Quinn Freeman had handed her the smallest patch of happiness, but it did the trick. "Thank you." She looked up at him, for he was a good foot taller than she if only a few years older, and thought that he was indeed clever to recognize a slapped-together toy would do so much good. "I did need to see this—you were right."

"Most people are afraid to really build anything here, thinking it'll make it feel like we'll be here forever, but even I know lads with nothing to do usually find something bad to fill their time."

"You'll be here another month?" Many families were talking of pulling up stakes and starting over somewhere else just as soon as circumstances would allow. Others refused to even think past their next meal.

"That's my guess. Don't pay much to peer too far into the future these days. God's got His hands full in the present, I'd say."

"He does." And he talks about God. In a *calm* way. Many people—her own family pastor Reverend Mansfield included—were shouting about the awful judgment

God had "sent down" upon the sinful city of San Francisco. It wasn't so hard a thought to hold. With dust and destruction everywhere, it was easy to wonder if the Lord Almighty hadn't indeed turned His head away.

By this time they'd reached the mail wagon, and Papa was standing with a sour and alarmed look on his face. "Thank heavens you're all right. Just what do you think...?"

"I've seen her back safely, Mr. Longstreet, and told her not to venture over here like that again," Quinn cut in.

"Papa, this is Mr. Freeman. The man who returned Annette's locket. Now you can thank him in person."

The announcement took the wind out of Papa's scorn. Her father stepped down off the mail wagon and extended a hand to Quinn. "Seems I owe you."

The two men shook hands. "You don't owe me a thing. I was glad to help."

Papa looked at Nora. "Don't you go needing help again. I'll not let you come back if you wander off like that again. It's only by God's grace that Mr. Freeman was here to keep you from any trouble."

"Grace indeed," Quinn said, shooting a sideways smile at Nora as he tipped his hat at Papa. "Don't let it happen again, Miss Longstreet." As he turned, he added quietly over Nora's shoulder, "At least not until tomorrow around two."

Nora climbed back on the wagon to join her father. Perhaps the mail would not be so perfunctory from now on.

Chapter Three

Ah, but she was a beauty.

Quinn stood mesmerized by the way she held her ground. Tall and proud, with defiant lines he wanted to catch from every angle.

Quinn was vaguely aware of an elbow to his ribs. "Nephew, ya look foolish just standing there like that."

Rough hands grabbed his face on both sides and pulled his gaze to the dusty, whiskered sight of his uncle Michael. "There's something wrong with you, man. It ain't natural, the way you look at buildings."

"Architecture. It's called architecture. I'd give anything to study."

Uncle Mike snorted. "You need a wife."

Quinn shifted his sore feet as his mind catapulted back to the rows of tiny black buttons that ran up the sides of Nora Longstreet's boots. He'd stared then, too, liking their lines as much if not more. "I need to *learn*," he said impatiently to his uncle, who simply rolled his eyes at the speech he'd heard every day even before the earthquake. "Apprentice an architect. Only there's no time to learn anymore. We need loads of builders, but we need them *now*." Everything took so much time these days. *Lord Jesus, You know I'm thankful to be alive, but this bread line feels two thousand miles long. I'm in no mood to learn no more patience, if You please.* He felt he'd die if he wasn't back at the camp edge by two. He had to see her again. Had to see that dented locket that he just knew would be polished up and hanging around her neck. He'd miss half a week's worth of bread to make sure he caught that sight—even if it meant he'd catch a whole lot more from his ma for returning without bread.

By the time the sun was high in the sky and the police officer on the corner said it was one-fifteen, Quinn still was looking at forty or so people in line in front of him. Without so much as an explanation, Quinn nudged his uncle and said, "I'm off."

"And just what do you think you're doin'?" the man balked as Quinn strode off in the direction of home, his feet no longer feeling the holes that burst through his shoes yesterday.

"I ain't sure yet," Quinn replied with a grin, tipping his hat as his uncle stood slack-jawed, "but I'll let you know."

Nora sat beside her father in the mail cart, her heart thumping like the hooves of the horse in front of them. Since the earthquake, she'd barely looked forward to anything or been excited about anything.

She wanted to see him. To feel that tug on her pulse when he caught sight of her. He seemed so *happy* to see her. She knew, just by the tilt of his head, that she brightened his day. There was a deep satisfaction in that;

something that went beyond filling a hungry belly. Still, that hadn't stopped her from bringing a loaf of bread she'd charmed out of the cook this morning.

He was a very clever man. He stood on the other side of the street, far enough from the cart to be unobtrusive, near enough to make sure she caught sight of him almost immediately. His eyes held the same fixation they had at the ceremony, and Nora felt a bit on display as she went about her duties.

He watched her. His gaze was almost a physical sensation, like heat or wind. He made no attempts to hide his attentions, and the frank honesty of his stare rattled her a bit, but not the way that man Ollie's stare had. She might be all of twenty-two, but Nora had lived long enough to judge when a man's intentions were not what they should be. Simply put, Quinn looked exceedingly glad to see her again. And there was something wonderful about that.

"You'll stay by the cart today," Quinn said, walking across the street when the line finally thinned out. "Mind your papa and all."

"I should," she admitted. "However, I would like very much to see the teeter-totter again. It seemed a very clever thing to do, and I wonder if there aren't some things back at my aunt's house that we could add to your contraption."

A bright grin swept over his face. "My contraption. I like that a far sight better than *that thing Quinn built*." He pushed his hat back on his head as he looked up at her, squinting in the sunlight. It gave Nora an excuse to settle herself down on the cart, bringing her closer to eye level with the man. "A contraption sounds important. I'll have to build another just to say I am a man of contraptions."

They held each other's gaze for a moment, and Nora felt it rush down her spine. It was powerful stuff these days to see someone happy—they'd barely left misery behind, and there was so much yet to endure ahead of them. She'd taken the streetcars completely for granted before. Now, everyone's shoes—and feet—had suffered far too much walking. She imagined his smile would be striking anywhere, but here and now, it was dashing.

"Still," he said, "it's best we don't wander off today. I wouldn't want your papa thinking poorly of me."

"Oh, I'm sure he couldn't do that." Nora fingered the locket now fastened around her neck. Something flickered in his eyes when she touched it. "You brought me back Annette's locket, and that was a fine thing to do."

"The pleasure's mostly mine, Miss. I think it made me as happy as it made you. And good news is as hard to come by as good food these days."

"Oh," Nora shot to her feet, remembering the loaf of bread tucked away behind her. "That reminds me. I know you said you didn't need a reward, but I just didn't feel right without doing something." She pulled out the loaf, wrapped in an old napkin. "Cook makes the best bread, even missing half her kitchen." She held it out.

"Glory," Quinn said, his grin getting wider, "You can't imagine how glad I am to see a loaf of bread. Especially today."

"Aren't you able to get any?"

She thought she saw him wink. "That's a long story. Just know you couldn't have picked a better day to give me a loaf of bread."

That felt simply grand, to know she'd done something he appreciated so much. "I'm glad, then. We're even."

"Hardly," he said, settling his hat down on to his head again. "I'm still ahead of you, Miss Longstreet. By miles." He bent his nose to the bread and sniffed. "I'd best get this home before it gets all shared away. Thank you, Miss Longstreet. Thank you very much."

"My pleasure," Nora said, meaning it. Taking a deep breath, she bolstered her courage and offered, "Tomorrow?"

"Absolutely."

The only sad thing about the entire exchange was that three months ago, Nora would have rushed home to tell every little detail to Annette. Today, she didn't mind the trickle of mail customers that still came to the wagon, for there was only Mama waiting at home. Nora laid her hand across the locket, hoping her thoughts could soar to where Annette could hear them. *Is heaven lovely? I miss you so much.*

Reverend Bauers tried to lift the large dusty box, but couldn't budge the heavy load at his advanced years. He huffed, batted at the resulting cloud of dust that had wafted up around him and threw Quinn a disgusted glance. "I'm too old for this."

Quinn wiped his brow with his shirtsleeve. It was stale and dusty down here in the Grace Mission House basement, and he'd already had a long day's work, but he'd be hanged if he'd let Reverend Bauers attempt cleaning up the rubble on his own. The man was nearly eighty, and although he showed little signs of slowing down his service to God, his body occasionally reminded him of the truth in "the spirit is willing but the flesh is weak."

"Didn't I just get through telling you the very same thing? Reverend, I don't think when God spared you and Grace House through the earthquake and the fire that He did it all to have you collapse in the basement. You've got to slow down. You'll do no good to anyone if you hurt yourself."

His long and fast friendship with the pastor—since boyhood, going on twenty years now—had given him leave to speak freely with Reverend Bauers, but even Quinn knew when too far was too far. And even if the reverend's insistence on ordering the Grace House basement was a bit misguided, Quinn wasn't entirely sure he should be the soul to point it out. People reacted in funny ways to the overwhelming scale of destruction. His own ma bent over her tatting every night, even though Quinn was certain there'd be little use for lace in the coming months. Many people focused on ordering one little segment of their lives, because they could and because so much of the rest of their lives was spinning in chaos.

"I can't seem to stay away," Reverend Bauers said, giving a look that was part understanding, part defiance. "I keep getting nudges to tidy up down here, and you know I make it a policy not to ignore nudges." Reverend Bauers was forever getting "nudges" from God. And Quinn believed God did indeed nudge the portly old German—he'd seen far too much evidence of it to dismiss the man's connection with The Almighty. Only no one else ever just got "nudged." God seemed to be shouting at everyone else—or so they said. People were talking everywhere about God's judgment on San Francisco or claiming they'd heard God's command to destroy the city—and/or rebuild it, depending on who you talked to.

Only, after twenty-six years, God had yet to nudge or shout at Quinn. Reverend Bauers was always going on about purpose and providence and such, and he'd so vehemently declared that God had spared Quinn for some great reason that Quinn mostly believed him. The reason just hadn't shown itself yet, nor had any of God's nudges.

Quinn sighed as Bauers slid yet another box out of his way, poking through the cluttered basement. "There must be something down here," Bauers said, almost to himself. "Over there, perhaps." He pointed to a stack of shelving that had toppled over in the far corner of the room and motioned for Quinn to clear a path.

It took nearly ten minutes, and Quinn was tempted to offer up a nudge of his own to God about how dinner might be soon, when suddenly Bauers went still.

Quinn looked up from the shelf he was righting to see the reverend staring intently at an upended chest. "Oh, my," Bauers said in the most peculiar tone of voice. "Goodness. I hadn't even remembered this was down here."

"What?" Quinn cleared a path to it.

"That's it, isn't it? And there should be another one—a long, narrow one—right beside it somewhere."

Quinn stared from Bauers to the pair of chests, his heart thumping as he recognized the shape of the long narrow box. He must have been, what, twelve? Surely not much older. He caught Bauers's gaze, the old man's eyes crinkling up when he read Quinn's expression.

"Mr. Covington's things." Quinn began tearing

through the boxes, bags and beams between him and the pair of chests. "Those are Mr. Covington's..."

"No, man, not just Mr. Covington's, and you know that. Those belong to the Bandit."

Quinn had reached the chests, fingering the latch on the longer box. He remembered what was inside now. He remembered thinking that that sword and that whip were the most powerful weapons on earth. He blew the dust off the box and set it atop a crate. "Do you think it lasted?"

"I see no scorch marks or dents. I'd venture to say it's in perfect shape." He picked his way quickly through the room until he stood next to Quinn. "But we'll not know a thing until you open it."

Chapter Four

With a deep breath, Quinn undid the pair of latches on either side of the long wooden box. Inside, carefully nestled in their places on a bed of still amazingly blue velvet, lay a pair of swords. Even with the patina of twenty years, they gleamed in the basement's faint light. "His swords," Quinn remarked, not hiding his amazement. "The Bandit's swords."

Reverend Bauers's hand came to rest on Quinn's shoulder. "So many years. Such a long time ago—for both of us."

Quinn could hear the smile in Reverend Bauers's voice, sure it matched his own as he remembered the daring heroic feats of the Black Bandit that had once captured his young imagination. A dark hero who roamed the streets at night, offering aid to those who had none, supplying food to needy families, even sending money once to fix Grace House. The Black Bandit legend had woven its way into San Francisco's history—everyone's mother and grandmother had a Black Bandit story—but Quinn and the reverend were two of the only four people in the world who knew Matthew Covington had been the man behind the mask. He cocked his head in the clergyman's direction. "Wouldn't we like to have our Bandit back now, hmm?"

Quinn picked up the sword, turning it to catch the light. When he was twelve, this sword had seemed enormous. Too heavy and long for a slight boy. Time and trials had done their work on Quinn, however, and he was a tall man of considerable strength. He wondered, for a moment, if he remembered any of the moves Mr. Covington had taught him. "Do you remember that day, Reverend?"

There was no need to explain "that day." Bauers would know Quinn was referring to the day he met— and marred—the noble English businessman. Bauers's smile and nod confirmed his understanding. "Evidently, I've remembered it better than you. You, who have the most reason of all to remember that day."

Quinn's introduction to Matthew Covington had been, in fact, by injury. He'd taken a knife to Covington's arm as the Englishman tried to stop a robbery. A crime Quinn and his buddy were attempting—stealing from Grace House. It was amusing, in a sad sort of way, to think they'd thought times hard enough to steal from a church back then. Those times were nothing compared to what they were now.

Still, Quinn was young, impressionable and desperate for decent food. His father's love of the whiskey bottle hadn't made for much of a steady home life. Trying to steal from Grace House Mission—an organization bent on helping his impoverished neighborhood—had been the low point of his life.

It had also been the turning point. Back in that garden, watching Matthew Covington bleed, Quinn had realized he had two choices in life: up or down. Dark or light. Hard or easy. And, when it came right down to it, destruction or redemption. That day Quinn chose to climb his way out of the mess his young life had become, and Reverend Bauers had been the first to recognize it. That troublesome day, and the tense ones that followed it, marked the beginning of Quinn's unusually close relationship with the reverend. Uncle Mike had been known to say that Bauers was the real father Quinn never had; and it was true.

Quinn swung the sword in a gentle arc. It felt so light now. "Do you think he knows? Everything that's happened here?"

Bauers smiled. "Matthew and Georgia wired money last week and asked that we wire back a list of needed supplies. His own son is fifteen now."

Quinn tilted the sword again, admiring it. Even though Bauers had only been able to secure him a year or two of fencing lessons, he knew it was an outstanding weapon. It had a graceful balance and tremendous strength.

As wondrous as the sword was, it wasn't the weapon most people associated with the Black Bandit. Catching Bauers's eye, Quinn flipped open the second chest. There it lay, on top, carefully coiled; the Bandit's leather whip. His mind wandered back to the summer afternoons where Quinn would swish a length of rope around the Grace House garden, pretending at the Bandit's skill with his whip. Quinn lifted it carefully—it hadn't survived the years as well as the swords. Bits of leather disintegrated with every flex, and the rich black braids were a stiff and crackled gray. He found himself afraid to uncoil it, simply moving it to the side to gain access to the rest of the chest's contents. It contained exactly what he knew it would: a pair of black boots with a small silver B imbedded in each calf, a trio of dark gray shirts—voluminous, almost piratelike in appearance— and a black hat with the remnants of a white feather beside it.

And there, at the bottom of the chest, lay the mask. An ingenious thing, the Bandit's mask was almost a leather helmet with a strip that could either come down over the eyes or fold up into the hat. Covington had let him try the mask on once, and the thing had nearly slid off his head. Quinn raised the mask into the light, inspecting it. It had held up much better than the whip, still surprisingly supple even after so much time. He couldn't help but smile at the memory of the Bandit's myriad of adventures. "Mr. Covington should have kept these."

The reverend's expression changed. "I don't think that was the plan. He gave those to *you*. And Matthew Covington did everything for a very good reason."

That made Quinn laugh. "I've not much use for a sword and whip, now do I? Although I could put the boots to good use."

Reverend Bauers leaned his heavy frame against a dusty chest of drawers. "It makes one wonder."

"What?"

"What else you could put to good use."

It took Quinn a full ten seconds to gain the man's meaning, at which point he dropped the mask. "You're not serious."

The sparkle in Reverend Bauers's eye was unmistakable. "Why not?"

Quinn squared off at the man. "I'm a bit old for adventure stories. And times are a mite harder now."

Bauers folded his arms across his chest. It was a gesture Quinn knew all too well, and he did not like the look of it.

"Matthew was close to your age when it all started. And it all started with a story." He caught Quinn's glare. "Stories are meant to be told. And *retold*."

"I'm not Matthew Covington," he said, because it needed saying. Covington was a clever, wealthy man who'd done remarkable things.

"No, Quinn. You're *you*. Matthew knew that, too. What if you are exactly the man we need? Do you really think we're down here digging in the basement for no reason at all?"

Quinn sank down on a crate. "I hardly think God brought me down to your cellar to ask me to be the Black Bandit."

It was a long moment before Bauers answered simply, "How do you know?"

"Because it's insane. I've barely enough food to eat, my shoes have twelve holes in them, the city's barely getting through the day, I've no money, no influence and barely a spare hour to think."

Bauers's face split into a satisfied grin. "But you found enough time to help an old man go through his cellar. You found enough time to build those little ones that toy you told me about. You know what I always say—there's always enough time to do God's will."

Even as the mail cart bounced its way a block from Aunt Julia's house, Nora could tell something was happening. The house seemed almost bustling, with Mama and Aunt Julia scurrying around the yard and porch with a speed and energy Nora hadn't seen in a while. A gracious table—or as gracious a table as one could manage these days—was set up on the porch.

Tea. Mama and Julia were setting out afternoon tea. And while afternoon tea had recently meant cups and saucers on mismatched plates with whatever crackers could be managed, this tea was different. It took a moment for Nora to realize what Mama and Aunt Julia were actually doing; they were entertaining.

"There you are," said Mama hurriedly as the cart rattled its way into the drive. "Goodness, I thought you'd miss it altogether. Run upstairs, find whichever dress is the most clean and put it on. She'll be here soon."

"Who?" Nora and her father asked at the same time.

"Mrs. Hastings."

"Dorothy Hastings? Here?" Papa asked. "I didn't think she was still in town."

"She's returned." Mama said it almost victoriously, as if it were as significant a societal achievement as the streetcar lines coming back into service. "And she's coming *here*."

The Hastings family was a social pillar of San Francisco. Mr. Hastings was on the Committee of Fifty—the emergency governing body that Papa served. Mrs. Hastings, like many of the city's finer families, had removed herself from the city to safer environs. Why she was in town at all, much less at Aunt Julia's house, Nora could only guess. Still, it was clear her visit was important to Mama. Perhaps even more than that, the opportunity to host someone, especially someone so important, seemed to light a spark in Mama and Aunt Julia that had been gone since the earthquake. A spark, when Nora was honest with herself, she hadn't been sure would return. That relief made Nora practically dance up the stairs to find whatever dress seemed the least tattered.

She found a frock—a deep rose that hid dust and dirt especially well and whose neckline showed off the locket to particular advantage—and a small pink flower that had fallen off a hatpin to tuck into her hair. It did feel wonderful to "dress up," even just this small bit. She had no idea how Mama and Aunt Julia could pull together any kind of tea under the circumstances, but they were highly motivated and resourceful women. And the combined skills of the two household cooks had managed some wondrous meals given the lack of foodstuffs. Half of Nora understood her father's amused scowl at the whole thing. She was sure Papa found the whole exercise to be simply a diversion for his wife. Even if Mr. Hastings was in charge of city services, tea seemed rather pointless.

Still, the other half of Nora understood how valuable it could be right now. To engage in something—anything—for the mere pleasure of it seemed a dear luxury. A tiny, beautiful shield against the endless, tiresome obstacles of rebuilding. Not unlike, she realized as she fixed the small flower into the corner of her chignon, Quinn's teeter-totter. Papa might consider that a pointless diversion as well, and yet she recognized the plaything's value.

Nora was just dusting off her skirts a second time when Mama entered the room. The *real* Mama, not the wisp of a woman who had seemed to occupy Mama's skin for the last few months. She'd been praying nightly for God to return the light to Mama's eyes. Today, those prayers had been answered.

For days after the earthquake, Mama had carried all her good jewelry around in a pocket tied inside her skirts. There was no safe place to put anything, and no one knew, as the fires ate up more and more of the city in an arsenal hunger no one could quite believe, when a hasty exit might be required. Over and over again during those first weeks, Nora had watched her mama lay her hand over the lump in her skirts. Checking to be sure it was still there or perhaps just shielding the trinkets from the horrors of the outside world. Eventually, Uncle Lawrence had produced a lockbox for Mama and Papa, and their valuables went in there. Nora thought it was far too tiny a thing to hold a life's valued possessions, but then again, Nora had had to rethink a lot about life's valued possessions in recent weeks.

Today, Mama had her pearls around her neck. And Grandmama's pearl ring—a piece that belonged to Mama and Aunt Julia's own mother—graced her right hand. It wasn't the beauty of the jewelry that made Nora smile, it was the way Mama carried herself when she wore it.

Mama came over and readjusted a curling tendril that fell from Nora's chignon. "You look lovely," Mama said. "But I think," she said delicately, "that it would be kindest to tuck the locket inside your dress."

Nora's hand came up to touch the locket. She'd already been gratefully amazed that Aunt Julia let her keep it. In her joy over recovering the locket, she hadn't even considered that Aunt Julia might want her lost daughter's necklace for herself until Papa brought it up on the ride home. He'd gone with Nora to show the locket to Aunt

Julia, and it had taken every ounce of will Nora had not to beg Aunt Julia to let her keep it. It would be wrong to deny a grieving woman any remnant of her daughter, but the necklace couldn't come close to meaning to Aunt Julia what it meant to Nora. She *needed* to have it. Needed to feel the only tangible evidence of that sweet friendship around her neck, close to her heart.

Aunt Julia had clutched the locket for a long moment that made everyone in the room hold their breath. Papa kept his hand on Nora's shoulder, as if to say, *be strong,* but said nothing. After a hollow-sounding breath, Aunt Julia let it slide back into Nora's hand. "You keep it, dear," she said with an unnatural calm. Nora and Papa waited there for a moment, thinking she meant to say something else, perhaps to cry or to say how glad she was to have the locket found, but she never said anything else. She just straightened her shoulders, touched Nora's cheek in a way that made her shiver and walked on to the porch to sit staring out over the city.

Nora went after her to thank her, but Papa's hand held her back. "Let her be," Papa said quietly. "It is a terrible thing to bury a daughter. And it is a far more terrible thing to not have a daughter to bury."

Of course Nora would tuck the locket out of sight. And Mama was right—it was by far the kindest thing to do.

Chapter Five

❧

"It's hopeless." Quinn's ma stood at the opening of their shack and rewound her graying red hair up into the ever-present knot at the base of her neck. "You can't expect children to run around such filth all day long without shoes and not cut their feet to ribbons." She looked up and saw Uncle Mike coming up the path. "Did you find any, Michael?"

"It's just as I thought, Mary. Only the sisters in the other camp have any iodine left."

His mother blew out a breath. "The sisters. Well, that's all well and good for them, but we're on the wrong side of the street to get much of that, aren't we?"

"And they don't come over here 'til Thursday."

Quinn watched his ma look at poor Sam. He'd cut his foot yesterday morning on a nail, and it was an angry red this afternoon—a bad sign. "It hurts you, don't it, boy?"

Sam, smart enough to see the bad news in Ma's eyes, put on a brave face. "Not so much."

Quinn sat down next to the boy. "Your limp says different, Sam. If it hurts a lot, my ma should know. Ma's are smart that way, besides. No use fooling them about things like this."

Sam swallowed hard. "It hurts a lot," he admitted.

"I reckon it does," Ma said, her smile softening. "You've got a man-sized wound in your foot, and you're just a tiny one, you are." She put Sam's foot back into the bucket, which was really just a large tin Uncle Mike had found and washed, and motioned for Quinn to stand.

"I'll take it you'd know where to find a shot or two of whiskey," she asked.

Quinn raised an eyebrow at his mother. Given the damage alcohol had done in this household, he knew his mother's disapproval of drinking. "For the *wound*," she clarified in an exasperated tone. "Iodine would be better, but we can hardly get persnickety now, can we?"

Uncle Mike put his hands into his pockets while Ma reached for the small pine box she kept under her trunk. Quinn knew they were searching for a coin or two—the man at the far corner of Dolores Park, who'd opened an undercover tavern, brooked no charity whatsoever. Even if he carried Sam bleeding and screaming in pain to the man, Quinn doubted the profiteer would spare a tablespoon for medicinal purposes. "I've got one," Quinn said, producing the silver coin he'd found under a beam two days ago. He'd had his eye on a pair of hose for his mother—her fifty-first birthday was next week—but Sam seemed a more pressing cause.

Ma sighed. "That'd buy a whole bottle of iodine before."

"Before." Quinn echoed her sigh, tucking the coin back in his pocket and tussling Sam's hair. "Before" didn't even need words around it anymore. It had become an expression unto itself. Everybody knew what

you meant when you said "before," especially when you said it that way. As he walked out of the tent toward the rowdier edge of the camp, Quinn wondered if the time would come when someone said "before" like it was a bad thing. Like things were so much better now. *That day will come, won't it, Lord?*

As he picked his way through the moonlit alleys—lamps or any other open flames were scarce and outlawed after sundown besides—Quinn was almost sorry he'd said that prayer. It kept ricocheting back to him somehow, as if the answer to it lay within his own reach. He was one man, barely able to scrape up enough whiskey to treat a boy's wound, much less make things better than before. Right now, with the wind rousting up an uncomfortable chill, San Francisco was a problem that felt even too big for God, and Reverend Bauers would surely scold him for thinking that way.

Reverend Bauers.

Quinn thought of the boxes they'd discovered in the Grace House cellar. Did he even dare think one man could make things better?

Bauers would undoubtedly argue that Quinn did know one man who had made things better than before. Quinn shrugged and pulled his thin coat tighter around him. Had he really? Or was he just remembering the daring Black Bandit exploits with the easily impressionable eyes of youth? He'd thought the Bandit's weapons giant-sized, but they weren't when he held them yesterday. Matthew Covington was clever, yet hadn't Nora Longstreet called him clever to realize the children needed playthings?

Am I clever enough, Lord? The question seemed to shoot right through him, like an electric current. Donated medical supplies were supposedly pouring into the city. They had to be going somewhere. Perhaps a clever man need only help get such things from one place to another. And these days, with as few people watching as possible. That, Quinn surmised with a low churning in his chest, was most definitely the job for one clever man.

Quinn Freeman couldn't really be the Black Bandit. That was fine, however, because San Francisco didn't need a Bandit. It needed a messenger. An invisible transporter, getting things from those who sent them to those who needed them. He could do that.

I can do that. Quinn had to stop for a moment, reeling from the weight of the idea. Actually, he reeled from the *lightness* of the idea. Quinn had just answered the question burning in the corner of his heart since the fires. The question everyone asked but no one dared to voice. The thing niggling at him, keeping him up nights, making him stare off into space for hours instead of sleeping: *Why am I still here?*

"That's why I'm still here?" His chest began to lift as he said the words aloud to himself. It made perfect, ridiculous sense. He knew the streets in a way a wealthier man never could. He had size and speed and the kind of wit that can get a man from one point to another without being seen. He had weapons to defend himself and the unfaltering faith of Reverend Bauers at his back.

And he'd been chosen. Decades ago. By the one man most qualified to choose.

That's why I'm still here. That's why I survived. That's why the chest survived and why we found it again yesterday. Quinn could almost feel God's eyes looking

down on him, waiting with a stare twenty years long.
Poised to launch him into an unimaginable adventure.

Quinn looked quickly around, somehow sure he'd
changed physically, that those around could see the
earth-shattering moment that just took place.

The world shuffled by dark and unawares. There
seemed no other words to use. Quinn squeezed his eyes
tight and prayed. *Here I am, Lord, send me.*

Nora examined Sam's injured foot as he poked it
toward her. An angry red gash ran down the soft pink
flesh; far too large a cut for such a fidgety, innocent
foot. And to call it clean was a bit of a stretch, given
the grime on the rest of the boy. She had no doubt Mrs.
Freeman struggled to get the boy as clean as he was.
"They make me sit here all the time," he pouted. With
youth's astounding flexibility, Sam pulled the foot up
practically to his nose and squinted at it. Nora's hip
joints hurt just watching the contortion.

Comically, Sam sniffed at his foot and wiggled his
toes. "Smells fine," he pronounced, giving the tiny jar
of whiskey on Mrs. Freeman's trunk a suspicious glare.
"I'm okay now." He put the foot down, stuffing it back
into the single enormous sock—one of Quinn's, Nora
supposed. Mrs. Freeman had tried to make Sam wear
it in a last-ditch effort to keep out the constant dust.

He made to stand up, until Quinn's hand came down
on his shoulder. "I thought you said you wanted a visit
from Miss Longstreet here. It took a fair amount of
promises and convincing to get her to come over here."
Quinn pulled the huge sock back off Sam's foot. "You
can't just up and leave now that she's been nice enough
to come and call, now can you?"

Sam's wiggles suggested that he intended to do just that, and Nora wondered if her visit had been meant to distract Quinn, not Sam himself. "Oh, no, Sam, I came to see you." Nora paid careful attention not to catch Quinn's eyes as she spoke that last bit. "I wanted to make sure you were all right. After all, you've entrusted your mail into my care, and that means we're friends now."

"It was fine of your father to let you come." Mrs. Freeman nodded toward Sam, who didn't relax until she put the jar of alcohol away back inside the trunk. She handed Nora a roll of makeshift bandages, much like the strips of sheets and cloth Nora had made with her mother and Aunt Julia nearly every week since the earthquake. Nora's family—and most of San Francisco's female population—was down to one petticoat in the name of bandage making. "He was just a bit less wild with the promise of a visit from you." She shook her head and motioned for Nora to begin wrapping Sam's foot. "'Tis a crime to be treating lads with whiskey." She spoke sharply as she slammed the trunk shut. "But I suppose we should say a prayer of thanks that we've got anything at all." Mama might have taken Mrs. Freeman's sharp tone as an accusation, but Nora could see it was just frustration at how slow relief seemed to be moving. Everyone—Nora included—had thought things would be so much more settled by now. Mrs. Freeman turned to Sam with a mother's piercing glare. "You say a prayer of thanks, young Sam, that Miss Longstreet brought you those fine sweets to suck on while we tended your foot."

"I did," Sam replied quickly. Under Mrs. Freeman's suspiciously raised eyebrow, he added, "Sort of."

Quinn hunkered down to Sam's height as Nora tied

off the end of Sam's new bandage. "I'd change that 'sort of' into a 'thank You, Father God' tonight, if I were you. My ma talks to God all the time, so she'll know if you don't."

Sam nodded.

"You've still no real bandages?" Nora asked, straightening up. She'd caught sight of Quinn staring at her hands as she wrapped Sam's foot. Even though it was a quick glance out of the corner of her eye, she found it unnerving. That man watched things far too intensely. "No things to treat wounds? My father said supplies like that are coming in from the army all the time." She handed back the bandage roll while Quinn tied the enormous sock in place with a piece of string. The makeshift footwear looked absurd, the toe of the sock flopping about as Sam jiggled his foot.

"Your father would know that more than I, miss, and it may be true." Mrs. Freeman opened the trunk once more, tucking the roll of cloth strips inside. "The nuns and the official camps have supplies, surely, but they only come over here once a week. You can't very well ask people to only cut themselves on Wednesdays, now can you?"

"It's just iodine," Nora said, amazed. "There must be bottles and bottles of it at the other camps by now. Papa says crates of supplies come through his office every day."

"And you can see how much of it makes its way to us out here." She softened her hard stare. "We can't all fit into the official camps, no matter what those men in suits say. But that's none of your doing, Miss Longstreet. I've not meant to grouse at you. I don't know where they expect us to go or how they expect us to get by. So much making do and doing without wears on a soul."

Obviously cued by Quinn, Sam stood up straight and extended a chubby hand. "Thanks for my licorice, Miss Longstreet. And for coming."

Nora shook Sam's hand with grand formality. "You're welcome, young master Sam. And thank you for the invitation. I do hope you're feeling better soon."

Sam was evidently feeling better now, for he tumbled through the door as soon as Quinn's hand released his shoulder. A limping tumble, but an energetic one just the same. Nora watched him go. "What else do you need? I have to think there is something I or my family can do."

Mrs. Freeman planted her hands on her hips. "What *don't* folks need? We need everything. Bandages, iodine, wood, water, socks, pins, string...I could rattle on for days."

"Wait a minute." Nora fished into her pockets for the bits of paper and the stub of a pencil she'd begun keeping in there during her mail cart visits. "Let me write this down." Mrs. Freeman rattled off the surprisingly long list of basic items needed in the makeshift camps. Many of these things showed up regularly in the official camps. How had things become so segregated?—everyone suffered. It made no sense. Two or three of the items she could provide from her own household. Surely in the name of Christian mercy Mama and Aunt Julia—with a little help from Mrs. Hastings, perhaps—might scour up the rest.

"Could you make another copy of that list?" Quinn asked, holding out his hand. "Reverend Bauers could put one to good use, I'd guess."

"Of course." Nora found another scrap of paper—this one a page torn out of a cookery book—and copied down the list.

Quinn folded it carefully and tucked it into a pocket of his shirt. He had the most peculiar smile on his face, as if he'd just learned a great secret. "I should get you back, Miss Longstreet, before your father worries."

Quinn stared at the list. Miss Longstreet did a funny, curvy thing with the dots on her *i*'s. A delicate little backward slant. He ran his fingers across the writing again, careful not to smudge it.

He had his first challenge. A list of basic supplies.

It was in her handwriting. That shouldn't have mattered much, but it did. There was a generosity about her that stuck in the back of his mind. She was kind to Sam, but not out of pity—the sort that he had seen far too much of lately. That version—a superior, ingratiating sort of assistance—bred the hopelessness that was already running rampant in the camp. Nora's kind of help was respectful. She grasped the truth that made so many people uncomfortable in this disaster: fire was no respecter of privilege. Those now without homes had done nothing but live on the wrong street corner at the wrong time. The firestorm and the earthquake destroyed nice homes as eagerly as they consumed shanties. Bricks fell just as hard on good men as they did on criminals. Certain people had begun to sort victims into worthy and unworthy categories. Official camp refugees and squatters. Implying reasons why the refugees were in the positions they were. It was, Quinn supposed, a perfectly human reaction to death and destruction's random natures. A desire to seek order amidst chaos.

It was just very irritating to be on the receiving end. And Quinn, like most of Dolores Park's residents, had come to see it a mile off.

Nora wasn't like that. And yes, he had come to think of her as Nora, even though he'd always address her as "Miss Longstreet," of course. Quinn felt as if he could read all her thoughts in those violet eyes. It seemed such a cliché to say "there was something about her," but he could get no more specific than that—something about her tugged at his imagination constantly. Little details, like the gentleness of how she bandaged Sam's foot. The delicacy of her handwriting or the way her fingers fluttered over the locket when she was thinking.

He could no longer lie to himself: Nora Longstreet had caught his eye.

Chapter Six

"I've laid it all out in my head, Reverend. It wouldn't be that hard, actually."

Reverend Bauers sat back in his chair, ready to listen. Quinn had once loved the meticulous order of the reverend's study—it had seemed to him like an enormous library, although he'd never actually seen a true library. Today, Bauers reclined between tall stacks of linens and a tottering tower of pots and pans. The neatness of his study had been overthrown by the new demands on the Grace House kitchen, which had suffered damage in the earthquake but now had even more mouths to feed. As such, the study now doubled as an extra pantry, so the books shared their shelves with tins of tomatoes, jars of syrup, and whatever foodstuffs Bauers had managed to find to feed his flock.

"I expected as much, Quinn."

Quinn again had the sensation of being the center of a story that had begun before he arrived. As if everyone around him knew more of his own future than he himself did. It was the kind of thoughts that could make a man edgy. And bold. "If we could get them from the army or the hospital, it'd be easy as pie."

Reverend Bauers frowned. "If you could get them easily from those places, you'd have them already."

Quinn leaned one shoulder against the wall. "You're right. And that's wrong. Even I can see we can't fit in those official camps. Why bother to divide us at all unless someone wants the groups to start fighting each other?"

"Just to make things clear here, man, stealing will not be an option. I admit we might have to stretch our definition of 'procurement,' but there will be no taking of supplies against the will of those who have them. You must become an agent of expediting, not a thief."

Quinn furrowed a brow at the long word. "Expediting?"

"The art of expediting is the art of getting things where they need to go quickly. Efficiently. And, I've no doubt in this case, rather creatively. You possess the creativity in spades. We just need someone very well-connected. And, you'll be happy to know, God has been kind enough to present us with an ally. Can you be at Fort Mason tomorrow afternoon at two?"

Quinn winced. There was only one place he ever wanted to be at two in the afternoon, and it wasn't anywhere near the army base. "I've got someplace to be at two, but make it three and I'll be there."

"Two minutes after three," said a dark-haired man in uniform with a precise mustache and an even more precise snap of his pocket watch. "He's punctual, at least. That's something." Quinn found himself nose to nose with a meticulously dressed man with dark, sharp eyes.

"I'm told you run fast." The man pocketed his watch.

"I do."

"Have you a steady hand?"

Quinn wasn't entirely sure where this was heading. "So they tell me."

"Quinn Freeman," Reverend Bauers cut in, "may I present Army Major Albert Simon. Major Simon, this is Quinn Freeman, the man I've been telling you about."

Major Simon walked around him, appraising him as if he were buying a horse. "Tall, strong, good reach, I'd expect." He turned to Bauers. "He's had some training in fencing?"

"Two years," Quinn stepped in, not liking the idea of Bauers and Simon talking about him as if he weren't in the room. "It was a long time ago, but I still remember most of it."

Simon stroked one hand down either tip of his mustache. "Ever shot a pistol, Freeman?"

"I've been fired at," Quinn offered, "but I don't own a gun."

"It's harder than you think."

"So is a lot of life, Major. Especially now."

"Which is why we're here," Bauers declared. "Major Simon," he said in a lower tone, "has agreed to be in on our little scheme."

Quinn looked at the man. He was fit but a bit on the heavy side, somewhere in his late thirties from the looks of it and alarmingly serious. He didn't seem at all like the scheming type. "The Bandit—"

"Is not a name I'd mention in loud tones around here,"

the major cut in sharply. "Not everyone in the army is a fan of such…resourceful measures."

"I think you'll find Major Simon a most extraordinary fellow." Reverend Bauers walked over to a large sack Quinn only just then realized sat on a table in the center of the room. "With some very considerable resources." He pulled open the drawstring and tilted the top for Quinn to peer inside.

The sack held half of what had been on his list. On Nora's list, that is. Bandages, iodine, salt, a few tins of meat, needles and thread and half a dozen other various supplies. Major Simon went up a few notches in Quinn's book, to be sure. More than a few.

"Where'd you get all that?"

"No need for you to know," Simon said slyly.

"You stole it. Why else would you answer like that?"

"Would you take it no matter where it came from?"

"I'm smarter than that. I don't know you, even if Reverend Bauers does."

"They were 'procured,' perhaps, or more precisely, 'diverted,' but ready for you to put to good use." Simon pulled the string shut, placing the sack into a crate that sat under the table. "And no, you don't know me. Yet."

"The major has arranged a discreet drop-off point," Bauers said, clearly enjoying the adventure of it all. With that look in his eye, Quinn could easily imagine the days when Reverend Bauers had been the Black Bandit's trusted accomplice. He seemed delighted to step into those shoes again. "You're to return tonight and get it back to camp by…well…whatever means you find necessary."

His first mission. It hummed through Quinn's veins.

Suddenly, he couldn't get the Bandit's old gray shirt on fast enough. He longed to strap on the sword and take the world by storm. Now.

"You have a fire in your eye, Freeman," Major Simon said to him. "I've found our friend the reverend is rarely wrong on such things. But you'll need far more than good intentions if you really want to do what you say. You'll need training and cunning and several very particular skills. Skills I've offered to teach you. But you'll have to be both patient and discreet."

"I am."

"You don't strike me as patient in the least."

"Would you be patient if your family didn't have enough to eat or a real roof over their heads?"

Simon chuckled and clapped Quinn hard on the back. "Bold as brass. You're right, Bauers, he's just the man for the job. If he doesn't get himself killed first."

"You've no idea where all this came from?" Nora asked as she peered at the supplies that had appeared overnight at the Freeman shack.

Mrs. Freeman squinted at the cut on Sam's foot, paused, and then dabbed it with a bit more iodine. "None at all," she said over the resulting protests from Sam. "Quinn said he'd put the list up on a fence post across the street last night, asking for help. That's all we know." She turned to the boy. "Hush, lad, it'll hurt far more than that if it don't heal properly." Her words were harsh, but her eyes were kind.

"It is amazing, isn't it?" Nora examined the items again, grateful her father had allowed her to come over to Dolores Park to inspect this surprise package—provided, of course, that she was properly escorted, which wasn't at all an unpleasant requirement. Nora turned over the tins of meats, looking for any clue. She'd shown the list to several people, and obviously someone else had now seen the list, but still no one seemed to know who'd found the rare items and delivered them to camp. It was a feat. As common as the items were, Nora could only manage to scare up two needles and three spools of thread. Before the earthquake, it might have taken her all of fifteen minutes to secure the entire list. How scarce life's necessities had become.

"You'd best listen to my ma," Quinn said, planting himself down on the chest next to a squirming Sam, whose bottom lip threatened tears at any moment. "You strike me as a smart lad. And a brave one. We'll need you fit and strong to help out. You'll be no use to me limping around like a goat, now will you?"

"I'll need you to escort me," Nora whispered to Sam, grinning. "I shouldn't trouble Mr. Freeman much longer. He's a busy man and he's likely to tire of leading me to and fro."

Quinn applied a mock frown, but his eyes told a far different story. While he'd refused her any details, she knew he'd gone to great lengths to meet the two o'clock mail run yesterday. When they were late because one of the cart's finicky wheels had jammed, she'd found him practically pacing the street in a state she could only describe as panic. And while he'd walked calmly— perhaps it wasn't too much of an exaggeration to say he swaggered slightly—back to the edge of the camp, she'd noticed he broke into a flat-out run once he turned the corner. Yes, sir, Quinn Freeman was very late for something yesterday, and she could not deny what his tarrying had done to that sparkling spot just above her stomach. He looked at her as if she were the best part of his day, and she was not at all certain she hid her own pleasure at seeing him.

"She's far too much work, this one," Quinn said. The sour notes in his voice were no match at all for the spark in his eyes. "Take her off my hands as fast as you can, man." He ruffled Sam's moppish hair.

Mrs. Freeman gave the quickest of glances back and forth between her son and Nora. "When the foot's ready, and not a moment before. Iodine and bandages are too rare to go wasting with foolishness. Put that sock back on, young man, and mind you stay out of the dust as best you can. Come back tomorrow and I'll have a look at it again."

"Yep," said Sam, sliding off the trunk.

Quinn snagged the boy's elbow as he went to leave. "Yes, *ma'am,* and say thank you."

"Thanks, ma'am." Sam punctuated his attempt at manners by wiping his nose on his sleeve.

Mrs. Freeman moaned. "I'm climbin' uphill both ways to keep anything clean here." She rubbed the back of her neck with her hand and sighed. "What I wouldn't give for a true sink and a clean set of sheets."

Quinn gave his mother a quick peck on the cheek. "You've worked wonders as it is, Ma." He pointed to the stock of supplies. "And somebody's taken notice."

"And wouldn't I like to know who?" his mother said, smiling. "And what else they've got. Father Christmas coming in July. Who'd have thought?" She wiped her hands on her apron and began loading the supplies back into the trunk. "Get her back now, Quinn, before her father starts to worrying about where she is."

Quinn shrugged his coat back on as they walked. "So

your father's office didn't deliver that package? I thought surely you'd done it. You had the list, after all."

"So did you," Nora replied. "And you posted it. Someone with the things must have seen the one you tacked up. Still, what showed up didn't really match up to the list we'd made."

"It's a mystery, to be sure." He went to do the button on his coat, found no button to do, and gave out a little *hrrmph* as he was forced to let it hang open. "I may have to beg Ma for a little of that thread, won't I?" They walked on, and Nora made a note to dig through her father's coats for a spare button tonight. "Everyone needs everything, it seems," Quinn sighed. "Reverend Bauers at Grace House can be a resourceful man, but he needs all of those things as much as we do, if not more."

"I've heard stories about Grace House. Is it still standing?

"It is," Quinn replied. "The building next door fell to the ground, but Grace House is mostly fine."

Nora let out a long sigh. "It's hard not to wonder how He's let all this happen and why. I can't get my mind around anything that makes sense, no matter how many prayers I say."

"No sense to be made, if you ask me. Some things just are. You could stand around all day trying to figure out why, and it still won't find you dinner or get your house rebuilt. It's not the *why*s we need to worry about now, Miss Longstreet, it's the *how*s that matter most."

"*How,* then, do you think those things found their way to your mother?"

He stuffed his hands in his pockets and shrugged his shoulders. "Don't rightly know."

"Someone, somewhere, has played the hero. I think it's perfectly grand. I hope everyone hears about it and twenty other people do the same. What a wonderful thing that would be, don't you think?"

Quinn laughed. He had a very delightful, forthright laugh. "I think you're getting ahead of yourself, miss. It's not smart to make so much of one good deed."

"One good deed like a teeter-totter? Oh, I think you know the power of one good deed far more than you let on." She didn't hide the broad smile that crept up from somewhere near her heart.

"Grace House does the important work, not me. But even they're busting under the load right now, or so Reverend Bauers says. He's got a few benefactors who can help out, you know, friends in high places and all, but not nearly enough."

Why hadn't she thought of it before now? "I can help with that."

He raised an eyebrow. "I think you're helping as much as you can now. Your pa'll be sore at your being gone as long as you have, if not worse."

"No, I mean with the benefactors. I know someone who can help. We had a wealthy woman named Mrs. Hastings to tea at the house the other day. She's wanted to see the ruined city but her husband won't let her come any farther than our house." Nora looked at Quinn. "What if we could get Mrs. Hastings to tour Grace House? Surely her husband couldn't object to something like that? Then she could meet people. She could meet Reverend Bauers. I've heard so much about him, even *I'd* like to meet Reverend Bauers. It's the perfect solution."

Quinn stopped walking and looked at her. "You've never met Reverend Bauers?"

He made it sound as if her social upbringing lacked a crucial element. "Well, of course I've shaken his hand at some city ceremony at some time or another, but I don't really know him. I only know of him. Papa knows him, I think, but not socially."

Those words came out wrong. As if people like Papa didn't socialize with people like Reverend Bauers. It was true, in some ways, but not in the way her words made it sound. Quinn had noticed. He stood up straighter, started walking again, and the set of his jaw hardened just enough for her to notice.

Nora reached out and caught his elbow. "I didn't mean it like that."

"No one ever does." The edge in his voice betrayed the wound her words had caused.

"No, really. It was a horrid way to put it. I just meant…" What did she just mean? She'd said it without thinking, without consideration, of what Mama would have called "their differences in station." Why consider some great foolish gulf between them—especially now, when all that seemed to matter so very little? She dropped her hand. "I don't know what I meant. But I've not met Reverend Bauers and I would very much like to. And I want to help. I believe Mrs. Hastings will want to help, too, if we can show her Grace House. Please. I know she will."

"If she honestly *wants* to help, and not just gawk at other folks' hardship. I've seen those types. Riding in carriages around the edge of our camp with hankies pressed to their noses. As if we're all some odd entertainment."

"Mrs. Hastings can be a bit stuffy, but I think she truly does want to help. She just doesn't know how. Or maybe just where to start. I know something good would come of it if we could just make the arrangements." Suddenly, it had become the most urgent thing in the world. Something large and important she could do to make things better. And surely, once she'd been to Grace House with Mrs. Hastings, Papa might let her do more than just sit around and wind bandages. Mrs. Hastings had loads of friends with all sorts of connections. Even Mama would be delighted to work on projects with someone of the Hastingses' stature. It was the most perfect of ideas.

Quinn's expression softened. "I'll see what I can do."

Chapter Seven

⌒

"You've left your side unprotected," Major Simon warned. "I could have run you through four minutes ago."

"So you said," Quinn panted as he wiped the sweat from his forehead with his sleeve. Major Simon was proving to be a merciless teacher. Just a moment ago he'd planted the tip of his sword over Quinn's pounding heart and declared with an annoying calm that in a *real* duel, Quinn's life would have come to an abrupt end. Something in his eyes made Quinn believe he could do it. Part of him suspected the major had taken more than one life—in battle or otherwise—but the wiser part of him decided he didn't really want to know.

"Die? Right here?" Quinn challenged as he regained his footing. It was useful to discover he didn't at all like being on what Mr. Covington had once called "the business end" of a sword. Quinn vowed to remember the unpleasant sensation of having a blade planted gingerly on his chest—and vowed it would never happen again.

"Hardly sporting of me, I know," Simon pronounced as he flicked the blade away.

"Speaking of sporting…" With a swift move, Quinn skidded down and forward, making sure his tattered boot collided with Major Simon's foot, sending the stocky officer off balance. With another kick, he knocked Simon's remaining knee sideways so that the major came down to the floor in a crash of weapons.

He shot Quinn a nasty look, then laughed. "One does not kick in fencing!"

Quinn held out a hand, telling himself it would be unsporting to enjoy the moment but enjoying it immensely. Simon had kept the upper hand for most of the hour, anyway. "Were we fencing?"

Simon took Quinn's extended hand and pulled himself to his feet. "That was entirely uncalled for. And downright clever. An old general of mine used to say that the best use for rules was knowing when to break them." He slid the foil into the holder at his hip. "I dare say it's a lesson you already know."

"Life can be a good teacher of some things."

"And not others. You kicked me because you were angry, not because it was a good strategy. It worked this time. It won't the next." He pointed a finger at Quinn as he pulled a handkerchief from his pocket. "You fight with too much emotion, Freeman. We'll have to work to cool that temper of yours. Give me your hand." He held out his hand to shake Quinn's.

Matthew Covington had insisted they shake hands at the end of every fencing lesson or duel as well. Quinn pulled off his glove and held out his hand.

At which point Simon grabbed it, held it, and before

Quinn could even blink, had produced a short dagger from his boot and dragged it sharply down Quinn's forearm.

"Ouch!" Quinn yelled as a thick line of blood pooled where Simon had scratched—no, sliced him. He just barely bit back a retort that would have made Ma's ears burn. "What the…"

"No broken rule goes without consequences. Every knife hurts, especially the one you didn't see coming." Simon handed Quinn the handkerchief. "Next time you face me, you'll think twice. A small price to pay for wisdom."

Quinn stood, staring at the man, unable to piece together the gentleman with the savage who'd just calmly cut him.

"It's but a scratch," Simon said, "and the first lesson I give all my best students."

"Some compliment," Quinn muttered. "What will happen to me if you really like me?"

Simon looked him straight in the eye. "You'll live."

As he stood in Reverend Bauers's study that afternoon, wincing at the excess of iodine the pastor dabbed over his forearm, Quinn recounted the major's painful lesson.

"I can't say I care for his methods, but Simon makes an important point." The reverend smiled. "No pun intended."

Quinn thought about the tip of Simon's foil skewered into his chest. "He's a wild sort, he is. Dangerous."

"No, I think that Major Simon is just a man aware of how dangerous a game we aim to play here. The moment you forget yourself in the name of playing hero, that's the moment any fool could come out of the shadows and take you." He put a clean bandage over the wound. "How'll you explain that cut to your ma?"

"I'll worry about that later." Quinn looked at the reverend. "Are you saying I shouldn't be doing this now? Changing your mind?"

"Not at all. I'm only saying we can't be too careful. 'Wise as serpents,' the Bible says. Taking on evil—even with the best of intentions—is always a dangerous endeavor."

Quinn muttered a thing or two about the snakelike nature of a certain army major as Bauers bound off the bandage. The wound smarted for a dozen different reasons, only half of which could be attributed to Reverend Bauers's enthusiastic doctoring.

"Think of it as a repayment," Bauers said, raising a disapproving eyebrow to Quinn's muttered insults. "You do remember the very nasty gash you gave Mr. Covington on your first meeting? The cut you lads gave Matthew was much bigger and twice as deep. All for his noble effort to try and stop you two hooligans from stealing from Grace House. Why, I stitched up his arm in the very next room. After twenty-odd years, has a bit of balance to it, don't you think?"

"No, I don't." Quinn flexed his arm. "And this hurts."

"Good. Now—" Bauers changed his tone as he put the medical supplies back in their box "—have you given thought to the message system?"

"It'll go up just before dark tonight," Quinn replied. "If I've got both arms to use by then. I found the wood yesterday, and with a bit of help I can have the post up in an hour. Right across the street from where the mail cart comes in."

Bauers smiled. "By the mail cart. What an extraordinary coincidence."

When the mail cart pulled up the next day, Nora noticed a large square post had been erected across the street. A sort of column made from pieced-together planks of wood now stood in the passageway between two shacks. People crowded around it, and it was a minute or so before Nora realized small pieces of paper and scraps of wood and material were stuck to the thing.

She'd heard about a fountain downtown that had become a message board of sorts. People fastened messages or notices or sad notes like "Can't find Erin Gray since Tuesday" on Lotta's fountain at Kearny and Market streets. It had become a vital communication place, a gathering spot for the lost and those who had been found. Logistically and emotionally the center point of town. Someone—someone very clever—had thought to do the same here.

When Nora looked out over the crowd, her suspicions proved correct, for her one raised eyebrow of silent inquiry was met with Quinn Freeman's grinning nod.

"The mail can't all be headed out of town," he said when he ambled across the street. "Folks here need to send messages of a smaller sort, too. Took all of an hour, once I found the wood."

She noticed he had a bandage on his right forearm. "It took a bit more than that, it seems," she said, pointing to the wound. "That wasn't there yesterday."

From behind her at the mail cart, Nora heard her

father make a grumbling sort of noise, as if he wasn't much fond of his daughter noticing the state of some man's forearms. When she turned, he shot a look of warning between them, as if telling her to stay on the cart while he climbed down to hoist another mailbag off.

"A fencing injury," he said, pleased at her concern. "I won the duel, anyway."

What a wit he had. "Now, Mr. Freeman, what sort of man has time for fencing these days?"

"You'd be surprised." His eyes fairly sparkled. He had the most extraordinary vitality about him. An energy, an inner source of power that stood out like the noonday sun in such a sea of weary souls. And when he looked at her like that, a spark of that power lit up inside her own soul. It was at once thrilling and dangerous.

Nora hid the blush she felt creeping up her face by changing subjects. "How is Sam?" she said brightly, fiddling with a stack of mail. "All healed?"

"Soon enough. He was asking to come over here this morning, but Ma held him off one more day. Fairly bursting to run around, he is. Ma threatened to put him on a leash yesterday afternoon after you left."

"How resilient children are," she sighed, sitting down on the edge of the cart. "I think they've fared the best of all of us." Mrs. Hastings's visit had cheered Mother and Aunt Julia for a little while after, but the dark melancholy had returned within a few days.

"We do fine. Well, as much as we can. You should come over and look at the post. There's happy news there, as well as the sad news." He pointed toward the wooden column and extended a hand to help her out of the cart.

Her father didn't look pleased, but neither did he voice an open objection—that would have to do for now. Nora took Quinn's hand, forgetting she'd removed her gloves, for it was nearly impossible to handle stacks of paper and the other odd forms of mail with gloves on. He clasped her hand, stunning her with the touch of his rough palms. They were working hands, large and calloused, yet strong and steady. Warm. Something unnamed shot through her, something far more alarming than what his eyes had done. Nora tried to brush it off as something from a dime-store novel, a juvenile thrill, but it felt so…important.

A touch. Quinn Freeman had touched her. Papa was undoubtedly cross, even though it was something as genteel as helping her out of the wagon. Still, she wasn't the least bit sorry she wasn't wearing gloves.

He winced, and she realized he had helped her out of the wagon with his injured arm. "Goodness," she said, "You really are injured there."

"Only just," he said, still smiling. "I'll be fine." She knew by the way he looked at her that he was as aware of their touch as she was. He held her hand for a fraction of a second longer than was necessary before letting it go and motioning toward the post. She felt that tiny linger—a trembling sensation in her hand—as if her palm would somehow be able to retain the feeling. Nora felt as if she would look at her hand an hour from now and find it physically changed.

She saw, out of the corner of her eye, that Quinn ran his thumb along the tip of each finger. He felt it, too. They walked quietly toward the post, each of them a little bit stunned, pretending at normalcy when nothing at all seemed normal.

Notes of every description, on every kind of material, had begun to cover the post, tacked and pinned or stuffed into cracks. One small corner of a newspaper held the message "Looking for Robert Morris." Another read "A.D.—I'm fine—M.T." One heart-wrenching note read "Josiah Edwards born Tuesday morning." Nora hadn't even thought about the fact that babies were still arriving. It was cheering to know life went on, but what sort of anguish gripped a mother bringing a precious new life into the wake of catastrophe?

Quinn noticed her eyes on the announcement and nodded at her. "I saw little Josiah yesterday morning. Fine and healthy and hungry as any baby ever was. He's hurting for a few necessities, but I gather he'll make out just fine."

Nora thought of all the soft, clean pampering that surrounded the last baby she'd seen. Babies should never know hardship—it was just wrong. "What's he missing?"

Adjusting his hat, Quinn pursed his lips in thought. "The usual things—diapers, cloths, jumpers and such. Soap, too, I suppose." Getting an idea, he began to walk around the post, one hand roaming over the fluttering papers. "Oh, here's one. 'Baby arrived. Need sheets, shirts, cloths and pins.' You know, that sort of thing. Ma found a clean pillowcase they cut down for Josiah to wear and a pair of little socks from a doll somewhere, so things find their way."

Nora began to look all over the post now, scanning for any requests like the baby's. There were half a dozen, maybe more, and the post had only been up one day. "I want to write these down, like I did the others. Surely we can find some of these things."

"Could you make me a copy, like you did before?"

"Of course I could. Do you have any ideas where we might find some of this?" The "we" had slipped out of her mouth unawares.

"I've a few thoughts," he replied. His eyes glowed again, and Nora felt surely Papa would storm across the street this very second and plant her back on the cart.

"Let me get a page from Papa's ledger," she said, needing to turn away from the way Quinn smiled at her, trying to wipe the smile from her own face as well.

Nora could barely keep her eyes on the page as she copied down the posted needs Quinn read out. There was an enthralling partnership in this, as though she were grafting herself into something far bigger than her own tiny problems. Here was something—something concrete and important—that she could do. The first list had been just a product of her being in the same tent as Sam and Mrs. Freeman. This felt more deliberate. *Help me, Lord,* she prayed as she worked the pencil and paper. *I'll move Heaven and earth to get these things to these people.*

Her plan hadn't worked. Quinn knew just by the set of her shoulders when the cart pulled into sight a day or so later. He'd feared as much, suspected that Nora Longstreet hadn't yet realized just how hard supplies still were to come by. And while a huge chunk of him wanted her to wheel in here victorious, his practical side knew she had always stood a far bigger chance of wheeling in here sad and frustrated.

She was even prettier when she pouted. Her delicate frown whipped up something fierce inside him, some heroic urge to see her smile again and to do whatever it took to produce that smile. She didn't know he had the means to do it. She didn't know how much he'd stared at his hand yesterday, trying to recall the softness of her palm and the distractingly soapy scent that seemed to float around her.

She didn't know her father was standing over her shoulder looking straight at Quinn, as if to say there'd be no wandering across the street today. That was fine— Quinn had another strategy to restore Nora's smile, and that strategy was currently tugging impatiently on his good arm. He didn't mind at all that Sam wouldn't take no for an answer in coming to see Nora.

The moment Quinn finally let go of his hand, Sam scrambled across the street and up onto the cart to give Nora an enthusiastic hug. Her laugh at Sam's exuberant, nearly tackling welcome made Quinn smile. Those two were a pair from the first moment.

He stayed back while Nora went through her usual business with the mail, which was hampered by Sam for most of her visit. Sam had obviously declared himself her assistant, and Quinn couldn't help but laugh as Sam's "assistance" made Nora's tasks that much more complicated. Every once in a while she would look up, catching Quinn's eye. Even at this distance—as they had at the rally not so long ago—her eyes could dazzle him. He could tell she was disappointed at not being able to provide the items they'd listed. He admired how important helping out had become to her, mostly because he shared the same urgency.

When her mail was dutifully received and Sam had been thanked, rethanked and thanked again for his "invaluable assistance," Nora tugged a small box from the back of the cart and then handed it to Sam while she climbed down. Quinn wanted to sprint over there and help her down again, if only to buy himself the fraction of a second it gave him to hold her soft hand, but he decided restraint was the better choice. No one used to say restraint was a characteristic of Quinn Freeman, but maybe the stinging cut on his right forearm was sinking the virtues of discretion into his thick skull.

After producing a piece of licorice for Sam from her pocket, Nora waved Quinn over. He forced himself to walk casually to the cart.

"Here. It isn't much, I'm afraid." She held out the box to him with a handful of bandage rolls and half a dozen dish towels inside. "I think the dish towels will make fine diapers if they're cut in half."

"Don't say it's not much," Quinn replied to the frustration in her voice. He took the box from her, resisting the urge to find a way to make sure their hands touched when he did. "Every bit helps out here. You're doing so much already. Josiah's ma will be thrilled."

The wind stole a lock of hair out from underneath her hat, and she reached up to push it back off her face. "There's just so much to do."

"Reverend Bauers says all we can really do is the bit God puts in front of us. With all he faces, I think he might know a thing or two about big problems."

"The post has twice as many messages as yesterday," she assessed, squinting across the street. "It was such a splendid idea. You really should be proud of yourself."

Quinn shrugged, hiding his pleasure at how obviously she wanted to go over and inspect his creation. "I just copied the fountain. Anyone could have done it."

Her eyes told him she thought otherwise, and he liked that very much.

She stared harder. "The post looks nearly full."

"And I need to talk to you about that." Quinn leaned in as close as propriety would allow. "I know someone. If we could write all these down, I could get the list to him and he might...help out."

"Someone? Who can find these things?" Her eyes grew wide, and he feared he'd blurt out his secret any second.

"Could be. A bit early to tell, but it's worth trying."

"Really? How wonderful."

"We'll have to be quiet about it. Careful. Things might get out of hand otherwise, there being so much need and all. Will you help?"

He had expected her to hesitate, to worry about the clandestine nature of it all. She didn't. "Absolutely," she said, taking in a breath. "How could I not?" Looking over her shoulder at her father, who was thankfully otherwise occupied, Nora asked, "But why do you need me?"

He hadn't thought about that. He'd just wanted to make sure she was involved. With clever moment's inspiration, he held up the bandaged right arm. "Hurts still. Besides, you've got more access to decent paper than I do." He'd thank Major Simon at tomorrow's lesson. Maybe.

"Oh, of course. I should make two copies again, like we did with your mother. That way I can look while your...friend...does his own looking." Resolutely, she brushed off her skirts and nodded back toward the mail cart. "I'll just fetch another piece of Papa's ledger. I'm sure he won't mind."

"You mind your pa, now. Don't give him any reason to decide it's not wise for you to be coming here anymore." Quinn didn't even want to think about how he'd endure the days if two o'clock didn't mean seeing Miss Nora Longstreet anymore.

"I'll mind." Her smile was as warm as sunshine. He had a partner. Actually, if Major Simon and Reverend Bauers counted, he had a tiny army. Quinn felt like he could take on the world if God asked him to do so.

Quinn felt himself grinning like a fool the entire time Nora ventured across the street and wrote down items from the post. She slipped him a conspiratorial smile as she climbed back aboard the mail cart and handed him his copy of the list. "Do you really think this will work?"

"No harm trying. Oh, by the way, I'm meeting with Revered Bauers to set up that tour you asked for."

"That's wonderful. I think Mrs. Hastings could be a grand patroness if she chose. And I imagine Reverend Bauers can be most persuasive. I do hope it will be all right with them that I come along."

Quinn wouldn't have it any other way.

Chapter Eight

As it turned out, Reverend Bauers was already familiar both with the Longstreets and the Hastingses, and it took little convincing to arrange a tour. The hardest part about it turned out to be accommodating Mrs. Hastings's packed social schedule and her limited visits to town. How anyone managed to do so much socializing in the wake of an earthquake, Quinn didn't know. That world was as foreign to him as the hatch-mark signs that used to hang in the Chinese quarter of town. And while Ma raised an eyebrow when Quinn asked if there was anything close to a clean, pressed shirt in the camp, she'd long learned to expect strange things from Quinn's association with Grace House. She'd only looked at him for a quizzical second when she handed him a surprisingly tidy shirt on the appointed day.

"There simply isn't enough space," Reverend Bauers said as he pointed the tiny tour group down the hallway. "With the camp right next to us in Dolores Park, the needs have been enormous. The army is doing a commendable job with the official camp, of course, but I think we can all see how much more help is still needed. He pointed to a row of long, narrow tables that now filled what used to be the front parlor. "We already feed sixty or so at a time at these standing tables. With a little help, we might be able to add benches, but that seems a long way off for now."

"Gracious," said Mrs. Hastings, gripping the hankie that had been her constant companion for the visit. "Eating standing?"

"When one is thankful to eat at all, sitting or standing hardly seems to matter," replied Reverend Bauers.

"It is an amazing thing," Nora said as they walked down the hallway. "You'd think feeding all those people would be chaos. But it seems quite orderly. People seem grateful and very kind."

"I suppose," Mrs. Hastings said, "that might depend on your definition of order. And they certainly ought to be grateful. Free hot meals." Her phrases were kind, her tone was not. Quinn bit back the retort he would have liked to offer.

Surprisingly, Nora stepped in where he'd been silent. "I think they'd much rather be paying customers, earning their own keep," she said. "They're no happier to be out of their homes and out of their jobs than Mama and Papa would be. They weren't even given tents like at the other camps. That's hardly their fault. Everyone has suffered."

Quinn wondered if Nora was as aware of Mrs. Hastings's expression as he was. The woman bore a look Quinn had come to recognize over the time since the earthquake. The unspoken theory that folks had brought the earthquake down upon themselves. It made no sense, of course, for the Grace House kitchen fell down just as fast as a brothel kitchen half a mile away. Reverend

Bauers said those society types had "hoarded their grace and left none for anyone else," and looking at the sharp angle of Mrs. Hastings's eyebrows as she surveyed the Grace House pantries, Quinn thought the description fit. He was trying not to judge, but it was mighty hard.

Reverend Bauers pointed to the near-empty pantry shelves. "Our need is great, as you can see. Even the staples are hard to come by."

"But I hear food and goods are pouring in from all over the country. They tell us the camps are in fine shape. Money has been donated," Mrs. Hastings argued.

"The official camps are indeed doing well, and it gladdens my heart to see it. But too many are struggling in places like Dolores Park, and we can't turn our backs on those souls. Distribution to those in need is still nowhere near fast enough."

Yet, Quinn's mind silently added. He had Nora's second list from the message post, and he had an appointment with Major Simon late this afternoon.

"Things have been finding their way, Mrs. Hastings," Nora offered. "Just this week I learned of some medical supplies finding their way into Dolores Park to help a little boy. Little miracles happen every day as people help each other out." She turned her smile full force to the woman, and Quinn felt a twinge of ridiculous hope that her charming smile would one day be turned to him. "Can you see the good a woman of your compassion and influence might be able to achieve? I just know you could work wonders." She reached into her pocket and pulled out the piece of her father's ledger. "There's a post in Dolores Park. People have been tacking up requests on it, and I've copied them down." She handed

Mrs. Hastings the list. "See? It's nothing so hard to get. Everyday things."

"I'm flattered you hold me in such high regard, Miss Longstreet. And ladies have been shredding petticoats into bandages since the first day. I'm not at all convinced there's that much to go around. And Dolores Park is..." The woman stopped short of the remark she was obviously thinking.

Nora simply stood in front of the lady, hands folded, silent. Quinn, trying not to get his back up over Mrs. Hastings's judgmental attitude, would have handed Nora the shirt off that very back were she to turn that look on *him*.

"But what kind of Christian woman would I be to turn down such a thoughtful request?" Mrs. Hastings took the list from Nora and tucked it into her fine silk handbag. "I shall see what I can do."

"Splendid!" said Reverend Bauers, clasping his hands. "I've no doubt you will indeed work wonders. Praise God for bringing you across our threshold, my dear madam. God will smile kindly on your charity."

Major Simon sheathed his sword with narrowed eyes. "The post was a brilliant idea. I'm not sure if I should be impressed or rather worried. You've too much a talent at deceit for my taste."

"Deceit?" Quinn asked, trying not to pant as he spoke. The major had just taken him through an exhausting series of exercises and Quinn was certain his arm— and lots of other parts of him—would be hurting in the morning. "I'm not trying to trick anyone. I'm keeping quiet in order to do what I think needs doing. I needed a way for folks to make their needs known that wasn't obviously attached to me. It's not like everyone can come tell me what they need." He took the towel Simon offered and wiped the sweat off his brow. "Besides, I didn't even think it up on my own. I just copied what I saw happening on the fountain downtown."

"Smart men don't bother rethinking good ideas. They just borrow them for their own use." The major took a drink from one of the glasses of water that had been set on a table at the side of the room, gesturing with his hand to the bandage that still wrapped Quinn's right forearm. "I stole that move from a particularly success-ful, if rather nasty general in the southern states. And I noticed you were far more thoughtful with your attacks this afternoon."

Quinn had to admit it had worked; the fact that his arm stung every time he thrust it forward made him more deliberate in his choice of offensive moves. Was it sheer pain or a learned lesson that had reined in his impulsive nature? Mostly, it seemed as if Major Simon wasn't out to get his goat today the way he'd been at first. Either Quinn was growing used to the major's larger-than-life persona, or Simon wasn't going out of his way to provoke him. It was for the best either way. "Lesson learned, Major. But I'd rather have done it without the blood, thanks."

Simon put down the glass. "Nonsense. Blood's a necessary part of the thing. And I imagine a clever fellow like yourself could squeeze a little sympathy out of a kind lady with that bandage…*if* you were so inclined."

Quinn might, under certain circumstances, have admitted to being pleased at the attention his wound seemed to garner from Nora, but neither here nor now.

"I manage," he said with what he hoped was an enigmatic grin.

Simon grinned back. It was times like this that Quinn could almost muster an older brother kinship with the man. A tentative friendship was forming between them despite Quinn's first impressions. "I imagine you do," Simon said with something almost like a wink. "And you've remembered more of your fencing than Reverend Bauers led me to believe. We may be able to start next week."

And start the next week they did. Major Simon had come through with flying colors. His supplies, along with some of Quinn's old connections to dockworkers and the men in the rail yards, had produced half the list of items requested on the post. The deliveries began. It had taken most of the night to quietly ferry the items from the secret storage location to the shacks in question, but the next day Quinn knew.

It was worth every risk. The look on folks' faces, the way they chattered around the post the next morning, the jolt of it all, was worth a month of sleepless nights. And the look Nora shot him as Sam rattled on about "the most amazin' thing that happened"? Well, that would have kept him up a week straight with ease.

"…and Missus Barker, she got soap, and some other lady got things for her baby, and no one knows how."

Unbidden, Quinn's memory brought back the morning he'd been sent to socialite Georgia Waterhouse's mansion by Reverend Bauers. He'd been assigned to fetch her back to Grace House the morning everyone discovered the Bandit's first delivery. The Bandit—whom Quinn would later learn was both the invention

of Miss Waterhouse and the surprising new alter ego of
Matthew Covington (although neither knew the other's
involvement at the time)—had nailed actual dollars to
the top of Grace House's doorjamb. It was more money
than anyone had seen in years in one place, and Reverend Bauers stretched those dollars as far as the eye
could see. By his first gift of funds—and the many
gifts of all kinds the Bandit gave after that—Quinn had
watched one man spark a tidal wave of optimism and
good deeds.

And now, it was Quinn's turn. This morning, standing among the folks' astonished buzz, Quinn felt the
legend come full circle, as if he'd been there way back
when just so he'd be ready to be here right now. As if
God really had lined it all up in perfect harmony just
the way Reverend Bauers always said He did. Quinn
felt the power Matthew Covington had spoken of, the
limitless energizing from knowing he'd ignited the rarest
and most powerful resource known to man: hope. He
knew now how Matthew Covington had forgone sleep,
ignored pain, defied odds and sometimes even grav-
ity to complete the Black Bandit's missions. He felt it
himself.

"It is extraordinary, Sam. A wonderful thing indeed."
Nora smiled. "We should all be very happy and very
grateful, don't you think?"

"Extra-extraordinary!" Sam's small mouth could
barely make its way around the large word.

There was a second, a sun-gilt moment when Nora's
eyes caught Quinn's overtop of Sam's continued chattering. She looked at Quinn as though he'd done something
monumental. As though the world spun on his command. No one, not even his ma, had ever looked at him

like that. The look she'd given him when he returned the locket had near stopped his heart, but this, this was even more stunning. It fired through his chest like a lightning bolt. A very addictive lightning bolt.

He stared at her for a moment, feeling the weight of the moment drive him to memorize its details. She had a splash of freckles starting on her cheeks, as though she'd spent too much time without her hat. He knew proper ladies weren't supposed to sport freckles, but he found them hopelessly endearing. They lent a natural-ness to her grace and breeding. He had the feeling he'd remember the slant of the sun and the particular scent on the breeze for years to come.

"Your post has done a world of good, Mr. Freeman," she said. Her words were pleasant and ordinary, but Quinn felt the world tilt and whirl like a shiny top all around him. She smiled, inclining her head in the direc-tion of his earlier contraption. "It's as clever as your teeter-totter, I think. Maybe more. You've a talent for simple things that accomplish great feats."

Her compliment swelled in his chest. "I just see what needs doing. Maybe clearer than most, but not by much."

"Seeing clearly is a great gift. Papa says if there's anything San Francisco needs right now, it's men with clear vision." She shrugged her shoulders. "Things have been difficult for him at the post office lately. Everyone seems to argue about everything and nothing gets done. But you, you see clearly enough to make a post and put it in the ground and look at all that gets done."

"No one is fencing me in with a load of rules or bick-ering about whether or not I can be trusted. Most men would have a time of it if they had to work the way your papa has to. Everybody's breathing down everybody else's backs these days. It's a wonder anything gets done at all."

Nora leaned in a bit. "Speaking of getting things done, I've managed a small bit myself." She produced a small parcel from her pocket and held it out to him. "There's some tea in there. It's not much, but Mama was saying there are days when her only luxury in life is a cup of tea with sugar, and I thought maybe you know someone who might need the same."

He'd almost grown used to choking down the concoction Ma liked to pretend was coffee each morning. And as for what passed for tea, well, it stretched the imagination, that's for sure. "Ma's birthday is this Friday," he said, "and she's been missing a decent cup of tea something fierce. I'll tell her you sent it."

"No, don't," Nora said. "Give it to her from yourself, not from me. A son should be able to give his mother a present on her birthday. If I made that happen, then that's thanks enough for me. Unless you had a gift already planned."

Quinn shrugged, trying to hide the surge of gratitude that was threatening to make him do something silly. "I haven't had a moment to sleep lately, much less scour up a birthday present for Ma. She'll feel like a queen having a real cup of tea with real sugar." He unfolded the handkerchief to see the little cache of tea and sugar. "There's enough here for a regular tea party I suppose."

She laughed. The sound of it fluttered through him like the flocks of birds that swirled around Union Square, perching somewhere just above his heart. "What's the world coming to when four spoonfuls of tea and two lumps of sugar constitute a tea party?"

"Nothing bad. Nothing bad at all." He held her gaze for as long as he dared, which was a lot longer than he ought to have.

After a flustered second, she reached into her pocket to produce another slip of ledger sheet and her pencil. "Well, should we make another list of what's on the post today?" She froze for a moment, as if a thought struck her. "Goodness, who'd have thought?"

"Thought what?"

"Well, now San Francisco has two kinds of 'post'—the kind you send and the kind you tack your needs to. Both are messages. It's really quite witty, when you think about it. Mr. Freeman, there simply is no end to your surprises."

Chapter Nine

You're being a loon, Nora chided herself after making that ridiculous remark about "posts." He must think her the most vapid creature to say such a thing. It wasn't even close to funny, and yet he laughed and smiled as though she'd made charming conversation. He'd made far too much of her tiny gift—surely a handful of tea and some coarse sugar weren't that handsome a present.

But oh, there was something handsome about him today. Yes, handsome was the word, even if she'd never speak it aloud to anyone. There was a confidence in him she'd not seen at Grace House. Something in the surety of his steps, even though his boots looked worse than ever. Mama would say something curt about the glint in his eye, but Nora saw it more as a spark, an energy that was so different than the weary glaze most men wore nowadays. "There's a new one over here," she said, pointing to a bit of shirt collar that had "hammer and nails" written on it with a name scratched alongside.

They went on for a minute or two, Quinn sorting through the messages and she recording what they found. Without ever really discussing it, they'd crafted

a partnership of sorts, and she liked the feeling of cama-
raderie that rose up as they worked their way around the
post. When she helped with the mail wagon, Nora was
always aware of her "assistant" status. Always cogni-
zant that Papa could deem it too dangerous or no longer
necessary and end her involvement there and then. But
here, she was an equal. They worked together, each
contributing important skills to the task.

She heard Quinn's breath catch as he squatted down
to look at a little strip of blue cloth tacked down low
on the far side of the post. "Isn't that the saddest thing
ever?" he said, motioning for her to peer down and
look.

In an unsteady script was the heartbreaking question,
"Can I have a doll again?"

Nora felt a lump in the back of her throat. The little
girl had dared to ask for a doll, but put her request on a
tiny slip at the very bottom of the post as if she hadn't the
right to ask for something so frivolous. But as Quinn's
teeter-totter had proven, sometimes the frivolous things
were the most important for survival. Her locket had
proven that. She raised an eyebrow in silent question,
and he nodded. "I'll take care of this one," she said, not
even needing to write it down.

Quinn squinted at the name. "Edwina Walters. She
had a baby sister. Died three days after the fires. They
had a little funeral, and her mama cried something horrible. Little Edwina just stared all quiet and numb. Broke
your heart to see her blank little face with all those folks
sobbing around her."

Nora ventured a look into Quinn's eyes as they stood
over the brave request, and she saw the same compassion
in his face that welled in her heart. She'd grown too old

for dolls, but she'd ransack every scrap of material in the house tonight to sew up a doll for little Edwina. Even if she had to cut up her own dress to do it.

"I could say a thing or two about simple things that accomplish great feats, Miss Longstreet," he said with a sad smile. "But I'm guessing you already know."

Nora tore the two duplicate lists apart and handed one to Quinn. "I'm learning. I have a gifted teacher, Mr. Freeman."

He took the paper with that thing Mama would call a glint in his eye again. "Is that so?"

"Miss Nora." Nora heard her father's voice call from behind her. He had been watching the two of them. "Best not to dally, your mother will be waiting."

Quinn's quick glance spoke volumes. Did he anticipate their daily meetings as much as she? "You'd better mind your pa," he said. "Everyone will be sorry if you can't come back." Nora was almost certain there was a meaning to the way he said "everyone." She hoped there was. Quinn tipped his hat, that breathtaking smile sweeping across his face, and said goodbye.

Two days later, Nora clutched the handmade doll to her chest as she scanned the rows of shacks for Edwina's. Papa had been called into an important meeting this afternoon, forcing a last-minute schedule change to the mail run, and she'd barely finished Edwina's little doll in time. She'd stayed up half the night sewing the crude doll, finding yarn for hair and embroidering a simple face. It was no masterpiece by any standards, but she was proud of it and prayed it would be sufficient to cheer young Edwina.

Which was, despite the dozens of reasons why she

shouldn't, why Nora found herself not at Grace House as she'd told her mother, but several blocks away, wandering alone into the unofficial camp. She was looking for Edwina's family shelter. As it was well before two, Quinn was not there to meet her. Papa wasn't even sure he'd make a mail run at all today, given this meeting he was attending, so Nora had asked to be driven to Grace House, thinking it would be easy to make it to Dolores Park and back without incident while her father was otherwise occupied. She could have waited until two for Quinn, or try to find him now, but it seemed presumptuous to assume he had nothing better to do with his time than escort her around on missions of mercy. He had devoted a great deal to accompanying her as it was—it would be both improper and inconsiderate to demand yet more.

Then again, it wasn't particularly prudent to be wandering Dolores Park alone, either. Yes, one little girl could easily wait for a doll she didn't even know was coming, but something about this entire process pulled at Nora so strongly that she couldn't rest until Edwina had her doll. And there had to be something behind that sense of urgency, didn't there?

Lord, Nora prayed as she walked down what she hoped was the final aisle, *I believe that urgency is from You. Am I wrong? Is this just me being willful? Please, don't let me regret this kindness. Guide my steps and don't give Papa reason to be angry with my foolishness.* A few minutes later, she found the shelter someone had described. "Hello, I'm looking for Edwina," she called, knocking on the broken shutter that served as an entrance.

"Why?" The sharpness of the male voice from inside

the shack caught Nora off guard. It still astounded her how suspicion had become the order of the day all over the city.

"I...have a gift for her."

A thin old man—too old to be Edwina's father, Nora guessed—slid aside the shutter. He peered suspiciously at Nora. "It ain't Christmas."

"No, it isn't. But I'd still like to give her this." Nora held up the doll. "Is she here?"

The man's countenance softened. "Edwina's asleep over by her cousin's. We put the little ones all together so they can nap. Her daddy's in the work lines and my daughter—her mama—well, she ain't been right since the little one passed."

"I'm sorry about your granddaughter," Nora said. "Edwina put up a little note on the message post that she'd like another doll."

The old man shook his head. "And here I was thinkin' that was just plain foolishness to let her put that up."

Nora held out the doll. "I'm afraid it's not much, but I hope this will do."

His eyes moved from the doll to Nora's face as he took the toy with careful hands. "And who're you?"

Nora shrugged her shoulders. "Just someone who could help. I got back something I lost, so I thought I'd do the same when I saw Edwina's note."

"Edie misses her baby sister," he said wistfully. "This'll help for sure. That's mighty kind of you. Thank you. I bet Edie'll want to thank you, too—how will she find you?"

Nora wasn't sure why, but she liked the idea of staying anonymous. Perhaps some part of her thought the mystery would make the doll's appearance more wondrous for the girl. On impulse, she said, "Do you know Quinn Freeman?"

"Shamus's son? Tall, sandy-haired, built that thing for the young'uns over on the other side of camp?"

"That's him. Tell Edwina she can thank Mr. Freeman if she wants to thank someone. He made the post that let Edwina ask for what she wanted."

He squinted at Nora as the sun pierced the afternoon clouds. He had the appearance of a once-strong man who had fallen on hard times. A weary, unshaven look that hung uncomfortably on his straight frame. "That don't make sense. She ought to thank *you*."

"I don't need it. Perhaps it will help your daughter to know that people care about what's happened to your family. I'm sorry for the terrible loss." Nora felt her hand stray to the locket around her neck. "I lost my cousin. And her mama, my aunt? Well, she hasn't been right since, either. It feels good just to know I helped, you understand?"

The man's face melted into a sad smile. "Well, what do you know? The world ain't entirely shot to pieces, now is it?" He held out a hand, and Nora noticed he was missing half a finger on his right hand. It was a recent wound, still bandaged. "Thank you kindly, miss. Edwina will be right pleased. Like I said, I didn't think it was such a good idea to write that note. When Edie asked her aunt to write it, I tried to stop her. And my daughter just cried and told her no one could care about one little girl's doll in all this disaster." He looked at Nora with such a tender heart that Nora felt as if she'd just received all the gratitude she'd ever need to make a dozen dolls. "I've never been so happy to see my daughter so wrong. I hope it helps the both of them." He managed a wider grin and put his hand on his chest. "Lightens my heart, that's for sure."

Nora nodded toward the wounded hand. "Is your finger healing? Do you need a doctor?"

The grandfather looked down at his bandaged hand and wiggled his fingers. "Me? I need a good steak more than I need a doctor. Who needs all ten fingers anyways? Don't hurt much anymore." It was as if he had transformed in front of her. His face had changed from the harsh man who opened the shutter to a fatherly man who thought it wasn't much to lose a finger. It made Nora wonder how many other people's faces would change with an act of kindness. It had been worth whatever risk she'd taken to be here now, delivering the doll. She wished the man well and smiled broadly as she made her way up the row of shacks out of the park. Despite the long walk, her feet hardly felt the ground.

Until she turned the corner.

She hadn't seen Ollie since the day he'd leered at her in front of Sam's shack, but she recognized him instantly. His eyes had a lazy, sinister quality one didn't easily forget.

"It's the pretty mail lady doin' her bit for charity again." He grinned and looked around them. "Way in here. You sure do get around, missy."

Nora felt her anger rise. She hated to have the satisfaction of her trip undercut by the nasty look in his eyes. "I've no business with you, so I'll thank you to leave me alone." She began walking faster toward the park's edge.

He followed. "But you're such a kindly type. There's *all kinds* of need in here. All kinds." His voice hinted at the kinds no one associated with charity. How foolish she'd been to think it would be all right to go this far into the park alone. She made her feet move as fast as they could. The way Ollie was following, she'd never make it as far as the street. Looking up, however, she spied the teeter-totter that told her Quinn's family's shelter was only a handful of rows away.

"C'mon, miss mail lady, there's no need to rush." He began closing the distance between them.

"Stop it!" Nora broke out into a run despite the tangle of her skirts. "Leave me alone." Praying for protection, she headed straight for the teeter-totter and the knot of children gathered around it, hoping even someone as awful as Ollie wouldn't lay a hand on her in front of children.

"Come on back here and…" Ollie managed to grab one elbow as Nora attempted to turn the corner at a run. She twisted out of his grasp and kept running. Angered, he came after her faster, not caring about the group of shocked young faces who now watched.

Just as they passed Quinn's contraption, Ollie caught her shoulder and tried to spin her around. With dread, Nora felt the chain of her locket tangle up in his fingers and snap off from around her neck. She grasped at it as it sailed through the air to land in the dust a few feet away. Nora lunged for it, ducking out of Ollie's outstretched arm.

"Leave her alone!" Sam's voice came out of the crowd, and running at Ollie full tilt, he knocked the startled man backward a few paces. "You're nothin' but a mean old goat."

Startled, Ollie backed off and let out a string of curses that made Nora wince and one of the younger girls start to cry. Nora was near tears herself, and she scrambled in the dust for the locket she couldn't bear to lose a second time.

"Get out of here. Pa! Danny! Missus Freeman!" Sam began howling a list of adult names in an effort to get one—or all of them—on the scene.

The locket was broken. It had come unhinged in the fall, and the tiny ovals of glass that held the pictures had slipped out. Nora's fingers tried to push the charred photos back in place, but they were too cracked and damaged to stay intact without the glass to hold them together. Annette's image, barely visible as it was, seemed to disintegrate under her touch. "No," Nora sighed, unable to hold back tears of fear and fury. "No, stay together, don't…"

It was useless. The photo crumbled into tiny black flakes that scattered into the dust at her skirts. Her last image of Annette, her locket photograph, was gone.

"Oliver McDonough, ye nasty excuse for a man, so help me if you don't get out of here this very minute…" Mrs. Freeman's sharp brogue cut through the gaggle of children's voices.

Nora felt the woman's strong hand on her shoulder as she bent down. "Miss Longstreet? Is that you? Did Ollie touch you? Hurt you in any way?"

Nora could barely even think about what Ollie had done in the heartache of losing Annette's image. The broken locket hurt much worse than any bruise Ollie had left by grabbing her. "I'm not hurt," she said as the tears overcame her. "He grabbed me and it…broke the locket." A small breeze stirred up the dust, setting the flakes flying and setting a panic in Nora's heart. It was somehow like losing Annette all over again. Desperately, she grasped at the tiny charred pieces before the wind took them forever, but it was impossible to do. "No," she cried, feeling helpless and foolish and startlingly wounded.

"Come now, hon, let's get you up." Mrs. Freeman crouched down beside Nora and took her by both shoulders. "There's nothing to be done about your bauble now." Nora let herself be pulled up, even though she felt as if she couldn't stand on her own. All the previous joy was gone—and then some, for she felt worse than ever to have lost the locket a second time. "You've gotten your fine dress all dirty now, but you don't look hurt. Ollie's a brute. Let's get you inside, Nora, dear. I just happen to have the makings of a cup of tea, and I think we both could use one."

The generosity—especially knowing Mrs. Freeman's fondness for tea and the scarcity of it—made everything worse. "Oh, no," Nora cried, the tears still coming down despite her efforts to stop them, "you couldn't use your birthday tea for this."

Mrs. Freeman stopped for a moment and looked at Nora before she pulled open the flap of leather that served as a door and steered Nora to the one chair inside. "And how is it that you know about my birthday tea, missy?" Her tone wasn't a suspicious inquisition, it was more of an amused curiosity. She began gathering things for tea, only taking her eyes off Nora for a few seconds here and there.

"Your son told me." Nora had to choose her words carefully for she didn't want Mrs. Freeman to know the tea had come from her. "He was delighted to find some tea to give you." The tears ebbed, giving way to a huge, shuddering sigh as Nora felt the panic subside. She brushed the worst of the dirt off her skirts—she would have some explaining to do when she got home. "He told me how much you loved tea and missed it."

Having sent Sam off to fetch hot water from a common fire pit down the way, Mrs. Freeman hunched down to assess Nora's condition with a mother's experienced eye. "You'll have a bruise where that knee hit, but I think that's the worst of it. On the outside, that is. Ollie get fresh with you, did he? He's all bark and no bite that one, but he can surely bark. He was no good before the earthquake, and now he seems to have plenty of chances to show us what a louse he can be." She pulled a cloth from her pocket. "Here, love, wipe your face. You've had a good scare, but thank the Lord it's no more than that."

It was much more than that, but Nora thought if she tried to explain she'd only end up flooding the shack with tears. And these people had endured losses so much worse than hers. It felt selfish to go to pieces over, as Mrs. Freeman put it, "a bauble."

Sam returned, and as Mrs. Freeman tended to her teapot, Nora wiped her face and then used the cloth to wipe the dust from the remains of the locket. It lay open and empty on her lap, as forlorn a sight as she'd ever seen. Both photos gone, glass gone, chain broken; it made her want to start crying all over again. Mrs. Freeman came back in, "I'll just tell Sam to run and get…" She stopped and looked around the shelter, one hand flying to her chest. "Mercy! Where's Sam? He was just here a second ago…*Sam!*" She pushed her head out of the shack and called "Where'd ya go, lad? Oh!" Nora couldn't see whatever it was that Mrs. Freeman saw, only watch her spine stiffen with the sight—whatever it was. "Glory! What happened to you?"

Chapter Ten

Quinn ducked into the shack a moment later, Sam ahead of him. Quinn's right hand was bruised and bloodied. He ignored his mother, heading straight to squat down in front of Nora. "Are you hurt, Miss Longstreet?"

Sam tugged on Mrs. Freeman's skirts. "Ollie sure is."

Mrs. Freeman rolled her eyes. "Oh, son, you didn't."

Nora felt Quinn's eyes lock on to hers. "Did he hurt you in any way?" he said angrily. "Any way at all?"

"He knocked me down, that's all." She tried to sound as calm as possible.

Quinn's intensity eased—until he saw the locket that lay broken in her hands. He returned his gaze to her eyes, and his simmering anger deepened into a look that held more sorrow and understanding than Nora thought her heart could hold. He, of all people, knew the significance of that "bauble." He seemed to know it was an almost unspeakable pain for her, for while he saw her own heartbreak reflected in the golden brown of his eyes, he said nothing. Were they alone, Nora felt she would have flung herself into his arms and cried for hours.

"Sam fetched more than water just now, did he? So you went and found Ollie," Mrs. Freeman said with an exasperated air. "And you let your fist say a thing or two on the matter?" She shook her head as she rummaged through that enormous trunk of hers for yet more bandages.

Quinn stood up. "Surely you didn't expect me to stand there and wag a finger at him. He had it coming, Ma. He's had it coming for a while."

"Oh, and that's *just* what we need in these parts," Mrs. Freeman scolded, "Grown men beating each other up in front of young lads."

"He had it comin'," Sam piped up, sticking his brave little chin out. "No one gets to hurt Miss Nora."

Mrs. Freeman leveled a "now look what you've gone and done" glare at her son and showed him precious little mercy with the stinging iodine. Quinn only sucked in a great deal of air between his teeth, winced and glared right back. "Ouch, Ma."

"I hope it stings 'til Sunday, ye great oaf." Anger thickened her brogue. Nora had to give Mrs. Freeman credit; Quinn had almost a foot on her, yet she held her ground fiercely. Of course, she had a bottle of nasty iodine to back her up, but Nora doubted that tipped the scales much.

"Are you badly hurt, Mr. Freeman?" Nora asked, mostly to change the subject. He'd defended her. Brutally, yes, but with such a ferocious loyalty that she felt it lodge deep in her chest and stay there. What a powerful thing it was to know he'd roared out as her champion like that.

"I'll be fine," Quinn said, flexing his fingers. From the look of things, his bleeding knuckles stung fiercely. "I only hit him twice." He looked up at Nora, the slightest hint of a smirk tugging at one corner of his mouth. "He deserved more."

"Enough in front of the lad," Mrs. Freeman said over her son's shoulder in a low monotone threat. "Now," she planted her hands on her hips, "this was hardly the tea party I had in mind, but since you're all here, have a cup and then we'll get Miss Longstreet back to her father before yet another man loses his temper in this place."

"I don't know who'll be more angry—your papa or my ma," Quinn said as he accompanied Nora on the long walk to her Lafayette Park home after tea. It had been the most ridiculous "tea party" in history—Ma seething and him all stinging and bandaged up so he could hardly hold the cup and Sam chattering and Nora so quiet. Quinn couldn't get out of there fast enough. Not to mention his insistent desire to steal a few moments alone with poor Nora so they could talk about the locket. Every time he thought about what Ollie had done, the urge to go find that snake and pummel him again surged up within him. Major Simon was right—his impulsive nature would lead him to trouble again and again. And trouble—even the righteous kind—was still trouble. He'd be no good to anyone locked up for brawling.

Nora nodded toward Quinn's hand. With his knuckles wrapped up just below the bandage still on his forearm from Major Simon's "lesson," his right hand was looking mighty worse for wear. "Perhaps Ollie is the most mad. It would certainly feel better to think he is."

"Whatever made you think it'd be wise to find Edwina

on your own? I'd have come if you asked—you know that. I *should've* come—and you know that, too."

Nora looked up at him with a tender smile. "Oh, and you've nothing to attend to all day but my whims? I've no right to ask you to be at my beck and call."

She had every right, but Quinn wasn't sure that was a safe thing to say.

Nora fussed with the dark smudge of dirt on her skirt. "It was a foolish thing to do, I know. But I couldn't seem to stop myself. I just kept thinking of poor Edwina. It was like I was choking on her wish until I could get that doll to her." She looked up at Quinn again. "And I met her grandfather. If you could have seen the way he changed—the way he literally changed in front of me when I told him why I was there. I felt like I was doing just what God wanted me to be doing. At just the moment He wanted me doing it. I don't know that I can explain it any other way. When I was walking back home, it was like I was walking on air."

He knew that feeling. He'd felt it walking back from his "delivery," wide-awake and deliriously satisfied even though it was two o'clock in the morning. He'd felt it as he drove that message post into the ground, full of energy even though it was blazing hot and he ought to have been exhausted. Reverend Bauers quoted that scripture about "soaring on eagle's wings," when he talked about feelings like that, and although Quinn found the description rather fussy, it did fit.

"'Til Ollie knocked you right off that air. I'm sorry that happened. Seems a double sin to take away someone's joy like that."

Nora's hand went to her throat, as it had done so many times since he'd given her the locket, and found only her neckline. "It feels awful to have lost her again like that. I know it's silly but it…hurts so much."

Her voice trembled again, cutting through Quinn. Without thinking, or perhaps it was more precise to say without caring, Quinn reached out and took her hand. He had intended it to be a light, momentary touch, but when she settled her hand into his he felt it ignite his heart.

"I'm going to fix that locket, just like I said. And mind you, don't go off like that without me again," he said. He hoped his voice didn't betray the storm going off inside him, but from the look on her face he knew it had. "We have to be careful," he felt compelled to add, meaning more than just her traveling safety. He was going to have to be very careful about her. She could drive him to impulses that were miles beyond unwise.

She pulled her hand from his, but gave it a squeeze before she did. "I know." He watched her run one hand across the other, and he knew her hand tingled the way his currently did. She did feel something. He knew he couldn't be the only one. There was too much between them to miss it.

There was *so much* between them. When they crossed Market Street, Quinn had the uncomfortable feeling that they'd shifted from his world to hers. Funny how life had made him feel like a trespasser in parts of his own city.

She felt it, too, for her steps became more determined. "Papa gave me a speech yesterday." She crossed her arms over her chest. "He went on about how the world wasn't the same anymore and how I ought to be sensible."

Quinn tucked his hand in his pocket. "I've never been one much for sensible myself. But he's your pa, that's his job." As they started up the hill toward the nicer part of town, Quinn tried to make a mental list of all the reasons he shouldn't be sweet on Nora Longstreet. He failed.

They walked on in a companionable silence for several blocks, looking up once or twice to catch each other's eye and offer a smile. More than once he had to stop himself from reaching out and taking her hand again. Impulsive as he was, he knew that would invite a host of trouble out here in her world.

A block before her house, Nora stopped and drew herself up straight. "Despite what happened today, I don't want to stop at Edwina. I don't think I'm *supposed* to stop at Edwina. I think there are more of these requests I can fill, but I don't know how it's all going to work just yet. I just know it's got to, and I suppose the 'how' will have to be God's problem."

Quinn thought he could not find her more endearing. Before today he would not have said something like tender bravery could exist, but it stood before him, her unsteady smile stealing his affections. "Well, then, you leave me no choice. I've got to help. I'm good with impossible problems. So consider me your partner."

"How?"

"Well, like you said, the 'how' may just have to be God's problem."

Her gaze held his eyes. "That would mean I am your partner as well, Mr. Freeman."

It was a step too far. It was not at all the proper thing to say, but none of that mattered. "My partners call me Quinn." Suddenly, it was the most important thing in the world to hear her say his name.

The smile on her face reached up into the violet

depths of her eyes. "Quinn. But very quietly and when no one else is around."

"It'll do." It would, but probably not for long.

Quinn thumped the list of requests he'd written down over the last day onto the table in front of Major Simon. "How many of these can you get?"

Simon peered at the list. "Are these from that post in Dolores Park? The one you put up?"

"It started with just messages, but then people began posting the things they need. It's perfect. They know I built the post, but they don't realize they're telling *me* what they need."

"Unless they watch you taking down notes every day," Simon cautioned.

"I make sure no one sees me take things down."

"You better be."

Quinn nodded impatiently toward the pile. "So tell me how much of this we can get."

"After you tell me how you got *that?*" He pointed to the bandage covering Quinn's knuckles.

Quinn told as fast a version of the story of Ollie and Nora as he could manage. "He deserved more. Mad as I was, he's lucky I stopped at two."

Simon let out a chuckle. "You should have stopped at one. Or none at all." The major planted his hands on the table between them. "Freeman, there are better ways to deal with louts like that. Think before you act. Rein in your impulses or you'll be no good to anyone."

Quinn scooped up the list in frustration, stuffing it back in his pocket with a loud grunt. "I'm in no mood to improve my character while things get much worse out there."

The major crossed his arms over his chest. "So get out your sword."

Quinn said nothing, just gave Simon the darkest look he could manage.

"Fight me now, while you're good and angry." With that, the major picked up a sword and readied his stance. He was so annoyingly calm and careful. Quinn wanted to take his sword and slash something to pieces—preferably the major's crisp, clean jacket laying across the back of a chair in the corner of the room. A warm coat had been one of the things on those notes—San Francisco's night winds could be freezing, even in July. Did fine, upstanding Major Simon even know what it was like to need a coat? To be so cold you thought you couldn't ever be warm again or so hot you thought you'd drop over? Quinn snapped open the box that held his swords.

"See if you can channel that anger. Make it a focus instead of a distraction. Fight smart, Quinn, not hard. *En garde!*"

Quinn took a set of lunges at the major, but Simon blocked his thrusts as easily as if he'd known which blows were coming when. "You're an imaginative sort, don't be so obvious."

Simon pointed the tip of his sword directly at Quinn's neck. "Stop," he said in a commanding tone. "Take a breath and look at me. Think about what I'm expecting, and then plan the opposite. Plan. Don't react, Freeman, *plan.*"

Quinn took a deep breath, willing the anger to settle down into something closer to resolve. He started off by moving toward the side but ducked around at the last minute to land a blow so hard to Major Simon's chest that it knocked him to the ground. The satisfaction of a calculated victory sung through his veins. He pulled off his glove to help the major up, only to find his knuckles and other wounds bleeding from the force of the blow he'd just struck. Smiling, he offered his left hand to the major, who took it with an equal grin.

"I haven't been knocked off my feet in five years. My only mistake, it seems, was to underestimate how fast you learn."

They went through several other lessons, the hour passing by so swiftly that it seemed neither of them had a moment to catch their breath. Wiping his brow, Major Simon snapped his pocket watch shut and pointed to Quinn's pocket. "Shall we have a look at that list again?"

Quinn put the list back on the table. His hand was still bleeding, and a corner of the list had a swath of blood across one side. "Go tend to that," the major said. "I'll look through these and see what I can do."

As he walked over to the side table and wet a handkerchief, Quinn hid his smile. "And not just that list. Anything and everything will help," Quinn offered. "If you've got it, I can find someone who needs it."

"You know a great deal of people, Mr. Freeman, of the good and the bad variety it seems. Miss Longstreet should be grateful for such a champion." Simon looked up and caught Quinn's eye with those last words.

"Ollie had no right to trouble her like that." Quinn tried to keep any hint of his affections for Nora out of his voice. "Or any other lady just trying to help," he added for good measure.

"Seems to me Miss Longstreet should well know the dangers of wandering around Dolores Park unescorted. It was a foolish thing to do."

"Some might say helping out a stranger is always a foolish thing to do, Major Simon. I'm fixing to do something mighty foolish, but you're fixing to help anyways, aren't you?"

Simon laughed. "You've a future in politics. You lack eloquence, but you've all the other tricks required. Still, I would advise Miss Longstreet to be more prudent in her efforts. I'll not say anything when I'm at dinner tomorrow night. As you seem to be friends, I hope you'll impress upon her to show more caution when you're not around to save the day."

Quinn evidently showed more shock than he would have liked, for the major nodded to his unspoken question.

"I've been invited to dinner at the Longstreet home tomorrow night. Mr. Longstreet seems intent on getting Miss Nora more involved in the ministries at Grace House and invited the reverend to dine. Bauers and I had a dinner planned, so he very kindly secured me an invitation as well. I must say I'm looking forward to it. Eugene Longstreet has quite the earthquake tale to tell, I hear, and I'd hardly object to a better acquaintance with Miss Nora. Can't say I wouldn't wallop a brute or two in her defense myself, Freeman. She's a fine woman, don't you think?"

Quinn said nothing and pretended to busy himself with the details of cleaning his cuts. He bristled at the idea of Simon having such access to Nora when he had to limit his visits to her the way he did.

When he turned his attention back to the table, Simon had written all over the list. "These," he said, pointing to circled items, "I can have ready for you tonight. I'll leave them in the same place. Make sure you come well after midnight or there'll be too many men rummaging around. These," he went on, pointing to ones with check marks, "may take a little doing. I may have one or two of them tonight, but the rest will take a few days at least. And these—" he pointed to three or four with dashes in front of them "—are near impossible. Be less bold Quinn. I'd hate to see 'shoot the messenger' come into play here."

Chapter Eleven

The evening reminded everyone that summer in San Francisco could feel far too much like winter by kicking up a stiff breeze and a good, heavy fog. *No one should shiver in July,* Quinn complained toward Heaven, flattening himself against one of the fort's walls as he waited for the last of a group to pass. Shaking off the cold, he reminded himself that one of the items he'd be delivering tonight was a blanket for a child.

The men walked into another building, the wedge of light that had spilled out into the alley disappearing behind the shut door. Quinn counted to twenty-five, just to be safe, then slipped in through the hatchway Major Simon had shown him. Following the instructions Reverend Bauers had passed down from his time working as the Bandit's accomplice, Quinn tied a dark bandanna over his sandy hair with a dark hat to obscure his face. He wore one of the Bandit's dark shirts, along with the many-pocketed trousers and the black boots left to him in the Bandit's chest. It felt ungrateful to cut off the tops of the boots, but they were too high for Quinn's liking and the silver *B*'s imbedded in the calf had a nasty habit of catching the light. They were about half a size too small, but since they lacked holes in the soles, they were still better than his everyday shoes by a mile.

Not that crawling on his hands and knees through a musty tunnel that led to the hidden spot where Simon left his "booty" was particularly heroic, but he doubted the shivering little boy would care how his blanket got delivered.

Quietly, Quinn loaded the items into his pack—a large drawstring contraption he'd devised out of an army duffel he'd darkened with ink and hot water. Slung over one shoulder, it held a lot—even bulkier things like tins of meat and such—but still gave him mobility. This time the pack was stuffed so full he had to pull it along behind him in the tunnel, making for an especially clumsy and undashing exit. No riding off into the sunset for this messenger—Quinn felt he'd spend most of his heroic efforts creeping in and out of shadows. Still, this messenger could creep mighty fast, and the entire trip into and back out of the hiding spot was accomplished in less than a quarter of an hour. Now for the more adventurous task of getting his goods into Dolores Park without notice.

All was going well until the last two blocks, when Quinn ran into a loud, drunken fellow brandishing a bottle in one hand and a gun in the other. Quinn made the mistake of thinking the fellow too far gone into his liquor to be very observant, but the man wheeled around as Quinn snuck behind him, waving the gun entirely too close to Quinn's head.

"Who're you? And what'cha got there, mister?"

"Laundry," improvised Quinn, lowering his voice.

"You're clackin'. Laundry don't clack." The man

narrowed an unsteady eye at Quinn. "You've got food in there, don't you?"

Technically, Quinn was redirecting relief supplies, but he hardly thought this was the kind of man to quibble over semantics. "Nah," he said, trying to casually walk on his way.

The fellow would have none of it. "You ain't got laundry in there, so I says you've got food. Or something else worth hiding." He cocked the gun. "How dumb do you think I am?"

"I got no opinion." Quinn held up one hand congenially while the other slipped to the knife tucked in an outside pocket he'd rigged into the sack. "I just want to get on my way."

The man gestured toward the sack with the point of his gun. "And what if I says no?"

Quinn drawled out his speech to match the southern twang of his opponent. "I ain't got no argument with you. I'll just be going."

"And I says *no*," the man growled, even as he stumbled a bit. Quinn considered that even a skilled swordsman couldn't best a drunk with a loaded gun. A fight was definitely not in his interest. Even if the scuffle didn't draw blood—which was a big if—it'd most definitely draw attention.

When the man clicked the hammer back on his gun, Quinn ran out of options. Drawing the knife, he flashed it towards the man's face, hoping to startle him just long enough to knock the gun out of his grasp. The man was big and quick, however, despite the drenching of alcohol, and things dissolved quickly into a dangerous tussle of arms, elbows, punches, and grunts. Quinn, weighted down by the pack, was seriously handicapped. After what seemed like hours but was probably only half a minute, Quinn managed to bring the heel of his boot down on the man's shin. In the handful of seconds the brute doubled over, Quinn ducked out of his grasp and set off running.

He'd gotten perhaps twenty paces when the heart-stopping sound of gunfire exploded through the alley. Quinn tripped as a hot sting tore in his left side, accompanied by a desperate whizzing sound. I'm shot, he thought with a clarity too sharp for panic. *Lord Jesus, save me, I'm shot.* He forced in a deep breath, discovered his lungs still worked, and set off at a stumbling run toward the darker part of the alley away from the shouts gathering behind him. He'd always imagined getting shot would hurt worse, always pictured it as an instant blackness stealing his life. Yet, he could still run, still breathe. Grasping his side as he willed himself to put one foot in front of the other, he reached toward the source of the stinging pain. Quinn's fingers discovered a gaping, singed rip in his shirt but surprising little wetness. Still running, still surprised that each breath came and kept coming, he pulled his hand up in front of his face, bracing himself for a bloody sight. A small amount of blood stained his fingers, even though his side stung worse than a gallon of iodine. Had he been only grazed? Had he indeed been graced by that providence Reverend Bauers never called "luck"?

After a minute or two of more running, Quinn ducked into a dark doorway and waited for his pulse to stop slamming through his chest. You are breathing, you are alive, he found he had to tell himself over and over. He'd heard of men who never felt their mortal wounds—whose bodies numbed themselves as the blood drained out. He looked back down the alley, scanning the bricks for a trail of blood. There was nothing. Quinn looked back down at his shirt and felt his side—which still bled a small amount—but nothing indicated the fatal shot he feared. He had, in fact, been grazed. Another handful of inches to the right, and he'd be lying in a heap in some corner of the city. It seemed bizarre to him to live through yet another close call. Perhaps it wasn't so far-fetched an idea that God was saving him for a special purpose. *If I were a cat,* Quinn thought dryly, *I'd only have seven lives left. Maybe six.*

The sobering thought of his survival just made Quinn's resolve that much stronger. It felt just like when he was dueling Major Simon. He could take the fear or the anger and force it into focus, channel it into an energy that strengthened his skills rather than detracted from them. *If I'm supposed to live,* he reasoned, *then I'd better do something good with that life.*

In all the chaos, he'd managed to keep hold of the sack of goods that had been headed for camp. A quick peek inside showed that while surely jostled, the contents hadn't been harmed. If he could calm himself enough to stay smart, there was no reason not to continue his mission. In fact, Quinn had new incentives to get these goods to the folks who needed them.

With quick steps, a long prayer and several deep breaths, Quinn set out toward Dolores Park.

Mama and Aunt Julia were simply delighted to be playing the role of hostesses. Although no match for their previous dinner parties, it still felt extravagant and celebratory. Nora was pleased to see Reverend Bauers again, even though she'd long since suspected her father's agenda for the evening. Papa and Mama had both made it abundantly clear that they much preferred Nora restrict her charity to the much safer confines of Grace House. Papa hadn't gone so far as to stop Nora's mail cart visits, but he was close. Of course, if Mama or Papa ever knew the full details of her scrape with Ollie, things would be much worse. Which made Nora wonder: how much worse would things get if they knew the way her heart jumped when Quinn took her hand? When she discovered Major Simon—proper, eligible and appropriate Major Simon—had been invited, Nora began to wonder if she hadn't hid her feelings as well as she thought.

"Oh, you look lovely." Mama smoothed a wayward lock of hair as Nora came down the stairs. "How good it feels to have guests on the way. It's such a simple dinner, one I'd be embarrassed to serve back…before…but still it is a pleasure just to set a decent table again."

"Major Simon is accustomed to army rations," Papa reasoned, "I'm sure he'll appreciate whatever you set before him. And Reverend Bauers's ample middle tells me the man simply likes to eat, so you've no worries about your meal. I admit," he sighed, letting Mama straighten his tie, "it is refreshing to do something simply for the pleasure of it again."

When the approach of the visitors was announced, Nora went to the front window to find a most amusing scene—Major Simon in full uniform, next to a humbly dressed Reverend Bauers on the bench of a dilapidated cart.

"Good evening and good welcome!" Uncle Lawrence greeted. "It feels wonderful to open our doors to guests."

Nora asked as many questions as she could devise about the ministries at Grace House. Not only did it provide for an entertaining conversation—for the reverend was always quick with an amusing or poignant story—but it pleased Mama and Papa. Still, for every story Bauers told about God meeting needs at Grace House, Nora recalled four similar notes up on the post. She admired Reverend Bauers, but to her his work didn't convey the affirming connection that she felt to the struggling residents of Dolores Park.

That she felt while with Quinn.

"I hear you are as brave as the good reverend in many respects," came the major's voice, pulling her from her thoughts as Reverend Bauers finished up yet another story of derring-do in the name of Christian charity. It came as no surprise that Nora found herself seated next to the major. "Tell me," he inquired, "do you think the Good Lord sends such adventures to Bauers, or does he simply go looking for them? I find I can't decide."

Nora had to chuckle, for in truth, she'd wondered the same herself. "God does seem to indulge his appetite for the unusual. He's only begun to tell me of his missionary adventures, and already he's described so many exotic places."

"The way I hear it, one does not have to travel far with Reverend Bauers to find adventure. Did you know he claims to have been an accomplice of the famous Black Bandit?"

"I had not heard that, for I've only just met him, but I must say it doesn't come as much of a surprise. He is very resourceful and not at all...shall we say... conventional?"

Now it was Simon's turn to laugh. "Not at all

conventional. I like that. Mind if I borrow your astute description?"

"After calling me both brave and astute, how could I refuse?"

He looked at Nora for a long moment. "You shouldn't." Up until tonight, Nora had seen the major's interest in her family as being purely the product of her father's position. They were, after all, partners in the logistical quagmire that getting goods in and out of San Francisco had become. And she had assumed that tonight's invitation had been at her father's instigation. Now, aware of the major's gaze, Nora began to suspect Simon had done a little instigation of his own. He was considerably older than her, but he possessed many of the qualities Mama would find "appropriate" if not downright "desirable" in a suitor. He was very formal—almost stiff— but managed an agreeable smile now and then. He was a steady, stable fellow, not dashing or charming, but friendly enough. He was fit but stocky, a barrel-chested, solid build that spoke of more strength than grace. Had the events of the last months not happened, Nora would probably have been open to the major's attentions.

The trouble was, the events of the last months *had* happened, and none of the ways in which Nora measured life—and men—survived the upheaval. Nothing in the major's interest ignited that deep, highly charged captivation every thought of Quinn produced.

Quinn. She used his first name with startling ease. Her mind played back to the power in the way he walked. The effortless grace of the way he moved, the corded muscles of his arms that showed when he rolled his sleeves up to work. He was an exceedingly handsome man, Quinn. She did not even know Major Simon's first name.

"What do you know of this post set up in Dolores Park?" Simon asked her, pulling her yet again from her distraction. Did he think her flighty, that he had to keep fetching back her attention? If he did, it didn't show in his eyes.

"It is the most amazing thing, Major. Brilliant, when you think of it. At first it was only to serve as a message board of sorts..."

"Like the fountain downtown," he said.

"Yes, but then someone posted a need—something small, I think, like nails, and someone saw that need and filled it. When all you see is need all around you, it's such a powerful thing to see a need being met."

"Hope is a very powerful weapon, Miss Longstreet. Even the army has nothing to match it."

He actually seemed to understand what she saw in the post. "I think hope may be the very best weapon we have."

"I'm sure Bauers would agree with you there. Even the army could take a few lessons in the hope-wielding department from him. We're good with logistics, and the whole business of keeping order, but we need some help in the morale department now and then."

Everyone simply expected the army to sweep in and take charge. Yet, it had to be frustrating and difficult for them as well—no one thought about that. They were, after all, men far from home living amid such destruction for months on end. "Has it been overwhelming?" she asked, turning toward him. "All the wreckage and supervision and sheer enormity of it all?"

His brow furrowed. "My men are exhausted. Some days I am astounded at what we are able to do. Other days, I find myself having trouble believing it will ever be enough. I've served several places, and this is by far the most devastation I've ever encountered. Were it not for the kindness of San Francisco's good people, I would surely lose heart." His smile hinted that perhaps he meant it in a more particular way than the mass support of the city's people.

"*Everyone* is grateful for what you do." It was better to keep such conversations out of particulars.

"Actually, some are decidedly ungrateful. But that is not a story for a young lady's ears. Tonight should be about hope and other pleasant things." With that, the major stood and offered a most eloquent toast to Nora's father, to Reverend Bauers, and the "many hopes for a pleasant future."

Mama looked pleased indeed.

Chapter Twelve

Quinn showed up early for the mail cart, taking his place across the street long before anyone else gathered. He told himself that it was to discreetly take down requests from today's messages at the post, to see if word of last night's deliveries had traveled around camp, but it wasn't that. Those things were necessary reasons to be there ahead of time, but Quinn's eagerness had far more to do with Nora's recent dining companion than any missions of mercy.

It irked him to think of Major Simon enjoying all the pleasantries of dinner with the Longstreets. Not that fine dining was ever a part of his life, but just to think of her chatting and laughing with Simon over dinner made him lose his own appetite. His imagination toyed mercilessly with him all evening. No doubt Mr. Longstreet offered Simon encouraging smiles instead of the stern glares he reserved for Quinn. How instantly, violently jealous Quinn was of the major's ability to waltz through the Longstreets' front door invited; his own appearance at that door would hardly meet with such a welcome. Simon had access to a world Quinn had never cared much about before. Now, Quinn felt his exclusion from it all too keenly.

Still, he knew that's not how Nora saw it. She saw *him*, his worth, his abilities. Not his status or his education or what he knew folks of that sort would call "prospects." In a perfect world, that'd be all the connection they'd need. Pity that these days, San Francisco was about as far from a perfect world as a soul could get.

And then again, were it not for the quake and all the destruction, would they have met at all? Could he be thankful for that course of events despite all everyone had lost? Reverend Bauers would probably have some wise remark about God turning evil to good, or as he put it, "turning the world upside down." He must be right, for Quinn could find no other explanation for his recent ability to feel on top of the world and at the bottom of it at the same time. "Upside down" surely was a good description of how he felt.

He felt a whole host of other things as the cart rolled into view, even though he caught a heavy exchange of glances between Nora and her father as they arrived. He hadn't seen her since the incident with that louse Ollie, and he worried that Mr. Longstreet would banish her from the mail run once he knew. Admittedly, things looked strained between Nora and her father, and it was clear her presence wasn't sitting well with Mr. Longstreet, but she'd either hidden the worst of what happened or managed to convince her father not to let it stop her from helping. Either way, Quinn found himself breathing out a relieved prayer of thanksgiving when the cart pulled to a stop and she caught his eye.

He squeezed his hand more tightly around the small object in his pocket. He was glad he had it to give to her today, even if it served his own selfish motives. Too wound up from the events of last night's close call, he'd spent the time he should have been sleeping managing the promised repairs to the tiny locket. And, in an act even his own mother would have called hopelessly romantic, he'd found a pair of tiny blue flowers and pressed them to fit where the photos had been. The locket looked so sad emptied of its images that he had to do *something*. At least it felt less foolish to think of it that way.

"You look worn-out today," Nora said when he finally crossed the street. "Was the weather awful last night?"

He slept in a shack. She slept in a house. Everything felt like a reminder of their different worlds. "I'll be fine." He changed the subject. "Edwina was running around the camp showing off her doll yesterday. You'd think the thing came from the finest store in the city to hear her tell it. I haven't seen a face that happy since... well, quite a spell."

"She liked it then?" Nora fairly beamed despite her efforts to keep her speech casual.

"She loved it. And why is it, by the way, that she came straight to me?" He scratched his head, mocking deep thought. "I can't recall making any dolls."

Nora reached to accept a sack-wrapped package from a family waiting beside them. "Ah," she said after the family had left, "but *you* made the message post. And no request for a doll could have been made without a certain post." She nodded at him. "So the credit belongs to you."

Quinn shook his head. "That note could have stayed there a hundred days and never gotten an answer if it weren't for a pretty lady with a very big heart. *You* made her happy."

"That's nice to hear. It makes it easier to forget about what happened…afterward."

It was as if a cloud passed right over her face—the glow left that quickly and that completely. It made Quinn want to go after Ollie again this very minute. "I can do better than that," he said, reaching into his pocket. For a moment he was ashamed of the coarse piece of string that held the locket instead of the fine chain that had broken, but the look on her face wiped that away. "It's not perfect, but it'll close now like before."

She took it with delight. Without his prompting, she somehow knew to open it, and he could tell when she caught sight of the two tiny flowers. If he'd been afraid that she'd find the arrangement crude—the flattened blooms were held in place with a tiny crisscross of wires because there was no way to replace the glass— he was wrong. The wonder in her eyes sunk deep into his heart.

Again, neither one of them seemed to have words big enough to fit the moment. A whole host of things passed between them in a silent exchange. She knew how he felt. He knew he had no reason to be jealous of Major Simon's access. He'd just gained an access of his own that no one could ever take away from him. While it made no sense and it offered no prospects and only a fool's chance of going any further, Quinn felt as if he'd gained the world in the space of seconds. God had given him the chance to give her some happiness, to restore the tiniest sliver of her world to rights, and it felt better inside his chest than the dozens of shiny medals Major Simon boasted on his.

"Mr. Freeman," she managed, and he wondered if anyone else could hear the tears lingering on the edge of her voice, "how is it you are always managing the most astounding things with lockets?"

"I'm clever that way." It delighted him to twist her words back on themselves.

"You are, indeed. And most kind." She looked as if she would have said a dozen other things if they were alone, and that hummed in his chest. "Whatever should I do without you?"

He managed a wink, sure he would overstep his bounds if he stayed a moment longer. He was dead tired, and she looked so breathtakingly beautiful. "Don't find out."

Tipping his hat, Quinn whistled as he walked back across the street, pretty sure his world had turned upside down yet again and not minding one bit.

"A gun?"

Quinn held up the shirt with the singed stripe just to the left of where his heart ought to be. It was only the grace of God, Quinn thought, that his heart was still around to keep beating. "I'm thankful to be alive this afternoon." He briefly recounted the details of his scrape the other night.

"Most of San Francisco could say they are grateful to be alive, Freeman."

"I'm telling you, that was too close a call. You said it yourself, I'm of no help to anyone if I'm dead." He pointed to the swords. "If these are all I've got to work with, it won't take long."

The major looked at him with an expression Quinn

couldn't quite read. "The Bandit didn't carry a gun that I know of."

"I'm not the Bandit." It was as if the concept, which had been vaguely bumping around in his head for days, had finally crystalized into clear thought. Quinn knew, somehow, that he wasn't going to be a second Bandit. A sort of bone-deep instinct that the Bandit wasn't what God had in mind. What God did have in mind, Quinn couldn't say. He'd be something else, he just didn't know what quite yet. In truth, he didn't like not knowing. Having only an insistent discomfort with the idea of stepping into the Bandit's boots wasn't nearly enough to go on. Certainly not enough to get killed over. He would rather God send a thunderbolt of clear suggestion down on him—and soon.

"I can't say I'm that surprised you want to be armed." He motioned to the swords. "These are fine weapons, but you're right—they won't be enough to accomplish your, shall we say, *unique* objective."

"So you agree?" Quinn suspected the major would object to arming him. Before last night, he'd have done his best to steer clear of adding a pistol to his weapons. But last night had been a harsh awakening. If armed assailants could take his cache, then he needed to be the right kind of man to stop them. To defend himself. "I want to stay alive, not to blast around the city taking down anyone in my way. I want to be able to shoot someone in the foot or leg. To wound him but not kill him. I want you to train me."

"I will. But as far as I'm concerned, you had to ask the right way first. I wasn't about to hand you a gun so you could…how'd you put it? 'Blast around the city taking down everyone in your way'? I make it a policy never to arm an impulsive man." Major Simon went to a shelf and flipped open the lid of a box to reveal a silver-colored Colt .45 pistol. "Here, take a look."

It wasn't that Quinn had never seen a gun before. It was just that it was a very sobering sensation to be looking at *his* gun. He glanced up at Simon, hoping he didn't look as taken aback as he felt.

"That's good," Simon remarked in low tones. "Honestly, I'd have worried if you snatched it up."

Slowly, Quinn lifted the firearm from its place in the box. He expected it to feel foreign and foreboding in his hand. Quinn flexed his fingers in a half dozen different configurations until they settled themselves around the handle.

"You know, it is easier to be careful with a gun than with something so dramatic as a sword. But a man has to come to that conclusion on his own."

Quinn eyed Simon, not quite sure what to make of such a remark.

"Can you shoot? Have you ever shot a gun?"

For a moment, Quinn second-guessed his impulse to tell the truth. He'd never needed one. He'd managed just fine by out-thinking anyone looking to harm him. "I know how."

"It's not that hard a concept. But knowing and doing are a mile apart. "Let's go outside to the firing range and find out just how clever a messenger you can be."

"I can't explain it," Quinn admitted as he put his shirt back on that evening after Reverend Bauers had mended both shirt and side. He'd come to Grace House not only because he couldn't safely explain the singe burn in his side or hole in his shirt to Ma, but because his thoughts were in tangles. "It was like the pistol was just there, waiting for me. But it's a gun. I own a gun."

"There's a difference between a gunslinging outlaw and a deliberate marksman." The reverend put away his bandages and mending supplies, shelving them in his study-now-pantry between a large book and a tin of beans. "After all, no one would compare the swordplay of the Black Bandit with that of a pirate. You're using it as a deliberate defense, not an impulsive act of aggression. You'll need to defend yourself if you're going to do…what you're going to do." The old man heaved himself down on to a crate. "Glory, but I think I'm getting too old for all this. Such drama is best left to younger hearts. Speaking of which…"

Quinn shot the old man a look. He'd seen this coming a mile off. Expected it yesterday, as a matter of fact. "Don't start."

"And here I was thinking I'd jumped to conclusions."

"You have."

"I don't think so." He held Quinn's eyes for a long moment, his expression so neutral Quinn couldn't say if he was about to be chastised or encouraged. Or both. "Miss Longstreet is an admirable woman, Quinn. Any man in the county would look at her twice. And you two seem to have much in common." There was an unspoken "but" in his tone. Bauers raised one eyebrow in silent invitation of a reply but didn't expound on what he was thinking.

Quinn was glad for that. Maybe. He fiddled with the box of noodles at his feet. "I can't stop thinking about her. No one else seems to see the things about her that I do. People dismiss her. Why doesn't anyone understand what's important to her?"

"And by that you mean her father?" It should have sounded judgmental, but it didn't.

"I know he's a friend of yours." On one level, Quinn knew Mr. Longstreet wasn't acting any different than most fathers. But he didn't seem to understand that Nora wasn't most daughters. She was so different…so amazingly, wonderfully different…that Mr. Longstreet's ordinary, protective behavior didn't sit well with Quinn.

"And he's a good man. He is a good father, too, even if that might be hard for you to see at the moment. After all, if something precious to you survived the earthquake, wouldn't you feel all the more protective of it? Isn't her locket—the one you found—even more valuable for surviving the fire?"

Bauers wasn't being helpful. Quinn needed no reminding of the mile-high wall between him and Nora. He thumped a tin of beans down on a nearby shelf with more force than necessary.

Reverend Bauers shook his head. "Your problem, Quinn, is as old as time. I find it rather encouraging to know some things will go on as they did despite all this. You and Nora come from different worlds. And while they may have come crashing down side by side, the distinction between those worlds hasn't altogether disappeared. You'd best remember that. But you'd also do well to remember," the reverend continued, turning away from Quinn and busying himself with a small stack of books, "that the truly extraordinary matches often make no sense whatsoever. If you're asking me, I'd take a reckless heart over a sensible one any day."

There was a long moment of stunned silence before Quinn replied, "Simon tells me reckless is bad."

"Of course he would. He's got the army teaching him how to live. You, you've got your heart and life and God guiding you. No sir, reckless has its uses. Messengers who go wandering around past midnight need to be a bit reckless."

Messengers. Midnight. The words clicked together in Quinn's brain to solve the one detail in all of this that still eluded him.

Quinn stared right at delightful, frustrating Reverend Bauers, who had no idea what he'd just done. "I know who I am now." No, Bauers had not solved the larger question of what to do about Nora, nor fixed the challenges of delivering goods, but he had just answered a small but frustrating question. "Thanks."

Bauers looked stumped. "For what?"

"The name. I'm not the Bandit. I never wanted to be another Bandit anyways. I'm the Midnight Messenger."

"The Midnight Messenger?" The reverend squinted up his eyes, as if trying the thought out for size. "It fits. It works. Yes, I believe you are the Midnight Messenger. Good gracious, what have I done?"

"Become an accomplice. Again." Quinn pointed at the old man. "I *knew* God wasn't done with you yet."

Chapter Thirteen

It was an unlikely crowd that gathered in the street between Dolores Park and the official camp later that week. Nora and her father stood with Major Simon, Reverend Bauers and Quinn Freeman, staring at the deluge of messages that now covered the post. While Nora was surprised that her father agreed to a further inspection of the notes when Reverend Bauers had asked, she was thankful he didn't seem to view the gulf between the two camps as wide as he had in earlier weeks. As it was, Nora sent up a prayer of praise that these five people could stand here together. She found herself thanking God daily for the wealth of experiences she'd had since that fateful Tuesday morning.

There was almost always a knot of people gathered around the column these days. Word of goods and foodstuffs arriving mysteriously in the middle of the night had spread quickly. Nora knew she had granted Edwina's wish for a doll, but that didn't explain how one family received the blanket they'd requested. Nora heard another story of a woman who tacked up a request for sewing needles, only to find them stuck in her door the next morning.

Suspicious, Nora had asked Quinn what he knew, but he denied any part in the thing. He had no reason to keep it from her, but then again she had no real claim to his confidences, did she? No matter who was behind it, the good news shot a sense of hope through the camp like a burst of sunshine after so much pain and suffering. Not every need was filled—from the looks of the column, perhaps only one request in twenty met with success—but even those odds seemed enough to fuel a surge of optimism.

Bauers folded his hands over his round torso. "From the looks of it, we'll need a second post by the end of the week."

"I had the same thought," Quinn agreed. "But a length of wood that big will be hard to come by. Folks are already saving every scrap they can find in hopes of rebuilding."

That gave Nora an idea. "Papa, what about the column you kept from our old house? We could use that, couldn't we?" It was charred and had a large chunk out of the top, making her wonder if her father had hauled it out of the rubble for purely sentimental reasons. It didn't look to her as if it could serve much use holding anything up anymore, so why not use it here where it could do a world of good?

"It was one of the few things we could save, burnt as it is." Her father pondered the idea for a moment, his reluctance obvious, and Nora thought of her locket, so precious to her even though it was battered almost to uselessness. Sometimes people just needed to hang on to something no matter how little sense it made. She was just about to take back her suggestion when Papa shrugged his shoulders and said, "I don't know why I saved it, to be honest. I suppose this is as good a use as any."

"You know, Longstreet, there's no reason to think it can't be returned to you later," Major Simon offered. "It might even be quite a conversation piece when you rebuild."

"I'm sure it would do good," Nora added. "We should do it."

"I could come over this afternoon and fetch it back," Quinn offered.

"Yes, then, why don't you?" Mr. Longstreet finally agreed.

Nora smiled. "Oh, Papa, I'm so delighted it's coming from our house."

Papa cleared this throat. "The question remains," he looked from Reverend Bauers to Major Simon, "*who* is it we are aiding? Reverend, do you know how the first requests were met?"

"Well, some of them have been met through Grace House and its benefactors, that's to be sure, but there is definitely another party at work. And no, I don't know who they are."

"I do worry that this 'generosity' is really the result of theft," Papa said, stroking his chin. "I'm not for helping out some misguided Robin Hood."

"I suppose it's always a possibility, but I'm inclined to think otherwise," Reverend Bauers said. "Until we have evidence that wrongdoing is involved, I choose to encourage this charity. Think of it as merely another version of postage—you are delivering communication, just by a means other than mail."

Major Simon cast his gaze up and down the first pole. It had so many notes upon it now, wood could no longer be seen. "Still, the postmaster has a point. Another column means twice as many notes. How many notes will be too many? Unmet expectations can be a dangerous tinderbox."

"We've already survived the firestorm," Quinn said. "What's a little more tinder if it might do some good?"

Papa sighed. "Mr. Freeman, I'll expect you this afternoon, if Reverend Bauers or the major can supply you with a wagon."

"Consider it done," Quinn said.

Nora tried to dismiss her twinge of excitement as simply the satisfaction of helping more people. That was a lie. It was far more about the prospect of Quinn Freeman coming to her house this afternoon. She just hoped her father couldn't tell the difference.

When Mr. Longstreet had mentioned he had a usable pillar stowed away in his backyard, he hadn't mentioned that it was hidden under a pile of other rubble and broken furniture. Hadn't Quinn stood on that far corner just days ago, bemoaning his lack of access to Nora's world? *I never learn, do I, Lord?* Quinn grunted and pushed a heap of old bricks out of the way.

Out of the corner of his eye, he saw Nora's face dart away from a window to his left. How long had she been watching him work? He pulled his shirt back on, suddenly feeling the effect of knowing her eyes were on him. *Does it have to be so hard, Lord? Do You set up a man's heart for this foolishness on purpose, or do we do this to ourselves? Surely You didn't bring me through a disaster only to watch my heart break, did You?*

"You look like you could use a drink." Nora appeared on the porch a few minutes later with a large tin cup in her hand. "We've not had ice for weeks, but the water's still cool."

Quinn thought he would have gladly drunk hot water just for an excuse to walk up onto the porch and catch a whiff of her hair. "I sure could use any kind of water. That post's heavier than it looks, I'll tell you."

He drained the cup quickly, glad to have the cool water slide down his parched throat. "Hard to imagine how a house full of sturdy wood came down so quick, isn't it?" He handed the cup back to her after spilling the last bit of the water on his hands and splashing it on to his face.

"The house across the street took three days to fall over. It felt like ours came down in half a minute." Quinn could practically see the memory darken her eyes as she leaned against one of the back porch's columns.

"I'm sorry," Quinn said, meaning it. So sweet a face should never bear that pained expression. "Some awful things happened in our neighborhood, too. A chimney fell on a man right in front of my mother. She has nightmares about it now and then, but it's getting better."

Nora eased herself down the length of the post to settle on the edge of the porch. She was quiet for a moment, fingering the hem of her skirts. "I used to dream about the ground swallowing up Annette every night. I'd wake up feeling like it all just happened, like it would never go away but just keep swallowing the both of us over and over. It was awful." She looked up at Quinn, who stood on the ground with one foot on the steps below her. "I haven't had that dream since you gave the locket back to me. Not even after I lost her photograph, although I cried when I got home." The tenderest of smiles fluttered across her face. "Thank you for fixing it."

It was a little thing, and then again not so little. He wanted to do so much more for her. "It's not the same. I'm sorry about that."

"I am, too." Her hand went up to the locket, and a surge of satisfaction came as her fingers traced his handiwork. She let out a sigh he felt as much as heard. "But nothing's the same, I suppose. We simply have to find the good where we can, make do."

Quinn couldn't help himself when her voice got that wistful quality. "There is good, you know," he said softly, daring a long look into those violet eyes. "More than I ever thought, actually."

She smiled. Not the frail smile of a moment before, but a warm, radiant one that seeped into him stronger than the sunshine. "There is, isn't there? Some wonderful things have happened. Things I can't help thinking wouldn't have happened if everything went on the way it was before. I had that thought just this morning as we were all standing around looking at your wonderful post. And now there will be two." She widened her eyes. "Did you hear the talk as we were standing around? People were saying the loveliest things. They were excited to be receiving gifts and to know that people cared about their needs. Reverend Bauers said that he thought maybe God was giving San Francisco a chance to show the world a good side no one thought was there. Do you think that's true?"

Quinn crossed his arms and leaned against the post

opposite Nora on the porch's back stairs. "I don't try to think what God's motives are. He knows what He's got planned, and I expect we wouldn't understand it much if He did tell us the whole scheme. I've got enough on my plate just working out my little part in it, much less the bigger picture."

"Oh," she said, "I think you have an enormous role in it."

Had Bauers told her something? Did she know his role in those deliveries? He didn't like that idea—the Midnight Messenger could be a very dangerous business, and he didn't want her mixed up in it, even if she did want to fill a few of the requests on the pillars. "How so?" he asked carefully.

"The posts, of course. I think God set you right there with that clever idea just like He set you in the camp with the teeter-totter. Like He set you to save me from Ollie. Or to find my locket." She looked right into his eyes, and Quinn felt his stomach drop out through what was left of the soles of his shoes. "You'll probably think it's silly, but you've been such an encouragement to me. Here I was thinking God had left me alone, and you do all those things—those little but very big things— that let me know He's still minding my path. You're an answer to my prayers, Quinn Freeman. How does that make you feel?"

He knew the exact moment his heart left his body. The exact instant it disobeyed all the good and solid reasons he had for not pining over Nora Longstreet and left to follow her of its own accord. He stared at her, knowing his affections had just overstepped all kinds of bounds and not caring. He no longer had any choice in the matter. "I'm thinking it might not be wise to answer that, Miss Longstreet."

She held his stare with an expression almost too bold for her delicate features. "Nora," she corrected quietly. "And what if I told you I think I might already know?"

"Nora," he said unsteadily, feeling the sound of her name play all kinds of havoc with his composure, "you do already know. I'm just not sure it will change anything." He waited a long moment before he added. "And that's a shame."

"I wish the world were different," she said. "Do you think the world can be different now? That the earthquake can change more than just…the buildings?"

Was she asking him if he was willing to defy all that stood between them? Did she realize how dangerous a question that was? "I know how I'd have things if it were up to me." He tried to tell her, without saying the words, how much that was true. He hoped his eyes showed her what her eyes were showing him. And at that moment, sore and sweaty with the sun beating down on his head, Quinn thought if the only reason God spared him was so that he could feel what he felt from her gaze, then he'd consider it a fair trade. He could do the work of twelve if he could see that look every day. "If God left it up to me…I'd…"

Somehow, some remaining shred of reason stopped him from finishing that sentence. As if it'd lose all its wonder if he tried to put it into words. But she knew. He could tell.

She, however, was willing to go further. "You're one of the very best things about all that's happened, Quinn." There was a power in her eyes that made him want to swoop down and carry her off to whatever future they could discover together. But he didn't want to steal her off her aunt's porch like some kind of marauder. If God ever gave him the chance to claim her for himself, he'd walk through the front door with the admiration of everyone who cared about her.

"You are a wonder, Nora Longstreet," was all he could manage, inadequate as it was. He covered the incredible longing in his chest with a teasing tone. "As big a wonder as they come."

"What will happen now?"

Quinn pushed off the porch steps and willed his feet to take steps in the direction of the cart. It'd take hours of hammering to squelch the humming in his gut right now. Tired as he was from all this work, he was glad to know more work—not to mention another attempt at a delivery—awaited him. He was lost, good and lost. "I've got to work that out," he said, snatching one last look at those memorable eyes, "but you'll be the first to know."

Chapter Fourteen

Nora sat gazing out her bedroom window that night, trying to make sense of her feelings. The warmth that surged through her when Quinn Freeman looked at her had yet to subside. His shoulders were so broad and his skin so tanned, she found her breath catching as she watched him work. Quinn was much more than just physically handsome—he had an energy about him, a presence that pulled feelings from her she'd never known before. Feelings so strong, in fact, that Nora was continually surprised that Mama or Papa hadn't noticed. She felt so changed that it must surely show.

Annette had talked about such feelings. She had been quite taken with a young man named Eric just before her death. Nora and Annette had stayed up many nights talking about him and, unfortunately, how Aunt Julia and Uncle Lawrence would react if they knew. Annette was a beautiful girl—the violet eyes they shared looked stunning against Annette's dark hair—and Aunt Julia had considerable plans to strike her an advantageous match. It was only Annette's fiery nature that had delayed such a match—her cousin had managed to sidestep many of her mother's attempts by proving herself "a bit too spirited." While Nora loved that about her, Aunt Julia considered it an unfortunate trait best stamped out at every turn.

Nora desperately longed to talk with Annette, to share with her the deep care growing in her heart for Quinn. A care she was sure would meet the same scorn as Annette's feelings for Eric. She'd lost so much when she lost Annette. Aunt Julia had moved her out of the pallet in the living room and into the room that had been Annette's—a touching and costly gesture for Aunt Julia, who had spent so many hours in Annette's room just after her death. Mama would find Aunt Julia wandering silently around the room, touching things, straightening the mess left by the earthquake, folding and refolding clothing. It was both comforting and harsh to be surrounded by Annette's things. As if she were all the more here and all the more gone at the same time. Without really meaning to, Nora found herself wandering the room just as Aunt Julia did, sorting through her possessions with aimless fingers.

She wasn't sure what made her look under the bed. Maybe it was the many times they'd played under there as girls. It was just no fun to explore alone.

As she poked her head under the dust ruffle, Nora noticed a whole host of articles that had been dislodged and scattered by the earthquake. Even the houses that suffered very little structural damage had been shaken like a snow globe with often disastrous interior results even if the exterior looked fine.

There was a small brocade sack. Nora recognized it instantly as the place where Annette kept her private treasures. She hadn't even remembered about the cache until seeing it just now. It would make Aunt Julia so happy to know she'd found it.

Until she remembered that it was where Annette kept her diary. And Annette's diary would surely be filled with entries about Eric. Nora didn't have the heart to open that Pandora's box up for Aunt Julia. What Annette had planned for her and Eric would only make Aunt Julia sadder, and what would be the use of that? She'd only just barely stopped moping around the room, only just begun to rejoin the world and resemble herself again.

Pulling out the sack, Nora peered in to find Annette's brown leather journal. Perhaps she had been sent Annette's companionship—even if only in her words and thoughts. Reading Annette's thoughts and feelings for Eric would be so great a comfort. Nora clutched the book to her heart, thinking it a gift from God. There were no issues of violating Annette's privacy. On the slim chance the diary contained no mention of Eric (which was possible if Annette truly feared her mother discovering the book) perhaps by reading it she would know she could turn it over to Aunt Julia with confidence. If not, Nora said silently, closing her eyes and hoping Annette could somehow hear, *I'll keep you safe to myself. It's the least I can do.*

Nora stayed up for hours that night, poring over the nearly year's worth of diary entries. Several times Nora found herself laughing at Annette's atrocious grammar or spelling. She had never been one to tend to her lessons, no matter how many times Aunt Julia scolded her for it. Her penmanship, however, was artistic and lovely, with lines as long and flowing as her onyx hair.

Annette had been in love. Dramatically—as one

would expect from such a spirited soul—and dangerously in love. She and Eric had been more serious than even Nora knew. According to her entries, the couple would have eloped by now. It struck Nora that earthquake or no, she'd have lost Annette—for the young couple would surely have run far away after their secret marriage. But I would have been able to say goodbye. To know you were happy. Aunt Julia, however, wouldn't share her good wishes. With a small smirk, Nora couldn't help thinking her aunt would see the elopement scandal as worse than a dozen earthquakes. Only you, Annette, could make me thankful for an earthquake in some ways. Yawning, Nora finally tucked the diary back into its brocade case and slid it to the bottom of the small drawer than held her nightgowns. God had sent her a bit of Annette after all. While it still stung to have known Annette kept such secrets from her, and her heart ached for the tiny photographs lost from her locket forever, her heart burned in a new, unfamiliar way for the man whose flowers were tucked in their place.

Now, it seemed, Nora had a secret of her own.

Ma stood in the doorway, staring holes in Quinn's back as he finished shaving outside and splashed the last of the morning's water on his numb face. "Did you think I wouldn't notice?" she barked finally.

Every muscle in Quinn's body ached beyond reason. He'd spent the afternoon sinking the second post into the ground, made a pretense at a few hours' sleep after dinner, then slipped off to make a few deliveries. He'd managed only three of the five requests before time and fatigue had caught up with him, forcing him back to bed if he stood any chance at making it through the day's paid labor ahead of him.

Heroes need better wages, Lord. Quinn prayed as he willed strength and reason to seep into his brain from the coffee cup he currently held. He needed to be three separate people in order to keep all this up.

"Notice what?" He didn't look at her, but he didn't even need the mirror's reflection to tell him his evasion wouldn't succeed.

Ma spun on her heels and turned back into the shack. "*Notice what?* he says," she addressed the empty shelter loudly enough for him to hear. "As if fooling his ma comes easy to him now. It's come to that, has it?" Quinn wasn't quite sure who she was conversing with, but it was clear that he shouldn't answer that question at the moment. He followed her inside, only to have her turn on him with angry eyes. "Who is it you're keeping all kinds of hours with, Quinn? Out half the night, carousing with the likes of Heaven knows who? There's nothing but drinking and gambling happens that time of night. I'm no fool." The look of disappointment in her eyes fell to the pit of his stomach like a dozen rocks. "You had such sense before, son. Where's it gone?"

She thought he spent his nights drinking. While it had never occurred to him she'd come to such a conclusion, once he thought about it there wasn't a single good reason she shouldn't suspect the worst of his midnight disappearances. Many a good man had let the stress and grief of the disaster lead him straight to the bottle. His own da had tripped along that path—to his own eventual end—years before with nowhere near the desperation that gripped the city lately. "No, Ma," he said, not having another excuse but not being able to bear the look in her eye.

She looked as if the loss of another of her men to the bottle would be her undoing. "Don't make it worse by lying," she said quietly. Her knuckles were white around the spoon she held.

Quinn took an enormous, burning gulp of coffee and looked her squarely in the eye. "I'm not drinking, Ma. I promise. I couldn't. Not with Da..."

One hand flew up to stop his words, as if even his name caused her pain. She turned away, shaking her head. Her disbelief stung him worse than the bullet graze he still nursed on his left side. In all his eagerness for secretive heroics, he'd never considered it would cost him Ma's trust to be the Midnight Messenger. Still, it had to be that way. Telling her where he really was would only place her in danger if things ever went wrong. But he couldn't bear her thinking he was slipping down to his father's ugly end at the bottom of a bottle. He had to tell her something, and quick. Blurting out the first thing that came to his mind—mostly because it never left his mind—he offered a sheepish grin and said, "You'd like her, Ma."

Ma went still, staring at him. "A woman?" she said suspiciously.

Well now, he hadn't thought through the details. What woman of decent character would keep the hours he'd been keeping? No woman of decent character. He could practically see his ma come to the base conclusion that his "woman" was no "lady." "No, Ma, not that, either."

Ma's hand went to her heart. "You're not giving me much hope to go on." She got a straight-to-business look on her face and sat down on her chair, placing her teacup carefully on one knee. "How about we try this again, and with the truth."

There wasn't another way. At least not one that he could see at the moment. "The truth is, Ma, that I can't say. That's the whole of it and the best I can give you. But I can tell you that it's not drink. But you can't know more than that, and I've my reasons."

"What kind of reasons would make a son lie to his mother?"

"I've not lied to you, Ma. And I'll make a promise to do my best never to lie to you. But that means you'll not get answers to some questions. At least not now." If he made enemies as the Messenger—which he most surely would—anything she knew would put her at risk.

She narrowed her eyes at him. "What in Heaven's name are you up to, lad?"

"You can't know, Ma, and it's as simple as that." He felt ancient this morning, and it had nothing to do with lack of sleep. "But you can know that I doubt I can do it well on an empty stomach."

Ma addressed the empty room again. "All secrets, but I'm to feed him breakfast. What's happening to the world, I ask you?"

"It's getting a little bit better day by day, Ma. And that's the truth of it." He reached out and gave her a hug, noticing how small she felt in his embrace. It felt odd to think of her as old, nearly impossible to think of her as frail, but the months had taken their toll on her much more than they had on him.

She opened the little tomato box that had become their pantry, pulling out a hunk of cheese he'd managed to procure the previous afternoon. "Is there really someone," she asked with careful words, "or were you throwing up smoke to your own ma?"

Quinn polished off the last of his coffee. "There is, and there isn't."

His mother cut the last of their bread into two thick slices. "What kind of answer is that to a simple question?"

"I suppose Reverend Bauers would say some simple questions don't have simple answers."

She only heaved an enormous, burdened sigh as she handed him the bread and cheese. "I suppose I can only pray for you. God Himself only knows what to make of the likes of this."

With a sad smile of his own, Quinn thought his mother was absolutely right.

Quinn slowly squeezed his finger and felt the gun's kick as it released its bullet.

Square into the straw target Simon had set up a good distance away. Quinn turned out to be an excellent shot. Within a week of training, Quinn already bested most of the regular infantry and half of the officers. While it surprised him that such a dark skill came to him so readily, he couldn't ignore the admiration and respect fellow infantrymen gave him when he shot as well as he did. He understood how the Wild West got so wild now—and why Ma had been so against him owning one. Guns gave very attractive power on very short notice.

Major Simon took off his hat and squinted down the line at the hit target. "I ought to enlist you," he said with a dark look. "This minute."

Quinn shook off the tired ache in his neck, aimed

and fired. A hole burst dead center on the second target. It rarely took him a second shot.

Simon shook his head. "You're wasted on the swords, Freeman. The pistol is your weapon by far."

It was the first compliment Simon had paid him in days. Things had been tense between them since the major's oh-so-well-received dinner with the Longstreets—but the tension had mostly been on Quinn's part. From what he could see, Simon was oblivious. Part of him knew the circumstances held immovable obstacles between him and Nora.

Another part of him refused to accept it. It was as if he and Nora were cut from the same cloth, but neither one seemed suited for their present circumstances. She was bolder than society cared to allow young women, and he craved more than what society cared to allow men lacking a formal education. It seemed unjust that neither of them be able to reach toward the middle ground they somehow seemed to share. He was not at all bothered by her boldness—something men like Simon probably considered unfortunate. He'd heard Simon speak of young, bold recruits as "loose cannons" or "liabilities." Quinn, on the other hand, was fond of Nora's boldness almost as much as he was fond of her eyes. No one should tamp down Nora's boldness any more than they should change her eye color. It was how God had made her.

"I'm not sure how you did it, but word is out," the major said once they returned inside, handing Quinn a cloth to clean the pistol. "People are talking about a mysterious 'Midnight Messenger.' Very dramatic name, by the way."

Quinn had "signed" one or two of the deliveries as the "Midnight Messenger." It was important that folks in Dolores Park knew someone was out there on their side. He'd done it as an act of reassurance more than any ploy for fame. "I wasn't shooting for drama. Just something people could remember."

"Oh, they're aware of you, all right." The major looked as if he didn't think that was such a good idea. "Now that you've got an identity, I'd venture people will be out looking for you. And not everyone will want to shake your hand, if you catch my meaning. I suppose the mask isn't such a bad idea after all." Simon nodded toward the ordinary-looking rucksack Quinn used. Inside were the costume and weapons of—now—the Midnight Messenger. Major Simon kept the bag inside a locked chest in a closet near his office, setting them alongside the supplies on delivery nights.

With Reverend Bauers's help, Quinn had fashioned a fabric version of the Bandit's mask—a sort of dark bandanna skullcap with a two-holed flap that folded down over the eyes to tie behind his head. It covered Quinn's visibly blond hair, hid his ears and brow, and worked just as well under a hat as without. Quinn could almost feel himself transforming when he put it on. Still, these people needed so much more than what he'd been able to give them. "These provisions aren't enough," he informed the major. "I'm going to need more."

"Don't overextend yourself, Freeman."

Quinn didn't care for his I-know-better tone. "I think I know how much I can do. I don't need you setting limits on me. If you can provide it, I'll find a way to deliver it."

"And your cocky attitude will fast find a way to get you killed. You're exhausted, Quinn. You won't be any good to me dead."

Any good to "me"? When had this become about Simon? "I'll admit I'm tired, but I'm not one of your liabilities. If I need rest, I'll get it. If you're so intent on my backing things down a bit, give me some extra provisions to take to Grace House. I'll let the reverend be the hero for the evening, feeding folks who need to be fed. A good meal's hard to come by, with cooking fires being outlawed and all."

Quinn pushed out an exasperated breath. Even he had to admit the last remark was an underhanded blow. Everyone hated the army's banning of open flame—necessary as it was to ensure public safety. It wasn't Simon's fault people couldn't cook for themselves. Maybe he really was too tired if he let the major's superior attitude get under his skin like that.

Simon looked annoyed, but didn't rise to Quinn's challenge. "I just took a delivery of some bacon, beans and even a little sugar. And because its kitchen is intact, Grace House can have flour for baking. I'll throw in three extra sacks. Bauers can feed extra mouths and keep everyone occupied for a day or so. Will that convince you to slow down?"

Quinn was smart enough not to let his temper get in the way of a good solution. He'd never admit it to Simon's face, but the prospect of a night off was sorely tempting. And although his cot called to him, Quinn knew exactly where—and with whom—he wanted to spend his newfound free time.

Chapter Fifteen

Nora stood in the living room later that afternoon watching glances bounce back and forth between her parents and Reverend Bauers. The reverend had just come to the house—under "major's orders"—to ask Nora to help with a last-minute army distribution of foodstuffs and supplies.

"I know Nora wants to help, but I need to be cautious about when and where she lends a hand, even at the request of Major Simon." Nora hoped her father wouldn't force her to decline such a perfectly good reason to visit Dolores Park.

"It is a testament to you that your daughter is so willing to be of assistance. She'll be back for supper, madam." Reverend Bauers folded his hands seriously across his chest. "You have my word. She'll only go to the very edge of the park, and she'll be escorted by Major Simon himself at all times."

Mama acquiesced first. "Please tell the major he is most welcome to stay for dinner when he brings Nora back."

They pulled up to the park edge to find Major Simon

smiling on the back of a large wagon mounded with a variety of clothing, blankets, building supplies and tins of various food. "How delightful to have your help, Miss Longstreet. It is a great pleasure to see you again. If you would be so kind as to sit behind this table and make a list of each family as they receive their goods? Just names please, as Sergeant Miller here will take note of the particular items over at the cart." He handed her a ledger and pencil.

She settled herself behind the table, and as the major attended to the other officer, Nora discreetly swept her eye around the gathering crowd. No Quinn. Not even after an hour's worth of listing names. It was foolish to expect him to find her every time she set foot near the park. She was chastising herself for giving in to such disappointment when Reverend Bauers came up to the table.

"Miss Longstreet," he said, "you'll be pleased to know I've persuaded the major to accept your mother's kind offer of dinner. I wonder if I could persuade you to offer me a moment of your time to help with the posts?"

"Please, Reverend, tell me whatever it is you need." Nora stood up and the reverend tucked her hand into the crook of his elbow. They had walked the half a block to the post when Bauers stopped and whispered into her ear. "What I need, my dear, is to get him what he needs."

Nora pulled back. "What who needs?"

Suddenly, Nora heard a voice from behind her other shoulder. "I need to see you." It was Quinn's voice, right behind her.

She moved to spin around and face him, but the

reverend held tight to her arm. "Quinn, can we at least *attempt* to be careful?"

Nora's eyes flew wide and her spine stiffened as she realized that Quinn had actually put the Reverend Bauers up to this meeting. "Quinn?" Nora fairly gasped.

"Mr. Freeman," corrected the elder minister.

"Quinn is just fine." Nora could hear the smile in Quinn's voice even if she couldn't turn to see it. "I had to see you." She heard him shift his weight and groan. "Reverend, give me a minute?"

The minister tightened his grip on Nora's arm. "Within eyeshot of the major? Certainly not." His voice was stern but Nora could clearly see the twinkle in his eye. "Nora, would you be so kind as to write down a dozen or so of these requests as I point them out to you? It should only take..." he inclined his head in Quinn's direction "...two minutes at the most."

"Five."

Nora was so flustered by the "conspiracy" and Quinn's nearby voice that it took her a moment to grasp the chalk and slate Reverend Bauers produced from his coat pocket. "Certainly. I had...very much...wanted to come back here and see...the posts." It was like trying to have six conversations at once. "Papa is so very cautious now."

"As well he should be," the reverend chimed in, at which Quinn produced an exasperated groan from somewhere just off her left shoulder.

"I need to see you."

Nora looked at the minister. How could she possibly answer such a question with a reverend inches away? As if hearing her thoughts, Reverend Bauers found something fascinating in the sky to look at and began to whistle softly.

"I...I don't know. I don't know how."

"I'll just talk to your father. Explain what's..."

"No," Nora countered. "He'd never listen. Not yet."

She heard him blow out an exasperated breath behind her. "I'd make him understand."

His determination made her heart pound. "Perhaps you could, in time. But not yet." The memory of Papa's scowl darkened her words.

"Your window is on the south side, right?"

Nora startled. "On my house? Aunt Julia's house?"

"Does it have a balcony?"

"Have you been reading *Romeo and Juliet?*" the clergyman asked in an exasperated tone.

Nora swallowed a laugh. The vision of Quinn Freeman scaling Aunt Julia's rose trellis made her want to giggle and sigh at the same time. "That's not wise."

"To say the least," Reverend Bauers said. He pointed out a message from the post asking for a hymnal and socks. "A meeting at Grace House is wisest. I told you that, Quinn. See here, Nora, there are three requests for dolls like the one you gave Edwina. I don't think the Ladies Aid society would see fit to provide those, but perhaps if Grace House supplied the materials you could make more."

"I told him," Quinn said. "Edwina was so happy."

"Her grandfather came to services at Grace House the following weekend. I gather he's not darkened the door of a church in ten years."

Quinn's voice was low and close. "You did that, Nora."

Nora's satisfaction ran so deep she could almost

soak in God's smile coming down on her from Heaven. "That's wonderful," she whispered, having to work hard to concentrate as she wrote down the three other names. "Of course I'll make more."

"If you bring them to Grace House, I can meet you there." The urgency in Quinn's voice made the back of Nora's neck tingle.

"I could be there Tuesday," Nora replied. Tuesday seemed like a million years from now.

"Tuesday." Quinn's single word seemed to echo her own frustration. Nora closed her eyes, feeling his gaze burn into her, sense his presence in the air just behind her, hear his breath. Her hand moved to grasp the locket around her neck.

"Tuesday it is. Take care, you two, we walk a knife's edge with this."

Nora felt Quinn's exit as much as she heard his footsteps. After a moment, the minister pointed out another two or three requests tacked to the post, and somehow she managed to write them down.

"Why are you helping us?" Nora had never used the word "us" before. It seemed terribly important that she had now.

Reverend Bauers turned to her with a smile that wiped years—perhaps even decades—off his face. For a moment she saw the dashing young adventurer he claimed to have been in his youth. God's provision over the years had made the reverend a very brave and daring man—Nora felt a stab of guilt at thinking of him as just a gentle old preacher. He was gentle, and old, but he was so much more than that. Nora wanted, at that moment, to know that at eighty *she* would look back on her life as full of God's adventures.

"Why? Is it not obvious?" He chuckled. "The man is absolutely relentless."

She smiled. "I believe I am coming to feel the same way."

They returned to the table and Nora did her best to wrestle her attention back to the task at hand. There was a moment, a frozen moment in time, where she looked up and caught Quinn's eyes as he stood at a distance. Even from far away, the gold of his eyes glowed like topaz, the intensity of his stare stole her breath and flushed her cheeks. She glanced around, sure the whole world saw the power of their locked eyes, but everyone bustled by unawares. Life pulsed by all around them, noisy and busy and ignorant of the air that hummed between Quinn and her. She could live to be a hundred and still be able to recall the amber glow of his eyes in that moment.

Suddenly, Romeo facing death to scale Juliet's balcony didn't seem so melodramatic. She had thought herself too old for such childish romance, but with her heart beating as wildly as it did, Nora felt perhaps the heart's distinction between brave and foolish was a very fine line, indeed.

A thud and a yelp dragged Nora from her thoughts. Something had fallen off the piles of goods that filled the cart. When white powder pooled out of the burlap sack, she could hear the reaction by those who saw. Flour ranked as one of the most coveted and least available supplies anywhere—everyone wanted some and it was nearly impossible to get any. As a matter of fact, the army was saying there wasn't enough to distribute outside of the official relief stations that were cooking for hundreds of refugees daily and supplying the endless bread lines.

"Flour!" one woman called out, pointing to the snowy mounds. "You've got flour in there! I want some of that."

Major Simon stiffened. Clearly this wasn't a good thing. "Sergeant?" he said in a cautionary but commanding tone.

"I don't know, sir, it must have been in there by mistake."

The woman who'd first cried out pushed her way to the front of the crowd. "They told us there isn't any flour to give out. Only there is, isn't there?"

Simon moved between the woman and the flour. "There isn't a way for you to use this. Baking requires fire, and fire is too dangerous right now."

"For who?" a man jeered. "You got enough to lose track of, then I say you got enough to let decent people do their own cooking."

"Who knows what else they been keepin' from us?" a second woman said, peering into the back of the cart. "I heard you been sellin' the flour rather than give it to us. Making profit off our need, are you?" This started a chorus of accusations against the army. Major Simon frowned and held up his hand to quiet the crowd, barely succeeding.

"We sell flour you can't use and buy things you *can use* with the money. One carelessly tended stove could start another fire. You know we can't have that. I know this is difficult, but…"

"Don't you get all fancy-worded on me. Ain't right to go profiteering off of folks in need. You think you know better than me, that's what I think. Well, you don't.

You're just another one of them, you are. Don't really care a fig for what happens to us so's long as you can keep us fooled."

"No one's trying to mislead you," the major said in a forced calm. "We're trying to give you what you need as fast as we can, but you've got to understand the dangers. The few common fire pits are the best we can do for now. We simply can't have you people using ovens. I'm sorry."

"Yeah? Well, I'm hungry. Which of us is better off?" some man called out from the back of the crowd.

"The Messenger could get us flour," the first woman declared.

"I'd hope the Messenger would care about the safety of your family as much as you do, ma'am, and he'd tell you what I'm telling you now." The major was trying to stay calm, but the crowd had turned on him.

"Hang your 'care,' captain. I'd rather have your flour. Wouldn't we all?" the man called out again.

"Let's try to see the bigger picture here," Reverend Bauers interjected, coming to stand next to the major. "Safety is absolutely vital. Times are challenging for everyone."

"Some more than others," a thin woman grumbled as she tossed the pair of shirts she'd just collected back on to the cart. Several others followed suit, and Nora could see the major's jaw clenching.

Nora felt the tension gather in the air like a storm. Suddenly, it felt as if all of Reverend Bauers's promises of a safe visit were going up in smoke. She looked up, needing to find Quinn's eyes, wanting to know he would step in and save her, yet again, if things got out of hand. But Quinn had vanished. Her pulse began to rise.

Forcing calm into her voice, Nora turned to Reverend Bauers. "Perhaps it might be best if we left now and saved the rest of our efforts for another day."

"Indeed. And perhaps it would be best not to ask the major to make good on his promise of escorting you home."

As voices rose, Nora craned her neck around against Reverend Bauers's pull on her arm, striving for one last glimpse of Quinn, who surely must be somewhere in that crowd. Tuesday felt years from now.

"That was a disaster." Major Simon let out a few choice words as he threw his gloves and hat down on the table in his office. He hadn't called for Quinn to come and see him, but it didn't take a genius to know that thanks to this afternoon's fiasco, the Midnight Messenger wasn't going to get the night off he'd planned. He and Simon stood in the major's office, staring at each other. It was the first time he'd seen Simon lose the edges of his slick control.

It was also the first time since he'd started that Quinn felt a pang of regret. Fear, even. It had been adventurous, a satisfying chance to make hope-sparking deliveries for people in Dolores Park. Now, Quinn felt the demands coming down on him like an avalanche. He was only one man—and yet the cries of that crowd seemed to expect him to do what even the U.S. Army seemed hard-pressed to do. "We set out to make a solution," the major continued, "and we've made a monster."

"The people want flour. Donated flour's coming in by the tons. How can we deny them things as if they're children?"

Simon sat down behind his desk. "And have them

burn the city down all over again? They've no real ovens. They've no safe storage. One careless spark, Freeman, that's all it would take. We've got to be vigilant. We've got to make decisions based on what's best for the entire city, not just one family's stomach. You heard me explain it—we've sold most of the excess flour to buy things they really can use."

"I heard you," Quinn replied, letting his tone show what he thought of that particular strategy. "You sold our relief supplies." It sounded wrong, no matter how the major put a shine on it.

"It's best." Simon's tone held a challenge of its own.

"And *you* know what's best?" Quinn felt as if that black shirt and mask were now made of iron, clamping down on him with heavy solidity. People expected the Messenger to give them what they wanted.

"Tight authority means life and death these days. We can't afford another rebellious mob scene like that."

Quinn forced civility into his words. "So what will we do?" He had a hunch he wouldn't like the answer.

"My grandfather taught me an old saying." Simon began writing something out on a slip of paper. "When you don't have what you want, make do with what you've got." He stood and called, "Private!" out his office door, handing the paper to the tense-looking young man who appeared seconds later. Quinn wondered, by the major's behavior, if he'd even remembered he was in the room.

"This is a requisition for two dozen blankets from the barracks warehouse. Tell them to make sure the blankets are in good shape and have the army markings

on them. I want them in my office within ten minutes.
Understood?"

"Directly, sir." The young man barely paused to salute
before bolting from the room. Simon pulled the office
door shut after his private.

"They want flour, so you're going to give them blankets?" Quinn had serious doubts it would be seen as a
fair trade. You could hardly eat a blanket, after all.

"No, *you're* going to give them blankets. Army blankets. It's high time we let everyone know the Messenger's on *our* side. You've lost your night off. I'm sorry for
that, but I'm sure you see the urgency of the thing."

Quinn wasn't liking this at all. "Wouldn't it be better
to get the people to understand why they can't have
baking fires? I don't see how tossing army blankets at
them helps."

The major frowned. "You cannot reason with a mob.
Only distract it. You watch—that post will be filled with
requests for flour tomorrow morning. Flour they think
the Messenger can find for them because they think
we've hid it from them. Nothing personal, Freeman,
but you've become a temporary liability, and we need
to recast you from rebel to partner. We can't have people
thinking the Messenger is out there outsmarting the
army. You saw how fast things escalated out there—the
Messenger has to be seen as working *with* us."

Quinn had the disturbing feeling that he'd been enlist-
ed without his consent. That he'd just been sucked up
into the army machine, forced—albeit kindly—to do
their bidding and serve their purposes. Major Simon
had done so much for him, and yet it was hard not to
feel as though it had all been for some convenient purpose. Like the small pawns in the chess game Reverend

Bauers was forever trying to teach him. Scooted about to serve some larger aim without much regard for his own health and safety.

Yet, Simon had a valid point—one careless spark could start the firestorm all over again. And Simon had given him weapons, training and was by far his best source for goods. Quinn couldn't be the Messenger without Simon's help—at least not yet. "And what are *you* going to do?"

"Oddly enough, the most important thing I can do right now is to do nothing. To behave as if all were well, as if there were no cause for concern whatsoever." He raised an eyebrow at Quinn, who tried to swallow the knot currently balling up in his throat. "Which means, thankfully, that it is in the city's best interest that I dine at the Longstreets' tonight as if there were not a single demand upon my time this evening."

Quinn hoped his mouth wasn't gaping open. It should have been.

"Word of my calm dismissal of any problem will travel through the city as fast as word of your deliveries will fly through camp. We're both making vital deliveries tonight. Just different kinds."

Quinn let his frustration grind a sharp edge on to his words. "So you solve this by eating a fine meal while I help you by spending another night hiding in shadows?"

Shrugging his shoulders, Simon said, "Would it help if I bought you a steak tomorrow night?"

"Only just." Quinn was glad no one required him to salute as he left. The Messenger was suddenly feeling less like a calling and more like a punishment.

Chapter Sixteen

Quinn stalked through the kitchen at Grace House. "I've had about enough of this. He's the one with the problem, so why am I the one staying up tonight to fix things? He's the one denying people what they want." He turned and glared at Reverend Bauers, not bothering to hide his frustration. "Yet he's with her, and I'm here."

Reverend Bauers gave out a lumbering sigh and put down the box of silverware he was shelving. "Except that he's right, and you know it. People can't have the flour, even if they think they need it. Simon is right, Quinn, but it's not really why you're rankled, in any case."

Quinn ignored that last remark. "We should be equals in this, but I've got the short end of the stick by far. I can't remember the last time I slept an entire night. Tonight I was..." He stopped himself. He was going to try and find a way to see Nora, that's what he was going to do with this evening. And now, not only had that opportunity been plucked from his hands, it seemed to have been handed—on a silver platter—to Major Simon. Really, if Simon had asked him to distribute army blankets on any other night, he would have donned the Messenger's black bag and gladly made the deliveries.

"You were going to what?" Bauers knew the answer. The knowledge in his eyes was disarming even if it was softened with understanding. "I was standing right next to you, you know. Balconies. You really do have a flair for drama, Quinn." He walked entirely too calmly over to Quinn, reaching up to tap Quinn's throbbing temples. "Use your eyes, man. You stare enough at her, surely you see it. You've no rival in Major Simon. She's as much drawn to you as you are to her. It's her parents who are your rivals. Their views and their expectations for Nora's future." He clasped Quinn's shoulder and returned to shelving the supplies that were finally leaving his study for their former places in the mission kitchen. "Why do you think God called you to be His messenger?"

His messenger? Quinn thought that made him sound a bit too much like the angel Gabriel. And Quinn wasn't feeling very angelic at the moment. "I don't know, actually."

"I do. Nora would too, if she knew. You're clever and quick and brave…and willing. Most times, all God really needs is a willing soul—he can always make up for the rest if a man is willing to step out in faith."

Quinn picked up a stack of plates and put them on a high shelf. "You make it sound noble. I doubt it will feel very noble at three in the morning when I'd much rather be home in bed."

"It *is* noble. And very few noble things in this world come without great cost. It cost you to help those people. It will keep costing you—probably more as this goes on. The question is, are you going to let that stop you?

Or are you going to keep on in the faith that God will keep on providing?"

"Simon's begun treating me like I'm some sort of secret army weapon. He's using me for his own end."

Reverend Bauers sat down on one of the kitchen's large wooden benches. How many times had the food Quinn had gobbled down in this kitchen been the only decent meal of the day in his childhood? The wood creaked under the reverend's weight—most of the Grace House furnishings were old and worn, leaving Quinn to wonder how much longer many of them would last. "You can always just quit," Bauers offered, resting his elbows on the table. "Stop. No one would be the wiser."

"And just let people think everyone's given up on them? Just vanish, even after people have come to have a bit of hope? What would that solve?"

"Exactly," Bauers replied. "What would that solve?" He motioned for Quinn to sit. "It wouldn't solve anything to your liking, Quinn. You care. Perhaps too much. But don't let some useless worry about Major Simon muddle your thinking here. You've a mission, and Simon's part of that mission. You need to trust God with the details, even if they don't seem to your liking. God knows what you feel for Miss Longstreet, and He knows what Miss Longstreet feels for you."

And that was the question, wasn't it? What did Nora feel for him? He thought of her eyes as she held his gaze on the porch the other day. He could dive inside those eyes and live a happy man forever. They seemed to pour courage and purpose into him—as if he caught the world by the tail just by catching her eye. She felt for him what he felt for her. He'd seen it, felt it. He knew she cared for him; he'd just let Simon's arrogant remarks fester a groundless doubt about it. "What is God up to here, Reverend?"

The question made the old man laugh heartily. "I ask myself that nearly every day lately. I've got an inkling, but if I knew for certain, well then there'd be no use for faith now, would there? Do I believe God sent an earthquake? Can't say that I do. I don't believe God sends evil upon us. But I do believe evil happens and then God works wonders to pull all the goodness he can out of those circumstances."

"Tell Him to pull harder. I'm running out of steam."

Bauers laid a gnarled hand on Quinn's forearm and bent his head. *"Holy Father, bless this man, your servant. Grant him strength and endurance. Keep him safe, honor his efforts to serve Your children. Tend to his heart as You tend to his soul. He is near and dear to me, Lord, and I would grant him the world were it up to my wisdom. But it is Your wisdom, Lord, that is always best."*

The reverend kept Quinn's arm in his grasp, and Quinn's breath caught at the surge of emotion that welled up in him. There was a time, when he was a young and angry teenager, when he'd tried to bolt from the house after an argument with his father. Ma caught him as he attempted to burst out the door, grabbing on to him with a fierce grip that seemed impossible for her size. She pulled him firmly to her, hugging him even though he struggled against it. He'd ended up clutching her to his shoulder—even then, he was taller than she— fighting the sobs that wanted to come tumbling out of his chest at how unfair the whole world seemed. It was as if she knew of the coming storm and made herself his anchor.

She'd settled something in him that day. Passed some kind of strength through from her heart to his, something that enabled him to stand firm when things got worse and worse with Pa. He felt the same way again, now, only deeper. As if Reverend Bauers had passed a strength of soul between them, lent him the steadfast faith it would take to see this thing through. Not a certainty, not a plan, not even a calm, but the steadfast faith that didn't need calm to stand firm.

Matthew Covington had once told him he was sure God ordained him to be the Bandit. Quinn thought it high-minded talk at the time. From out of the mist of his memory, a verse came to him. A blessing, as it were, from within. *"Be confident of this very thing, that he which hath begun a good work in you will perform it until the day of Jesus Christ."*

Major Simon was staring at her. Not in the open, unabashed way that Quinn had, but in glances and gazes over the conversation he held easily with her father. Ease. It was the single strongest word Nora could use to describe Major Simon. He was at ease with himself, at ease with his position, at ease with the chaos he'd been chosen to supervise and at ease with the obvious eagerness at which the Longstreet family welcomed him into their home.

That same eagerness made Nora uneasy. Despite her "advanced" years—most of her friends had been married off by now—she had never felt pressure of any kind to wed. Her parents had always patiently expected the right man to simply present himself in a matter of time.

Now, the earthquake's brush with death had made them anxious. Not in the "imminent disaster" kind of way, but more of a "life must be accomplished as soon as possible" outlook. As if Nora had managed to beat the odds by surviving, but had best grab the elements of life— husband, children and such—quickly, before the odds caught up with her. In fact, record numbers of couples had married since the earthquake. Albert Simon, with his charm and credentials, seemed to Nora's parents to be the perfect solution to all life's problems. The way Mama fussed over him, one would think they'd been betrothed since childhood.

"Nora," Mama said as if she'd been impatiently waiting for Nora to come up with the idea on her own, "why don't you show Major Simon the garden?"

"The garden" was a stretch of the term. In truth, it was a scratched-out patch of the backyard where Mama and Aunt Julia had managed to coax a few flowers into sprouts. Aunt Julia only had a kitchen garden before the earthquake, whereas Mama had tended a variety of overflowing flower beds. Nora wasn't sure if the new flower garden was for Mama's comfort, or just the only way Mama could think to engage Aunt Julia's increasingly withdrawn disposition. Either way, it struck Nora as the same intent as Quinn's teeter-totter—a "luxury" that was, in fact, very much a survival necessity. It was a pathetic display by Mama's former standards, but then everyone had had to redefine their standards lately, hadn't they?

"You've a garden?" Nora wondered if the major's impressed tone would survive the tour of the tiny seedling patch. She thought of Quinn's frequent reply of "only just," but swallowed the urge to use it.

"We've done what we could, given the circumstances," Mama said, smiling at Aunt Julia. Behind Mama's forced smile, Nora could see the hints of longing for her own garden, for her own home. Papa had begun the process of rebuilding just last week, but it would be weeks if not months before they were back in a home of their own, and Papa had decided to move them farther away from the bay. They'd be farther from Dolores Park and farther from Grace House once they left Aunt Julia's. Nora couldn't help but worry how Aunt Julia and Uncle Lawrence would fare, wandering around in their own freshly empty home once her family left.

Major Simon gave that grandly easy smile of his. "I'd like very much to see it." He looked right at Nora when he said it. The directness of his gaze ought to have disturbed Papa, but instead Papa looked supremely satisfied with the major's obvious interest. For the first time in her life, Nora felt the social expectations of a young woman's future tighten around her. As if she were standing with her feet in a fast-moving river, facing the very real threat of being pulled out into the rapids.

Chapter Seventeen

"I find them rather eager, don't you?" Simon surprised her when they'd closed the door behind them on the back porch. "Is there some sort of horrid fact about you they've yet to disclose? I can't possibly be the first caller you've had." He'd identified himself as a "caller"—knowing all that the term implied—with an unnerving confidence. As if they'd spoken of it for years instead of days, if not hours. As if there was no question how things would proceed from here. "They do seem in a hurry all of a sudden." It seemed the most neutral thing to say.

He tucked his hands in his pockets and walked out on to the lawn toward the rows of green shoots surrounded by a makeshift fence. "Many are, you know. It's a natural reaction to a shock such as the disaster."

Yes, he had several years on her, but even aside from that, Major Simon looked as if nothing ever shocked him. She had a sudden vision of him standing amid the roiling army barracks, legs braced wide on the shuddering ground, timing the earthquake on his pocket watch. "Were you frightened?" she asked. "When the earthquake struck?"

He raised a dark eyebrow, stumped by her sudden change of subject. He left his inspection of the fence to look at her for a moment. "I'd not be much of an officer if I panicked in a tight spot, now would I? I must be ever the stoic and fearless Major Simon."

Nora leaned back against one of the fat pillars that held up the porch. "I'm not at all sure I'd trust a fearless man. There are many real things in life to be afraid of. And after all, 'fear of the Lord is the beginning of Wisdom.'"

"I leave those ponderings up to the reverend."

"You're not a man of faith, sir?"

"All men pray in battle, Miss Longstreet."

Nora crossed her arms over her chest. "And that is not an answer, Major Simon."

He looked at her for a long moment. She could see him think, see him weigh her question and analyze its intent. "That is an important question for you, isn't it?"

"Yes, it is."

Simon clasped his hands behind his back. "Faith, to soldiers, is a luxury. Obedience and survival are our anchors." He returned his gaze to her. "I suppose the best answer I can give you is that I *could* be. Perhaps that is one of the things I might learn from you. If we were to…pursue things."

"I could never give you faith, Major. That is something only God can do."

"Perhaps," he said, his smile broadening. "But there is something I know you could do."

"And what is that?"

"You could call me Albert." He looked around. "At least, in less formal circumstances."

How had her parents, who never seemed to view her "spinster" circumstance with any anxiety before, suddenly become so focused on marriage? She supposed the great, awful lesson on life's fragility they'd all had was at the root of it. It wasn't hard to grab at happiness with both hands when even the slightest prospect of it rose. The number of marriage licenses issued since the earthquake proved there was an overwhelming, unspoken fear that destruction could happen again at any moment. That the whole world could shake and tumble off into the ocean tomorrow morning. It made some people desperate to do "what's right." It made other people desperate to do whatever it was they most wanted.

Calling him "Albert" should have come easily. Still, Nora found the only reply to his request she could manage was to say, "Perhaps someday." When his face fell at her response, she added, "Soon."

He crossed his arms over his chest, narrowing his eyes as if she had just become an objective. She could literally see him setting, as Mama would say, his cap for her. "You'll find I'm a persistent fellow."

Nora lay awake for hours, pondering her life's current complexities. She'd stayed up at first to merely read more of Annette's journal, her guilt at opening the private book overcome by the joy of just hearing her cousin's thoughts again. Annette was gone forever this side of Heaven, but reading the diary, Nora could imagine her sitting on the edge of the bed, recounting the dramatic details of her secretive meetings. Annette's life was such a tumult, it made her own life seem settled by comparison—even with the sudden social acceleration going on. Why were Mama and Papa suddenly eager to marry her out to a man she'd just met and a dozen years older than she? Stability? Protection? To simplify the rebuilding of their own home and lives? Suddenly, everyone had layers that weren't there before—Annette, Mama, Papa, Major Simon, even Reverend Bauers and Quinn—and clarity eluded her as surely as sleep did.

Quinn. She welcomed the use of his first name, clung to it, even though she'd resisted with…Albert. She tried his given name out in her thoughts, inspecting how it felt. It failed to hum in her head the way Quinn's name had. As if the word itself had colder, sharper edges instead of the curled warmth of Quinn's. The two men couldn't be more different. From a sheerly practical standpoint, she had no business even considering Quinn Freeman at all. Then again, Annette had been beyond impractical in her association with Eric. And yet, it had made her desperately happy. Ready to risk all she knew and loved to make a future with such an unknown, inappropriate man. It was romantic. It churned up a vibrant sense of adventure Nora had almost lost in all the day-to-day survival of the post-earthquake city. Everything had been so very serious for so very long.

What am I to do, Lord? Nora sat back, clutching Annette's diary tightly to her chest. *Surely, You've spared me for some reason. Let me find Annette's journal for some purpose. Is it fair to ask for more guidance? For some sign as to where I go from here?* It was larger, even, than the two men. She was powerfully drawn to Dolores Park and its courageous occupants. The desire to help them was like a pulse in her head, making her look at every scrap of food or clothing with keen new eyes. Could this be used here? Could that be put to use there? The world, which had tucked itself neatly inside the confines of her house and social engagements, had suddenly expanded outward with connections and relationships feathering out in all directions to a variety of fascinating people. *You want me to do something, Lord. I feel it. I think I've grasped on to it a time or two, like with Edwina or Sam, but I can't see the whole of it.*

She thought of the woman, Sister Charlotte, that Reverend Bauers had told her of the other day. The frail nun, now older than Reverend Bauers, had once been an outrageous diva of the stage. A societal maven, one of those people whose parties ended up in society pages from a grand time when Nora was young, according to the reverend. When her husband had died, Charlotte had opened up her huge estate as almost a public haven, helping just about anyone who came knocking.

Evidently, Sister Charlotte still raised eyebrows, for Mama's nearly shot into her hair when Nora asked if she could go with Reverend Bauers to meet her. God had certainly charted a wild course for the woman— even after decades in the church, people still tittered about how any woman like that could take vows. Had Charlotte heard God crystal clear to make such risky choices? Or was she just groping her way through the fog as Nora seemed forced to do? *There must be something I'm supposed to do. Some difference I'm destined to make.*

Nora went to her window, wanting to see the expanse of stars. They weren't always visible in San Francisco's fickle climate, but the vastness of them was a comfort to Nora when she could look up and see them. Great swaths of them were visible in between patches of clouds tonight. It was as if God was reminding her they were always there, even when the clouds hid her view. It was not much as signs from Heaven went, but it would have to do. Sighing, Nora peered down into the little, optimistic garden Mama and Aunt Julia had made. It would have to do, too.

She noticed it, just before she turned to go to bed.

A small bouquet of blue flowers, tied to the post that held up one side of the makeshift fence. Larger versions, Nora realized, of the tiny buds Quinn had fastened into her repaired locket.

He'd been there.

Yes, of course some other explanation was possible, but somehow Nora's heart was sure Quinn had left those flowers. The thought of him staring up into her window in the moonlight was so potent it stole her breath. They'd talked about how her window looked out on to that garden. She was even sure he'd caught her watching him as he removed the house column that had become the tent city's second message post. Quinn had been here. Tonight.

She yearned to dash downstairs, throw the back door open and peer around to find him waiting on the edge of the lawn in the way he waited across the street. To find those golden eyes amidst all the blue cream of the moonlight. Surely he must be awake, waiting, imagining. It was as if she could feel him out there in the night.

Quinn slumped on to his cot with such force he was sure Ma would wake from the sound. There must be some psalm filled with ache and misery to describe his current state, but he hadn't enough energy to recall a single verse. *It's too much, Lord,* he lamented in silent prayer. *There's just me and so much need. I've never been so tired.* So tired he'd almost been caught. The fog of his fatigue had made him sloppy, and he'd almost walked headlong into two men with guns. In that hollow gap between his mistake and his safety, he mind went straight to Nora.

I don't want to die without kissing her. That had been his thought. There, in the dark, his longing galvanized into something almost reckless. She would know, however he could manage it, what she meant to him. He would never take a kiss that hadn't been freely given, but if she gave him her affections he would grab at that treasure with both hands. *If you grant me her heart, Lord, I could take on anything.*

He walked out of that close call steeled to one purpose: letting her know.

How, exactly, does one man let a woman he can't see know what she can only guess, in the middle of the night? Quinn looked up, as if to dare Heaven to solve this whopping riddle, and saw his answer: in the flower box above his head was a collection of blue flowers. Nora's flowers, as he'd come to think of them.

It probably took more time, but it felt like mere seconds before he'd cut half a dozen from the flower box, pulled a handful of threads from the woven edge of the blanket, and ran all the way to Nora's home. A smile swept across his face when he saw what Nora must have thought of as the "rose trellis"—it was merely a fence post around the tiniest of gardens. Even if it held his weight, it would have provided four feet of altitude at best—hardly enough to reach the corner window he knew opened into Nora's room. He stood staring at the window for a while, willing her to come to it despite the lateness of the hour. Imagining what he would say, what he would do if she appeared.

It was probably God's grace that she didn't, for he was sure all his restraint would be lost if he saw her. Just before he left, Quinn ran his finger along one of the blooms, wishing it was Nora's cheek he touched. *She'll know.*

He repeated that thought—the half declaration, half desperate prayer that she would know his heart—as he lay on his cot. *I can't bear it if she never knows, Lord. Even if she doesn't feel the same, I need her to know.*

But she did feel the same, he was almost sure of it.

He fell asleep praying for God's mercy to find some way through the multitude of hurdles that kept them apart.

Chapter Eighteen

$\smallsmile$

By Tuesday, Nora felt time had crawled to a halt. She was grateful to have the task of doll-making, for the days seemed to lumber by, mocking her impatience. A struggle raged inside her: she needed time to assemble the dolls well, but she couldn't get to Grace House fast enough. Nora knew the flowers were a gift from Quinn, even if her mother persisted in her belief that Major Simon left them as a token of his coveted esteem. It seemed an act of God's kindness that Albert's schedule kept him from a visit—Nora wasn't at all sure what she would do when she faced him again. She had no idea how to handle his advances when she felt such an impossible and unlikely longing for Quinn Freeman.

And she did long for him. By the time she finally sat beside Reverend Bauers on his cart as it wound through the city, it had grown close to the desperate craving that Annette described in her diary—a nonstop fixation. But then again, it seemed entirely different. Annette talked of Eric's physical characteristics, things he did that made her feel special. Nora did find Quinn exceedingly handsome, but her attraction to him ran far deeper than that. It was his character, more than his eyes, that stole her breath. His thoughts, how he saw the world, how tenderly he treated Sam or Edwina. Certainly his eyes were capable of taking her breath away—even from a distance, as they often did—but it was the soul she glimpsed behind the eyes that captured her heart.

He *had* captured her heart. No matter how appropriate her parents found Major Simon, Nora's heart was no longer hers to give. Marriages for love did happen, but rarely. Did every woman let go of her heart in order to marry a suitable husband? It just seemed so wrong—so far from what God surely meant for His Holy Sacrament of Marriage.

"I need your help with a most peculiar problem," Reverend Bauers remarked jovially as they turned the corner toward Grace House. "What should I do about the persistent man pacing in my study? He's been hounding me daily regarding a certain woman. Miserable that Tuesday has taken so long in coming. I'm besieged."

"How unfortunate," she teased in return, delighted to know Quinn found the gap between this meeting and their last as unbearable as she had. "Tell me, Reverend, do you believe them well-suited for each other?"

"Oh, aye, I do indeed. It's true, they are worlds apart in life, but a perfect pair in spirit. Were they any other pair, I would count the obstacles between them as insurmountable."

Insurmountable. It was the perfect word for the sadness that overtook Nora at times when she thought of Quinn. It did seem as if the social chasm between them loomed insurmountable. *Were they any other pair...*She loved how Reverend Bauers had phrased it. "So, you do hold out hope for their prospects, then?"

"Oh, my dear, there is always cause for hope. Hope can accomplish the most amazing things." The reverend turned to look at her for the first time in their journey, and the knowledge in his eyes sparkled deep in her chest. "Yes," he said, at what must have been her desperate expression. "I am on your side, Nora. And his."

She wanted to wrap her arms around his shoulders and plant an affectionate kiss on his round cheek. "Reverend," she said, gazing into his amused eyes, "what are we to do?"

"Beyond prayer?"

"Yes, Reverend. Beyond prayer. I have prayed until my soul hurts and still feel like a storm surrounds me at every turn. It feels as if everything is against us. So if you have encouragement for me, I'd very much like to hear it."

"You have great reason to be encouraged, my dear. You have the heart of a relentless man of astounding character. Quinn will find a way. He found a way for you to meet today and will continue to vault over every hurdle between you, if I know him." A twinkle lit the old man's eye. "He simply can't bear to be separated from you, and as you know, your Quinn is not the most patient of men." He leaned in. "But you must take care, too. You will not be able to hide this for long, and I fear your own challenges once your family finds out. Society has some walls even an earthquake can't tear down."

Your Quinn. No, she wouldn't be able to hide this for long. His name hummed in her chest, and her hands tightened around the bouquet she seemed unable to put down since this morning. "He did arrange this, didn't he?"

"Of course he did." The old man laughed as if it were obvious. "And he tried mightily to convince me to fetch you yesterday—and the day before that. I was hard-pressed to get him to see reason and be patient. Even so, he has been at Grace House since sunrise, and I fear he won't last the day if we tarry much longer." His face grew more serious. "I'll be honest, my dear. I fear the strength of his affections may drive him to act unwisely. The two of you face so many challenges." He directed the cart around a corner, clucking his tongue as if he'd been negotiating rubble-filled street all his life. She wondered if it was age or faith that enabled him to face all that chaos with such calm. "Major Simon, among other things."

"Major Simon," Nora repeated, trying not to let her heart sink. "You know about him?"

"Albert Simon is an ambitious man. When he knows what he wants, he gathers every ally he can find to get it. Yes, he has asked me to speak to your father on his behalf. He is most taken with you. And I don't have to tell you Quinn is most disturbed by the rival." He leveled his dark brown eyes at Nora. "Should he be?"

She supposed a more sensible woman would have considered the situation carefully. As it was, "Not at all," came gushing out of her as if she were a schoolgirl. She felt her cheeks redden and cast her gaze down into the now-wilting flowers. She should have pressed them, but she couldn't bear not to have them near.

"Tell him so. You have much to say to each other." He winked. "But I believe he needs to hear that most of all."

Nora leaned over and gave Reverend Bauers a kiss on his cheek. "You are a dear, dear man, Reverend."

"Nonsense," he said, his smile warm and broad. "I am an idiot who doesn't know when to stop tilting at windmills. It is a good thing God suffers fools gladly, don't you think?"

"You are no fool," she said, wanting to get out of the cart and run the last few blocks while at the same time needing a host of hours to calm her nerves. "You are a very wise man."

"Remember that when we are all knee-deep in trouble."

Quinn looked at his reflection in the small, round mirror above the fireplace in Reverend Bauers's study. He wished mightily for a better shirt, for an unmended pair of pants. He looked at his bruised fingers, the ones that flexed so easily around the Bandit's sword, and willed himself to have Matthew Covington's elegance. That man was dashing and well-spoken. He? He felt like a joke of God's purpose, a fluke born of disaster and circumstance. More than anything at this moment, he wanted to feel worthy of Nora Longstreet.

It was, as Reverend Bauers was fond of saying, a God-sized wish. He heard the cart coming up the alley, and shut his eyes for a moment, drawing in a deep breath to slow down the cannon fire going off in his chest. He could have been sixteen instead of twenty-six the way his pulse was thundering. He was going to see Nora, alone. Not glancing over his shoulder or hers, but saying freely the things that had hung in the air unsaid between them. How he felt.

Hearing her say—and, mercy, he didn't know what he would do if he didn't hear her say—that she felt the same way about him.

The creak of the back kitchen door sounded her arrival, and Quinn dashed to the kitchen. She was looking down as she stepped through the door, her hat hiding her face, but when she met his eyes, a glow flooded his chest and banished every hint of worry. He understood now why men conquered the world for love. He remembered thinking Matthew Covington had gone mad when he watched that heroic man go completely foolish around Georgia Waterhouse. Back then, at his tender years, he'd thought Covington a fool. He didn't think so now. Had she asked him, in that moment, to lasso the moon, he would have said yes without thought or doubt.

"And hello to you, too, Quinn," the reverend said, having a grand time with Quinn's current speechless state. "Glory, it is worse than I thought. Why don't we all sit a moment and have a cup of tea. I'm sure cook has made some, and if not, I do remember how myself."

"I'm not thirsty," Quinn said, not taking his eyes off Nora.

"Perhaps Miss Longstreet…"

"Not at all, Reverend." After a dumbstruck second, she blinked and added, "Thank you."

Her eyes said everything he needed to know. He longed to sweep her into his arms that very second and defy the world to ever part them again.

Reverend Bauers stepped into his sight, mock sternness on his amused face. "I was thinking about how very nice it would be for Miss Longstreet to see the volume of Shakespeare sonnets Mr. Covington sent over earlier this year. The binding is exquisite." Quinn stared for a blank second. Reverend Bauers's foot gently tapped Quinn's boot. "Get out of the kitchen before you make a fool of yourself, man," he said in low tones. Raising a conspiratorial eyebrow, he returned his voice to a more public volume. "I simply haven't the time to show it to her properly. Do you think you could manage?"

"I'm sure I could, Reverend." With a grin he had no hopes of hiding, Quinn extended an elbow to Nora. "Reverend Bauers's study is just down the hall." As he turned to leave the kitchen, feeling the rush of having Nora's arm on his elbow, he caught sight of Reverend Bauers holding up ten fingers and mouthing the words "ten minutes."

Not likely. There'd be no rushing this moment, not for all the danger in California. Quinn forced his feet to move through the hallway at a casual pace, as if he were about to show Nora Longstreet the most mundane object in all the world.

Instead of showing her his heart.

Nora had thousands of thoughts tumbling through her head, feeling half her age and almost weightless as they walked down the hall. "You're hurt," she remarked, noticing new bandages on his left hand, just as the right hand's wounds were healing. "How hard you must work to always be nursing wounds."

Quinn opened the study door. "Many are hurt worse."

After a quick glance up and down the hallway, Quinn closed the study door behind them. It wasn't as if Nora hadn't been unchaperoned with a man before—she'd been ostensibly alone with Major Simon just days before—but Nora's heart was pounding so hard she fought against the urge to put her hand to her chest.

Her chest, where her locket lay. The locket housing the tiny buds Quinn had given her. Her hand found its way to the locket anyway, and she felt Quinn's eyes on her hand. On his gift. "Where is this book?" she managed to choke out.

Quinn's eyes glowed. "There is no book."

"So, I've been tricked?"

"I hope not." He looked at her, a long, unguarded gaze that sent her pulse skipping. "Have I?"

"I don't think so." Surely, the air had been cooler in the kitchen. "Those flowers, they were…"

"…From me," he finished for her, taking one step toward her. She'd known it all along, of course, but it felt so different to hear him claim them out loud. "I knew you'd recognize them." He took another step toward her. "I'm done hiding it, Nora. I don't want to talk around it or pretend it's not there or pretend I don't think about you all the time or want to show you every pretty thing I come across. There's so much awfulness around right now not to…" He flushed, as if he hadn't meant to be so forward.

Nora felt for the chair back behind her, suddenly needing something solid to hold on to. "Not to what?" She wasn't even sure she'd managed to say it out loud. His straw-colored hair refused to stay the way he'd combed it. He was standing close enough to her that she could smell the soap he'd used.

"Not to grab at the one thing, the one amazing thing that's come out of it." His face broke into that deep-down confident smile of his, a "count on it" quality that made her believe they could do anything if they were together. "It is amazing, isn't it?"

For a second, propriety made her consider denying it, but it would be useless. Even if she told him there was nothing between them, Nora was sure her

eyes and her very breathlessness would give her away.
"Surprising."

"Don't you think there's something planned here?
I found your locket, I found you, all the ways you've
helped?" He paused slightly before adding, "All the
ways you've cared?"

He was right. It was as if forces had been pulling
them together since that horrible morning. As if God had
handed her some glimpse of dawn after so much darkness. Now, looking at the blaze in his eyes, it seemed
completely useless to fight against it for a moment longer.
And she didn't want to fight it. She wanted to be with
him, to spend time with him, to share in the things he
did and the thoughts he had. A determination—a defiance, even—sprung up where all the denial had been.
"Yes," she said, a surprising strength in her voice. "Yes,
Quinn, I'm sure I…"

She was going to finish that thought. Just as soon as
she remembered what it was. At the moment, the look
in Quinn's eyes sent every shred of logic packing. His
smile broadened. He closed the distance between them
and put his hand to her cheek. His hand was warm and
rough and exquisitely gentle. Nora thought the room
would dissolve away to nothing around her, felt as if
the floor would give way and the walls would fall over.
She closed her eyes for a moment, hoping to memorize
every detail of his touch, sure this stolen moment would
be the only one they had. Life was too sensible to allow
something like this to endure. This was fantasy and
folly and…and she'd fight to keep it with everything in
her power. "I'm sure," she said again, whispering it this
time as she opened her eyes to see him gazing at her.

She brought her hand up to rest atop his, desperate to hold on to him as he touched her face.

One thumb traced a slow arc across her cheek. "I don't know *how,* yet." His voice held the same determination that drummed in her heart.

"There has to be a way."

"I'll find it. After all, I found you, didn't I?" He looked at her with wonder, as if the thought just struck him anew. "In all the city, I found you. After all this, I found you."

Nora let her head fall against his strong hand. "Find us a way, Quinn."

It was as if the topaz in his eyes ignited, as if she'd unleashed something fierce and powerful in him. He took both her hands in his and kissed them gallantly. "There's not a thing can stop me now."

She had to laugh at his exuberance. "What about Reverend Bauers and his ten minutes?" She held up her fingers the way the reverend had.

He laughed as well. "Never you mind that." He pulled her a bit closer. "Say my name one more time. Say it." He looked like he would spin them around the room any moment.

"Quinn, be careful."

"Not at all. I'm done being careful. Can't you see that?"

His defiance lit fire to hers. She brought both his hands to her lips and kissed them tenderly. He began to pull her closer. Neither one of them heard the knock on the door until it opened and Reverend Bauers cleared his throat with mock alarm.

"Good Heavens, I see I've come just in time."

Quinn scowled. "Go away."

"I think not."

Quinn's eyes closed. "Go *away,* Reverend, sir."

Nora felt flustered. "Reverend," she interjected, squeezing Quinn's hands, "You've been so kind to us. How can I thank you?"

"By taking this fine thing God has given you and being wise. Keep our friend here from crossing the line from brave to foolish. I'm afraid I haven't had much success in that department."

Surrendering to the interruption, Quinn reached out and clasped the old man's shoulders. "You've got too much of the fool in you yourself, old man. And I'm glad of it, I am." His gaze wandered back to Nora, as if he couldn't take his eyes off her for more than a second or two. "And grateful."

"And one or two other things I won't go into, I'm sure," Bauers said. "But time's not on our side. Part ways, you two, before anyone's the wiser or I'll live to regret this more than I do."

Quinn's eyes conveyed a million things, even if he only returned his hat to his head and said, "Soon." She found his smile the most remarkable sight; the glow of it seemed to settle beneath her ribs and warm her from the inside.

"Soon," she almost whispered. Even a second earthquake wouldn't prevent them from being together again.

Reverend Bauers folded his hands together across his stomach after Quinn left. "He's a most remarkable young man, but I gather I've no need to convince you of that."

"No, Reverend." She sighed. "I'm quite convinced."

The clergyman's voice fell to an oddly serious tone.

"He faces more challenges than you know. And I fear things will only get more difficult for him in the coming days. He'll need to draw strength from you." He walked toward her, clasping her hands in his. "But I see great strength in you, too, so I think that perhaps God does indeed know what He's up to."

Hadn't she wondered the same thing?

Chapter Nineteen

Quinn lay the list on Major Simon's desk. "I don't know whether to be flattered or worried." People's faith in the Messenger's abilities had expanded to some rather challenging requests. Pins and basic medicines were one thing. Some of the items on the posts this week made for tall orders. One man had actually asked for lumber—the largest request yet.

"Lumber is gold at the moment," Simon responded. "I can't get enough to fill my own needs much less extra. Besides, I don't much like the idea of people building on to their shacks. We can't have people thinking of Dolores Park as anything but temporary."

"Temporary? After three months?"

Simon gave Quinn a hard look. "You think I don't know most of these people don't even have two timbers left of their old homes to nail together? I know I'm not dealing in reality, Freeman. But I've got to work as hard as I can to give the right impression." He looked down for a moment and swore for the first time since Quinn had met him. "The general got a wire from the president yesterday. The whole world is watching." Major

Simon was normally such a cool-headed character; it was more than a bit unnerving to watch him fray around the edges. If the pressure was getting even to him, it must be huge.

"All right then, no lumber. I don't know how I'd carry it anyway." Quinn scooped the bits of paper back up.

Simon let his head fall into his hands and heaved out a sigh. "Their wants aren't your fault." He looked up, attempting a weak smile. "Now look who's gone off and shot the messenger, hmm? You've done an amazing job."

Again, Quinn was glad for the praise, but just a bit leery of Major Simon, who seemed to think the Midnight Messenger was an army recruit. He'd made a point to call them "partners" earlier in the discussion, but the relationship was feeling more lopsided day by day. Quinn had already decided it was time to seek out a few sources other than the army. *Lord,* Quinn prayed as he tucked the batch of papers into his pocket and said goodbye to Major Simon, *if You can bring water from a stone, and manna from Heaven, a dozen tins of peas should be easy, right?*

Actually, it was. For all the talk of scarcity, Quinn had secured half of what he needed from sources outside the major in the space of two hours. Things could be found with a little clever trading here and there. It took time, connections and creativity. The last two Quinn had always had in abundance. Time, however, was growing as scarce as sleep. By dinner, Quinn only had left the last four items on his list: two Bibles and two revolvers. He'd already decided not to even attempt the revolvers, and he had a pretty good idea where he could manage the pair of Bibles. He needed a safe place—other than Major Simon's cache or his own shack at the camp—to stash his Messenger "booty" anyway, and the Grace House basement was ideal.

"Glory!" Reverend Bauers remarked when Quinn came up the basement steps in the full Messenger gear he'd pulled from its hiding place at the army base, suddenly uncomfortable with it staying there. "You look dark and dangerous. I venture even the Bandit would be wary of you with that pistol at your side."

"I haven't used it yet," Quinn remarked, adjusting the large duffel that was beginning to wear permanent bruises in his shoulder.

"I pray you never do," Reverend Bauers said, "but that's optimistic, I fear." He handed Quinn the two Bibles he'd requested. "I feel much better knowing you've gotten even two requests for God's word. I know it's my weapon of choice against all we face these days." He stopped for a moment, considering Quinn with a wistful look. "'Blessed are the feet of him who brings good news,'" he quoted.

"Maybe, but sore are the feet of him who brings canned peas." He shifted the sack again, straining under the weight, cringing when the tins inside the sack clanged against each other despite the careful packing he'd done. "I'm delivering those first. No one had better ask for potatoes this week. Or anvils." Quinn turned his back to the reverend so he could untie the top of the duffel and tuck the pair of Bibles inside.

"You've still your humor about you," Bauers said as he retied the bag. "I'm glad of that." He gave Quinn's shoulder a quick clasp. "And you have much to be glad of, especially today."

"I'm glad of *you*." Quinn was pleased to have an ally in the old man, especially in terms of Nora. "Thanks."

"The glint in your eyes is thanks enough." Bauers moved aside the scraps of cloth that had been hung in the mission kitchen as make-do curtains. "It's good and dark out now. Off with you, and take care. Come back when you need anything else."

Quinn settled his hat down over the mask. "That won't be long, you know."

The night was thick with mist, hiding the slip of a moon that had appeared earlier in the evening. It made travel easier in some respects, with more shadows for hiding and bad visibility. The lack of vision, however, seemed to amplify sounds so that Quinn stilled and flinched every time the tins clanked against each other.

Inside Dolores Park, deliveries were always challenging. Close quarters granted all kinds of nooks in which to hide, but it meant eyes were everywhere. The camp never really went to sleep—someone was always up somewhere—but the lack of lanterns, fires, or streetlamps made concealment easier. Quinn had become so acquainted with Dolores Park's cracks and corners he could probably find his way blindfolded.

Saying a prayer of thanks for his gift at memorizing things, Quinn ticked down the list of who got what in his head as he peered down the next aisle. Two tins of peas to the third shelter on the left, one of the Bibles to the last shack on the right. Just before setting the tins down outside the structure, Quinn wet the nub of charcoal he'd found yesterday and used it like a pencil to add his new flourish—a large "MM" on the top of the tins. Not quite the Black Bandit's calling card of a white ribbon—frankly, he found that a bit overdone—but a mark of his own. Something to let folks know it wasn't just the United States Army looking out for their welfare. He did the same in the dedication page of the Bibles, and on every other item he'd procured himself rather than from the army stocks.

It was near three o'clock when Quinn finally folded the dark duffel and the other Messenger items into their new hiding place at Grace House, yawned, and headed for home. Just before turning in, Quinn removed a small square of lavender soap from his pocket, marked its muslin wrapping with the double M sign and hung it with a set of pins to their door for Ma to find.

Nora came downstairs later that week, still smiling from a bouquet of blue flowers that had once again found their way to the backyard garden fencepost. Even better, attached to the flowers this time was a large lump of sugar—something nearly impossible to get lately, and she had no idea how Quinn had acquired it. How clever he was—it was an ideal token to offer to her parents.

The packet fell from her hands on to the hall table, however, as she turned into the front room. Mama and Aunt Julia had the most dreadful looks on their faces. She hurried into the room, worried as to what could have made them so upset.

Until she saw what Aunt Julia clutched to her breast with brittle, shaking hands. She remembered now. She had heard a rustle in the garden last night, and had stolen out of bed to find the flowers and sugar tied to the fencepost as the bouquet had been the last time. It had been nearly impossible to fall back asleep, and instead she had stayed up until nearly dawn, reading.

Reading Annette's journal, which had become a treasured companion to all the emotions roiling around inside her. And she had fallen asleep, journal in hand, sleeping late into the morning. She had not realized, until just this horrid moment, that while the flowers and sugar were still on her coverlet, the diary was gone when she awoke.

Of course it was gone. It was now in Aunt Julia's hands. They must have found it when her mother came in to wake her. Nora squeezed her eyes shut against the wall of remorse that stole every drop of the joy she'd felt only seconds before.

"Yes," came Aunt Julia's tight, sharp voice, "I found it. Or rather, your mother did."

"Nora." Her mother's voice was laced with disappointment. "Why did you not bring this to us earlier? How could you have kept all this from us when we might have prevented…" Nora was glad Mama thought it too cruel to finish the sentence.

"I only just found it," Nora admitted, "I didn't know… before. I had no idea."

"You two shared everything." Aunt Julia jabbed the words at her. It was a fair accusation.

"I thought we did."

"You thought." Aunt Julia seemed to be a coarser, angrier version of the gray ghost she had become on the day of the earthquake when Annette's body could not be found. Annette had been sleeping at Nora's house the night of the earthquake. No one could ever understand why she had wandered off in the melee. It had been assumed, for comfort's sake Nora supposed, that she'd made her way home more quickly than the others in a desire to see her mother and father safe. As she stood there, watching her aunt's spirit seemingly die right in front of her, Nora realized that it was more likely Annette went looking for Eric. Which, according to the hints in the diary, was right into the heart of the destruction. It seemed so terribly, inexcusably cruel for Aunt Julia to know this now, when it did no good at all.

"Heedless child!" Aunt Julia hissed, her fingers nearly scraping at the bindings. "My own flesh and blood, capable of such…such *wanton* behavior." It was as if the very words left a foul taste in her mouth. Her face pinched tighter as tears reddened her eyes. Mama reached for her hand but Aunt Julia knocked it away. "And they've paid for their sins, her and that…shiftless cad. What snake of a man lures a young woman like that into plans to abandon us? It's this city, I tell you. This vile, sinful place…"

"Now, Julia." Mama reached out again, to no avail.

"Reverend Mansfield is right. We shouldn't be surprised. How much longer did we expect God to endure such blatant, sinful ways?" The pastor from the church Aunt Julia and all of Nora's family attended had been vocal in his condemnation of the city's sin. He was one of those people who saw the earthquake as God's judgment sent down upon an evil city. Nora could never see his viewpoint, especially now.

"God struck down the city," Aunt Julia continued. "And now I have to live with the fact that he struck down *my own daughter* with it."

Reverend Mansfield would surely see it that way, too. Nora's heart burned with regret for letting the secret slip when only pain would come of it. There was too much pain already.

"You've had a terrible shock, Julia," Papa said, coming into the room behind Nora. Land sakes, did everyone in the house know it all by now? "We all have."

"I want to leave. I want to leave this horrible place and never look back. There isn't a thing left here to want."

"That's not true," Nora said before she thought better of it.

"What do you know, you silly thing!" Aunt Julia snapped, making even Mama and Papa flinch. "You didn't even know enough to stop your cousin from walking into her own doom. We've taught you nothing about what's right, *nothing!*" With that, she threw the book on the divan next to her and left the room, her sobs wafting through the house until they all heard her door slam shut upstairs.

Nora went to pick up the journal. Awful as it was, she couldn't bear to think what Aunt Julia might do to it, and it was her last piece of Annette. On her knees in front of the divan, Nora slid the book to her lap and looked up at her mother. "I didn't know, honest. And once I found it, I only thought it would hurt Aunt Julia worse to know."

Papa came up and sat on the other side of the divan, so that Nora kneeled between her parents. "You really had no idea what this man was planning? You knew nothing of Annette's…" She could tell Papa was trying to think of a delicate term, "indiscretions?"

"I suppose I suspected something. She told me she fancied some man Aunt Julia and Uncle Lawrence wouldn't like. But running off with him? I never dreamed she'd keep something like this from me."

Mama laid her hand on Nora's arm as it stretched across the divan's thick brocade cushions. A color Annette had helped to choose, Nora suddenly remembered. She was so fond of burgundy. They'd planned to have a portrait of her painted this summer, sitting on this very spot. With a sad twinge, Nora realized it would never have been painted either way. For either way, Annette would have been gone.

But gone was not the same as dead, even if Aunt Julia would disagree right now.

"It is one of life's great tragedies, the things that have been done to innocent young ladies who do not guard their way. You see, now, why your father and I have been so very careful with you. So much can be lost."

Nora's heart shuddered.

"It is a horrible thing to think, but I can't help wondering if God has been kind in taking Annette when He did."

"Papa!" Nora said, pulling back.

"I know it seems harsh," Papa said, "but do you have any idea what kind of life awaited your cousin if she'd have gone through with this mad plan? A man from the docks? It's a terrible squalor of a life, Nora. Why do you think I'm so worried about you at Dolores Park? These are coarse, desperate people. Full of violence, drink and disease."

She'd never heard her father talk so. "But they aren't all bad. You help them. Papa, you spend *every day* helping in the official camps."

"It's my duty to serve those camps." He said it as if his mercies were an unpleasant but necessary task, like swallowing castor oil. "It's the duty of every good Christian to help those in need." The words didn't seem to include those in need in Dolores Park.

Nora ran her hand along the book. "Annette loved him." It was an odd thing to say, but she felt that someone ought to at least make it clear that Annette was not duped or kidnapped or stolen in the night. "He loved her—or she believed he loved her."

Mama reached out and smoothed Nora's hair, much as she had done when she was a small child. On the floor, at their feet, it did feel as if she'd become small again. "It isn't a fairy story, Nora. This would never have ended well. Only pain and heartache and much worse would have come to Annette. She must have known how dreadful it was to keep it even from you." Mama's eyes looked from the book to Nora. "You can't keep it, you know. And you must never speak of it." The warning in Mama's eyes made Nora clutch at the diary involuntarily. "I suppose it's up to Julia and Lawrence, but I wouldn't fault her if she chose to burn it."

"Burn it?"

"It's far better if no one else knows." Papa seemed to actually agree with Mama on this terrible suggestion. He looked at Nora. "Reverend Mansfield might make an example of Annette if he learned of it, and how could you put your aunt and uncle through something like that? Haven't they been through enough without adding such disgrace to their pain?"

A startling panic grabbed at Nora. "No one will know. I'll hide it. I can't bear to lose another piece of her."

Mama looked at her as if she were a petulant child. "I think you meant to hide it now, and we all see what has happened. Surely you won't put your needs before Annette's own mother and father's?"

Papa reached down and took the book gently from Nora. It took an enormous amount of willpower not to snatch it back out of his hands and run from the room. Everything seemed to be crumbling around her, and just at the time when things seemed to be springing to life. Any chance of Mama and Papa's ever approving of Quinn slipped through her fingers as she knelt on the parlor floor. "Perhaps," Papa said in a quiet, managerial tone, "this is best decided in a while. Everyone has a lot to think about."

Nora leaned back against the divan, feeling drained. *If only you knew how much there is to think about, Papa.*

"What was that you were holding when you came down this morning?" Mama's voice held a forced brightness, as if she were packing up all this unpleasantness to stuff away in a closet and wanted something nice to take its place.

"Sugar," Nora said, still too stunned to evade the truth.

"Oh, my. Received a trinket from our dashing major, have you?"

Of course Mama would think the flowers and sugar came from Major Simon. He'd made a spectacle of himself bringing sugar when he came to dinner—Mama was beside herself at having a "true cup of tea" after dinner. Nora didn't answer. She had no idea what to say, especially in light of all that happened.

"Now, don't make Nora blush," Papa said, smiling. It was clear from the look that passed between him and Mama how pleased they were at the major's attentions.

And yet how was she acting any different than Annette, sneaking around, whispering affections behind closed doors? "Perhaps you should come on the mail run with me this afternoon after all. I'm sure I could send word to Major Simon to meet us, and I'm equally sure he'd prefer to hear your gratitude in person."

Any chance at seeing Quinn—however small—was a treasure. She needed his help to figure out what to do next.

Or did she? Was she simply letting some insipid passion pull her off the sensible course? She had never been one to second-guess things, had always thought of her decisiveness as a quality, not a fault. She'd loved it when Annette called her bold.

And where had Annette's even greater boldness— which Nora had always admired—gotten her? The urge to see Quinn now vied with an equally strong mistrust of her instincts. The result was a frustrating paralysis.

Papa laid his hand on her shoulder. "Come now, you mustn't let Annette's misfortune weigh down your own future." It was the oddest thing to feel his offer of comfort, knowing he had no idea of the true reason for her upset. Like having two conversations at once. Now Papa was encouraging her to visit the camp?

Not the camp. The major.

Chapter Twenty

Dolores Park buzzed with talk of the latest Midnight Messenger visit. One sack of goods—well, actually two, for Quinn had to make a second run with all those cumbersome tins of vegetables—had launched a fast and ever-exaggerating chain of gossip. As he stood in a bread line for unofficial camp residents after several hours' work cleaning bricks this morning (gratefully, a seated task; his feet throbbed), Quinn heard the pair of men behind him boast that the Midnight Messenger had brought an entire ham to a shack in Dolores Park. The truth had been slightly less heroic—a can of some sort of luncheon meat—but it made Quinn smile just the same. He smiled for a good half an hour, until it came to him that perhaps he ought to worry about what kinds of requests would turn up today. Someone had even come from another unofficial camp several blocks away, pinning a handful of requests to the Dolores Park message posts.

Major Simon had advised Quinn to only pull a handful of requests on an irregular schedule, but he'd long since begun augmenting his army-supplied runs with

Messenger deliveries of his own procurement. There was just so much need.

"Beware expectations," the major had warned. "When unmet, they can be dangerous things."

"Kind of odd when you think of it," the man behind Quinn said. "We got us a whole army what's supposed to be lookin' out for our needs, and turns out one fella in a dark suit bests 'em all."

That made Quinn raise an eyebrow and listen harder.

"How do you know the Midnight Messenger wears a dark suit?" the other asked suspiciously. Evidently, he suspected his partner knew more than he was letting on.

"I hear tell. Besides, what do you expect someone called the Midnight Messenger to wear? Pink?" He lowered his voice. "I heard he's a big fella. Over six feet."

Quinn hunched.

"With long, flowing dark hair, like one of those pirate types."

Quinn straightened up again, laughing at his own prideful caution.

"I reckon he works for the army," the second man suggested. "So's they can cut corners and all."

"Or spy on us," the other countered. "He's got to be a sneaky one if no one's caught up with him yet." Quinn bent down, pretending to have something wrong with his shoe, so that he could angle his face just enough to catch a glimpse of the pair. He thought he recognized the voices, but the faces were unfamiliar. Never mind, he knew which aisle they lived in by the can of meat he'd delivered there.

"Of course, if he works for the army, no one's *gonna* catch up with him, are they?"

"I hope they don't. My wife needs a tin of powder for her stomach troubles, and I don't hardly think an army that won't give us flour will give us medicine for my Laura." The man grunted. "I'm fixing to put a message up on the post. I figure it's the postmaster who's got something to do with it. He don't ever cross to our side of the street, but his pretty daughter does. I seen her write things down once."

"I heard someone tell that Major Simon fella to expect the postmaster and his daughter at today's mail run. Could be you're right, Mack."

Only sheer strength of will squelched Quinn's urge to turn and look at the pair. Who was sending word to Simon that Nora was coming? And why? Had her father suddenly decided to encourage Nora's visits to Dolores Park? Or had Major Simon stepped up his efforts regarding Nora?

Nothing, not the longest bread line in history, not even the throbbing of his tired feet, would keep Quinn from today's mail run. He forced patience into his fidgety body as the line inched along by reciting, "Mack and Laura, stomach powder, same row as the ham."

Nora looked upset. She smiled pleasantly, casting her eyes out over the crowd with every piece of mail, but Quinn held back, suddenly unsure if her quick, searching glances sought him or Major Simon. He'd thought she'd be beaming after the flowers and sugar. After their declarations in Bauers's study. He'd felt like nothing would come between them after they'd spent that time together. Himself, he'd been walking on air for the hours since she kissed his hands. Now, he felt sore, exhausted, and naggingly uncertain. What he wanted, what he *needed,* was to speak with her. He thought of the pirates, the buccaneers the men in the bread line had likened to the Midnight Messenger. If I were a pirate, I would steal her away, he thought. Take her to some foreign shore where no one cared what cut of coat a man wore or who his parents were. Or weren't.

When Simon came to the mail cart, it only got worse. Mr. Longstreet beamed over the major, offering jovial smiles and knowing glances that lodged in Quinn's gut and simmered there. The only thing that made the whole scene bearable was the sure sense that Nora wasn't really happy to see Major Simon. Oh, she feigned it well, all smiles and downward glances, but the way she held her head and the way she flailed her hands gave it all away. When Nora was happy, her hands were calm and graceful. When she was upset, they traveled about like bees, flitting from her neck to her waist to her skirts. And he, he knew that about her like he knew a thousand other little details his heart had memorized. Because he knew *her*—the true Nora, the Nora inside what other people saw.

He lingered on his side of the street until she'd finished her pleasantries with the major. Then, as Simon and the postmaster exchanged confident looks—he disliked the sense of negotiation their glances gave him, as if Nora were a spoil of war—Nora went back to taking in the mail. Watching how she served those in line, his resolve grew stronger. She was in his life for a reason, and he in hers. All the conventions in the world couldn't alter that truth.

She looked his way, finally, catching his eye. For a

moment, there was the unchecked affection he'd seen in Bauers's study. Her eyes glowed, her lips parted just the slightest bit and he could almost hear her suck in a breath. For the tiniest moment the world fell away around them.

Then, as if a drape came down, he watched caution come over her. While she still held his gaze, it was with doubt rather than joy. Her eyes told him a sort of war was going on inside her—the possible fighting the probable. Affection and longing and fear and sadness all stuffed themselves into those few seconds.

Something had happened. He didn't know what, but he did know he couldn't let her alone. He pleaded to her with his eyes, hoping he could tell her to hang on, to give him just a moment to work something out. He held up a finger, arching his eyebrows and mouthing "wait," then ducked around the corner to find Sam.

It took all of ten minutes to contrive a reason for Sam to bring Nora to the teeter-totter, but Quinn was pacing madly by the end of it. His imagination had come up with a dozen scenarios—each more catastrophic than the last—as to what had happened to make Nora look at him with such worry.

"What's wrong?" His effort at a conversational tone failed miserably.

"Nothing."

Already she was lying to him. "That's not true. Something's wrong. I can see it."

She looked up at him. "This can't work. Quinn, surely you know that. We're foolish to think it can."

"You didn't feel that way earlier. You've never felt that way. What's happened?"

She glanced around nervously. "Annette. She kept a

journal, and I found it. She was…involved…with someone and they were going to run away together just as the earthquake…" Her hand went to the locket again. "Everyone is so upset. Her parents are furious, they're saying she's better off dead."

"We're not them, Nora. I'll go to your parents." The conviction roared up inside him. "I'll make them see. And if they don't…well, I won't be without you. We belong together and they'll just have to see that."

"They won't," she nearly wailed. "You should have heard them, Quinn. They said the most horrible, judgmental things."

"Do you believe that? What they said?" Suddenly, he needed to know that more than anything. Needed to know if she could defy them and their thinking.

Nora looked at him with stormy, sad eyes. "It's not just them. What kind of future could we possibly expect?"

"The same future anyone's got a right to expect. To be happy. To be with someone you care about. Nora, we'll never be running off in the night, I'll tell you that right now." He wanted to grab her hand and shake her, knock this new layer of fear off her spirit and bring her back to the courage he'd seen before. Instead, he gripped his hat and tried to hold her with his eyes. "I'm sorry about your cousin. But your parents are wrong. And we're right. I don't know how I'll convince them—how *we'll* convince them, but we will."

"I can't see how. Not now."

He reined in his frustration. "Not yet. Maybe you're right, and now's not the time, but soon enough *we will*. Do you trust me to work it out? Do you trust us to work it out?"

"I don't know."

"I do." He held her eyes, wanting desperately to hold her to his chest but knowing this wasn't the time for it. "I do know. Sure as anything. We'll find a way, Nora, you hang on to that." He locked her in his gaze until she straightened and nodded.

Hold her in Your palm, Father, Quinn prayed as he motioned for Sam to come walk her back. *She's my whole world now.*

Nora walked back across the street clutching Sam's hand. It was the mirror image of the first time they'd walked together. That first trip, Sam had grasped her hand tightly, all his fear clenching his fingertips as he led her to his father's shack. Now, she felt as if Sam led her through her fear back to her father's cart. She was grateful for the tiny escort—her mind was in such a tumble she didn't know how she'd have found her way alone.

She had fooled herself that it would sort itself out. That she would see Quinn and suddenly know her course. Instead, her heart tottered like the toy Quinn had built—one second thinking the safety of Major Simon and her parents' approval was so wise, the other second falling into a rush of emotion when she looked into Quinn's eyes. When he looked at her so fiercely, with such a command to trust him, she felt what surely must be passion. An overwhelming, powerful sense of need and "rightness" that let her believe they had a future. That the two of them had been uniquely paired in all the world, uniquely completing each life to the betterment of the other.

And a life with Major Simon? The most she could say was that it felt stiflingly arranged.

Why did life suddenly have such urgency anyway? Why, if she had gone on unpaired for this many years, did her heart and her parents suddenly demand upheaval?

The ground has shaken things up enough, Lord, she prayed as she gave Sam a hug goodbye and walked up to the mail cart. *Must You shake up my whole soul in the process?*

"Major Simon left something for you while you were gone," Papa said, as he offered his hand to let his daughter up onto the mail cart. He smiled with undiluted pleasure as he pointed to a small package on the bench of the cart. It opened to reveal a stack of cloth in various bright colors, small samples of yarn, a few bits of lace and a handful of buttons. Along with a small package of lemon drops. She read the accompanying note:

Reverend Bauers told me you needed more supplies to make dolls. I hope these will help. The lemon drops are for the dollmaker, from her admiring major.—A

"Why are we meeting here?" Quinn looked at the desolate corner of the scrapyard where Major Simon had asked him to meet. Even for their unusually discreet relationship, this seemed a bit much.

Simon picked up a tangled piece of steel and spun it to catch the orange sunset. "Because I have an important question to ask you. A sort of unofficial question on a rather unconventional matter. Not exactly army protocol."

Quinn didn't think anything he and Major Simon did fit within army protocol. "And what's that?"

"Are you ready for things to get complicated?"

Sitting down on a barrel, Quinn had to laugh. "They already are."

"True." The major stuck the shaft of steel upright in the dusty ground and sat down on a second barrel. "I suppose I mean, are you ready for things to get *quite* complicated?"

"Why?" Quinn replied. "What is going on?"

"I don't have to tell you," Simon began, "that a whole lot of people are watching how relief efforts get handled around here. If things go well, it could not only mean help for many people, but things could go well for me, personally. And," he added, looking straight at Quinn, "you as well. If we go about it in the right way."

"Our way isn't perfect, but it works."

"It could work better, I think. But like most good things in life, it's going to be a bit risky and I daresay unconventional." He shifted his weight on the barrel and gazed at the sun as it began to dip into the water. "Do you know how the great fire was eventually put out? Why we used all that dynamite?"

Quinn knew the basic concepts. "To burn things ahead of the fire so it didn't have enough fuel to move on. Starved it rather than drown it, I heard one man say."

"Exactly. We fought fire with fire. I'm proposing, Freeman, that we do the same here. Only the fire I'm fighting now is grift. Corruption. People abusing the relief system for their own good. It's making my job harder and your job more necessary. I wouldn't need the Messenger if things got *where* they were supposed to *when* they were supposed to. I'd like for the army to be out of the relief business, but not if it means the marketeers are all that's left. Despite my best efforts, relief is ending up in greedy hands."

Quinn thought Simon didn't need the Messenger as much as the people in the tent cities needed the Messenger, but he got the major's idea. "I don't want the marketeers to win either, Major. It's not right. All the generosity we've seen shouldn't be ending up in the places it is."

"I'm glad you agree. And I think your unique talents put us in a place to do something about it. A real something that gets results. But we're going to have to bend the rules a bit to get what we need."

Quinn smiled. "I'm no stranger to that."

The major laughed. "That much I knew. But for what I'm about to ask, you need to come out on top of this as much as I."

"Go on."

"I don't think I can stop the thieves in any conventional way. But they'll stop each other in the name of greed. That's what I mean by fighting fire with fire. I've got a pool of money—gold, to be exact—at my disposal. We're going to offer gold for information on how supplies are slipping out of army hands. Pay these grifters to turn each other in. Or, rather, turn their information in to the Midnight Messenger. Then you use the information, get the goods and deliver them to the people who needed them in the first place. You know parts of this city I don't. You can go places I can't, can do things that...well, let's just say fall well outside of army protocol. I supply you the gold to pay the informants, with any extra means you need to get and deliver the relief supplies and everybody wins."

Quinn took off his hat. "Except me, when I get shot for playing both ends against each other."

"There is that. It'd be far riskier than what you're doing now. But eventually, you'll make it unprofitable to steal from the army while still getting help to the unofficial camps I'm not really allowed to service. Think of it, Freeman. You could be the single most beneficial man in San Francisco."

"Only no one will know. They'll just know the Midnight Messenger did it."

"I've considered that," Major Simon said with a wry grin, "and I've a plan for that, too. I think that once the tension has died down and we've gained the upper hand, that we should reveal you as the Midnight Messenger. With, of course, a whole lot of army gratitude, a public commendation and a commission in the Corps of Engineers for you to get a draftsman's education and apprenticeship. It's never been done, but then again I don't think a lot of what I have in mind for you has any kind of precedent at all. You'll be a hero."

Quinn pulled in a surprised breath. The Army Corps of Engineers would have a huge hand in rebuilding San Francisco. He'd be building, fulfilling that dream of studying architecture if what Simon said was true. He'd never considered signing up, fearing they'd never grant a real education to a man of his status. Why haul bricks for the army when a civilian firm paid just as well and no one shot at you? He could never reveal his role as the Messenger on his own—it'd be far too dangerous—but with the army at his back, he could take real credit without risking harm. If he lived through double-crossing half of San Francisco's underbelly. "It's a big risk."

"It's a big reward. I'm offering you an entire new

standard of living, Freeman. For you and your mother. You'd be able to provide—very nicely—for all the people you care about. Isn't that what all this is about, anyway? Providing for them?"

Most of the people in Quinn's life who had power had gotten it by dark means. Influence that was more about fear than respect. The docks were a system of predators, a jungle that had finally consumed his pa and lots of other people he knew. Wasn't it worth any risk to escape that? To count for something in the world, be educated and have a real hand in rebuilding this city? It called to the deepest part of him, answered a need so basic he hadn't even named it until now.

And then there was Nora. What price wouldn't he pay to be able to be seen as "a man of prospects" by her family? To lay aside all the secrecy?

It was the opportunity he'd survived for. The reason God had spared him, had given him the talents he had and the past that now made him so useful.

"I'm in," Quinn said, without a shred of doubt.

Chapter Twenty-One

"Were these with the other supplies?" Quinn watched carefully to ensure his conversation went unobserved, and made his voice husky so that Leo, a man who most people knew as the butcher but was known to Quinn to have many other well-connected occupations, wouldn't guess his identity.

"No. Finding those'll take some asking around," Leo replied. His current target was a shipment of hospital supplies that had gone missing from Fort Mason yesterday. Personally, Quinn was in search of crutches for a young woman from the northern part of Dolores Park. The army hospital had a storehouse of crutches, but Quinn wanted to see if he could secure a pair on his own, outside of army influence, as long as he was casting about for information on the missing supplies. He'd been successful. The young lady would find the pair of crutches, with a MM carved into one side, lying outside her shack when she woke tomorrow morning.

"I've heard of a man with tents for sale," Leo said. "Army tents. Along with some ether. I think he might be who you're looking for. An awful lot of things seem to wander off the official camps when he's around, seems to me."

That's exactly the information Quinn was after. "Like I said, I can pay well for information like that," Quinn said quietly. "And do something about it besides."

Leo was the first man who dared take the Midnight Messenger up on his offer. The offer had been out on the dock's unofficial grapevine of gossip for a handful of days with no results. Folks were right to hesitate. Men who hoarded supplies for the black market weren't the kind of people to take kindly to exposure. Quinn had been forced to offer a whole lot more gold than he'd originally planned before Leo finally came forth. "Ain't cooperation a profitable thing?" Leo said, keeping his back to the Midnight Messenger as instructed. "Tomorrow, two o'clock. You bring the money, I'll bring a little map showing you where you can find 'im. But I'll need twice what you offered."

Quinn winced. Until folks realized they could deal with the Midnight Messenger and not get shot themselves, it was going to take a whole lot of convincing—the shiny metal kind—to gain conspirators. Success was getting very expensive. "Done." Quinn tossed a single gold coin at the butcher's feet. "For your time."

"Pleasure doing business with you, Mr. Messenger." Leo picked up the gold and tucked it in his pocket. He walked slowly away, whistling into the night.

It's started, Quinn thought to himself. Let's hope I'm alive to see it finished.

It had been an insufferable week. The unspoken tension in the house choked the sunlight out of the air. Nora did not see how Annette's unfortunate romance altered the sorrow of her death. In fact, Nora took some solace in knowing Annette had been so happy before her life was cut short. No one—most especially Aunt Julia—shared her point of view. Everyone clipped all mentions of Annette or romance or secrecy from their words, lest Aunt Julia fall into another of her crying spells upstairs in her room.

Her own parents took all the regret as fuel to watch *her* with excruciating caution. One more not-very-well hidden sermon on the values of propriety and familial respect, and Nora thought she'd burst. It was odd to have one's life boxed up like a curated museum piece when one had just survived one of the most devastating disasters in history. She couldn't persuade her mother or father that she was not a fragile lily on the verge of being crushed by the slightest misstep. Did Mama and Papa think that all her sense and intelligence had fled at Annette's words?

She knew better. Her chafing came from the inescapable fact that her parents had good reason to worry. She would close her eyes and try to imagine Major Simon kissing her hand in the tender way Quinn had. But she could not recall the color of Major Simon's eyes. And she saw the particular gold of Quinn's eyes in all sorts of things: sunsets, leaves, this color silk or that painting.

Albert Simon was a respected man, and a foundation for a solid marital future. Quinn, for all his impossibility, was a storm she could not escape or contain. He had character but few prospects, passion but earned little respect—at least from those who did not know him, for she knew him to be highly respected and loved throughout Dolores Park. At best, Simon had a space he held open for faith, whereas Quinn had a faith that seeped into every part of his life.

It could not be denied. She was, quite irresponsibly, in love with Quinn.

Nora had somehow become a different woman. The combination of disaster, Annette's death and secrets, and the laid-bare world she now saw had added a new layer to the old Nora Longstreet. Life wove complexities and consequences into threads she hadn't seen before. Her world had expanded, deepened, and her emotions had undergone the same transformation. She needed time, space and interactions with people to help her work through it all.

All she had were relatives, prayer, confines and the poor distraction of making a dozen or so rag dolls.

It was nowhere near enough.

Her prayers for a chance to get out from under the stifling supervision of her parents were answered, oddly enough, by Major Simon. Word had reached him, evidently through her father, that the supplies he'd given her had been made into dolls that were now ready. As such, he'd sent a young officer to oversee a trip to Grace House so that she could meet with Reverend Bauers to see about their distribution. She would much rather have been escorted to Dolores Park itself, but she knew that to be unlikely. Still, she hoped Reverend Bauers might know more about someone called the Midnight Messenger. For several weeks now, Papa had brought home tall tales of blankets, medicines, foods and such that had been snatched from the hands of marketeers and delivered to those in need. How this dark hero managed to slip in and out performing such deeds of bravery and compassion without anyone discovering his identity amazed her. She imagined he worked somehow with Quinn's posts, and that pleased her immensely. This hero sounded amazing enough, even if Papa's talent for exaggeration did leave some room for doubt.

"I think Simon's behind it," Papa had told her last night after seeing her eyes go wide with the latest recounting. "Finding a way to expand the relief efforts outside of the boundaries the army has set for him. He's denying it at every turn, but there's something behind the man's eyes. It's a pity you won't see him today. I suspect you'd be able to charm the truth out of him."

Whether or not Albert Simon was involved, Nora was grateful for the major's latest heroic act: getting her out of the house. She was utterly delighted to climb into the army cart with her basket of dolls.

"Marvelous!" Reverend Bauers exclaimed upon her arrival at Grace House. "I have missed you greatly, Miss Longstreet." He gave Nora a hearty kiss on the cheek as if she were his granddaughter. It was a pity the man had no family of his own. Then again, perhaps God had granted him a whole neighborhood as his family precisely because his heart was large enough for the task. "There has been so much commotion about lately. Politics and accusation and midnight deliveries. It is a sorry thing that no one here has any appetite for discussing adventures. I've been starved for good conversation."

He took one look at the very dutiful-looking private who stood by the cart as if his career hung in the balance. "The good major's not told you to stay the entire visit, has he?"

"Yes, sir."

Bauers waved him off as if he were an insect. "Glory, how wasteful that man can be. Surely there are more important things to be doing these days than guarding a young woman in a house of worship. Go find yourself something to eat in the kitchen and tell Major Simon I wouldn't hear of your staying and shall return Miss Longstreet safe and sound myself. Tell him I insisted." He gave the private a wink. "My boss has more authority than even his."

When the private hesitated, Bauers nearly bellowed, "Off with you, then!" and chuckled when the young man fairly scrambled in the direction of the kitchen.

"I've no mind to be supervised," Bauers said, tucking Nora's basket into one arm and her hand into his other elbow. "Nor, I gather, do you. Captured our good major's attentions, have you?"

"I fear it's more the work of Mama and Papa than anything I've done. I hardly need to add two words to their efforts. I've not had much opportunity to do anything. Mama and Papa have kept me under lock and key since…" She stopped herself, realizing she'd said too much already.

"Since what?"

She shook her head. How could she heap more shame on to Aunt Julia and Uncle Lawrence by telling a man of God what Annette had done? Then again, this man of God was not the sanctimonious Reverend Mansfield. She couldn't help thinking Reverend Bauers probably would have helped Annette and Eric if they'd come to him. Here, out of Aunt Julia's parlor, with all Bauers knew, she could at least speak freely and sort out her thoughts. Hadn't she just prayed for some help in dealing with the storm swirling around inside her?

"It is a long and private story, Reverend. But perhaps it is best that I talk to you about it."

"Let me attend to a quick matter, and then we'll have tea sent into the study," Bauers said. "We can talk for as long as you'd like."

Quinn was asleep when he felt his mother push at his shoulder. As he pulled his aching body upright on the bed, she handed him a note. "Come to Grace House?" he yawned aloud, looking up at her.

"Don't you be lookin' at me, boy," Ma said sharply. "No one tells me anything." She wasn't at all pleased, and she had good reason. Notes and messages and generally suspicious behavior had been the norm for Quinn for weeks now, and when she'd see him—which wasn't often—she'd look at him with disappointment and anger. Quinn knew she thought he was up to twelve kinds of no good, and it pained him to let her think the worst of him.

Hurry up the day, Lord, Quinn prayed as he avoided Ma's glare. *I'm tired of waiting for everyone to know what I'm up to.* After a particularly close call the other night, Quinn had begun to say prayers for his safety nightly and had asked Reverend Bauers to do the same. Bauers knew he was the Messenger and was storing additional supplies at Grace House for him, but even Bauers didn't know how far things had gone.

"It'll be all right, Ma." It was a poor excuse for a response, but Quinn had no other. "Just a little while longer."

She narrowed her eyes. "Isn't it funny how those same words come out of every mouth these days. If I go to my grave never hearing again about how everythin's coming soon or on its way or in just a while, I'll die a happy woman."

Quinn pulled on his boots and kissed his mother on the cheek. "Just mind it's not that grave that's coming soon. I need you."

Her gaze softened. "Aye, that you do. There'll be no rest for me until I see you off and settled with a family of your own. And high time it is for that, too. Not that anyone can make plans for any kind of future while we're here." She waved her arm around the shack while she pushed out a disgusted breath. "Oh, for a real roof over my head again."

Quinn grabbed his hat and two of the biscuits that sat on a tin plate by the door. "I'd say soon, but you might cuff me."

"If you were goin' anywhere else but Grace House, I just might, but for the size of ye."

These days Quinn actually had enough money to occasionally ride the streetcars, so he arrived at Grace House in one-third the time it would have taken to walk the trip. Bauers met him at the door with an assessing stare. "It's as bad as I thought," he remarked, crossing his arms over his chest. "How much have you slept this week?"

"Just enough."

"You can't keep this up for much longer. You know that, don't you? Exhausted men make foolish mistakes." They walked into the hallway toward Bauers's study. "Simon pushes too hard, I think."

"He's enough of his own worries. I'll be fine, Reverend. I doubt it'll be much longer."

"Until what?" The reverend regarded him with a narrowed eye. Bauers was clever enough to sense he hadn't been told the whole story. He might have worried less if he knew the entirety of the Messenger plan, but that wasn't safe. Quinn had already decided only he and Major Simon would know all the elements of how the goods found their way to refugees. Everyone else got only pieces.

"Now, you know better than to ask me that." The constant evasion was wearing on Quinn, tired as he was.

Bauers's worried look mirrored Ma's. "I'll just have to content myself with a safer question, such as, can you stay an hour or so?"

"I can." Bauers must have had some request of him to send the note. "What did you need?"

"It's not I that's needing. It's you. When was the last time you've spent more than two minutes in prayer, man?"

"You'd be surprised. They might be short prayers, but there's heaps of 'em every day."

"The chapel is a healing place to be, Quinn. I want you to spend some time there. I want you to know you're right with God while you walk this perilously thin line. And don't think I don't suspect just how thin it is."

Quinn had seen Reverend Bauers force folks into the chapel before. Bauers had actually barred the door behind him once when he went on the one and only drinking binge of his youth, and he didn't doubt the good reverend would do it again if he felt it necessary. Truth was, he did need to pray. He needed to pour out his hopes and fears to his Father in Heaven. Right now the thought of an hour in the chapel's cool, peaceful darkness seemed like the only thing that would keep him going. Quinn smiled at the wise old man. "How is it you always know what I need?"

Reverend Bauers smiled. "I listen to the One who really does know what you need."

"You won't have to bar me in this time. I know where I need to be."

"You know—" the reverend's smile broadened into a look of fatherly pride "—I believe you do. What a man of faith you've become, Quinn. I couldn't be more proud of you." He punctuated his smile with a wink. "But I'll still come check on you in half an hour. The spirit may be willing, but I suspect the flesh may fall asleep, at the rate you've been running."

Quinn could only return the smile as he walked off toward the chapel, knowing he was indeed headed in the right direction. Twenty minutes later, with a world of weight lifted off his shoulders, Quinn turned at the opening of the chapel door behind him to find the most beautiful reassurance God had ever sent.

Chapter Twenty-Two

Ｈow he'd gotten Quinn inside Grace House without her knowing, Nora couldn't guess. But when Reverend Bauers pushed open the door to the chapel and the wedge of soft light revealed that head of sandy hair bent over the front pew, Nora's heart tumbled. When he turned and looked at her, his gold eyes shining their surprise, the connection was as powerful—and unsettling—as it had been that first day at the ceremony.

She somehow managed a quick glance back at Reverend Bauers, who merely offered the most knowing of grins and pulled the door shut behind her.

Quinn stood. The chapel was so small that even though they were on opposite sides of the room, she could hear him clearly when he whispered, "You're here." The grateful amazement in his voice unraveled something in her chest. Something she'd been clutching tightly but now couldn't hope to contain.

"I've been here for most of the afternoon," she said, wondering how long he'd been here and exactly how much planning Bauers had done.

Quinn laughed softly and shook his head. "I wonder if God realizes how devious our good reverend can be."

She laughed herself. "I believe He does, and makes good use of it besides."

He looked as if he were a thirsty man drinking in the sight of her. She felt the same sensation—the very sight of him soothed her. Her heart was at once both pounding and wonderfully settled.

"Glory, but I've missed you," he said, crossing the distance between them. "I haven't slept a whole night in forever, but every time I close my eyes, I see you."

She knew now what drove Annette, for if he told her to take his hand and run away at this moment, Nora would have done it. "I…Quinn, I'm frightened." And she was. This thing between them seemed so much stronger than she could control. And so much of her didn't want to control it.

He took another step toward her. "We'll be together. I know it, now more than ever."

He closed the distance and reached up one hand to brush a thumb across her cheek. "If I tell you that in a little while, if you just keep your fight alive, there will be a way, will you believe me?" He feathered his fingers along the side of her hair, and she reached up to hold that hand against her face, treasuring his touch. She could believe there was a way. That tiny spark of determination leapt from his fingers and lit the fire waiting inside her.

"Yes." And she did want to. With a power she didn't know her heart possessed. Without another thought, Nora threw herself into his embrace. His arms were warm and strong and she knew they could hold the world at bay.

She felt him shudder at the contact and knew it sealed for him what it had sealed for her: their fate. Only it felt more like stepping into a wonderful, adventurous future God had yet to reveal.

She kissed him. The gentle kiss went through him like cannon fire, shaking him so deeply he could never hope to describe it. All the doubt, the envy, the worry fell away in the heady bliss of knowing she was his. He sighed and wrapped his arms more tightly around her. Nora Longstreet was in his arms. It was beyond imagination, and then again, it seemed as if it could never have been otherwise. She was so perfect within his embrace, so absolutely, wonderfully near him, that all his efforts to return the kiss gently were lost. It was not a gentle kiss. Fierce was the wrong word for it— although it seemed to wield the power of the universe. Passionate was too coarse a term. His meager education failed him any vocabulary save the thought that pounded throughout his body like a heartbeat: I love her.

The vitality she'd lost roared back into her eyes. When she threw her arms around his neck, he picked her up and spun her for the sheer happiness of it all. He kissed her again, just because he could. He could fuel a hundred Midnight Messenger missions on the surge it gave him.

"I've been so worried about you," she said when they finally pulled away to sit breathlessly in the pew, his fingers threaded between hers. He couldn't stop his thumb from tracing the back of her hand. "There seems to be so much going on. Papa has been bringing home the most incredible stories."

"Really?" Quinn worked hard to hide his amusement, pretty sure where this was heading.

"This Messenger fellow, he's filling requests from your posts, isn't he? You must know who he is. That might become very dangerous for you. He's made some people very angry, Papa says."

You've no idea how dangerous or how angry, Quinn thought. He hung on to the decision not to tell her, even though the spark in her eyes was making him work hard to do so. She would be so astounded once she knew. And then there was the very tempting prospect that revealing his role as the Messenger might raise his standing in her parents' eyes. Pleasing as that was, it came at too high a cost. If he revealed himself, even to only Nora and her family, it ran the risk of the secret getting out. He'd lose every advantage anonymity gave him, not to mention placing them at risk.

As Nora recounted a few of the stories she'd heard, Quinn grew shocked at the amazing deliveries folks credited to the Midnight Messenger. Exaggeration had stretched the truth far and wide in camp gossip. His heart was so full at the moment, however, that he felt capable of the astounding feats she listed. "He is a very clever man with some powerful helpers—or so I'm told," he offered. "I don't know that much."

"He uses your posts." She looked up at him with admiring eyes and he thought himself the most blessed man on earth. "Doesn't that make you feel wonderful, to know your idea is doing so much good?"

"You use my posts, too, for your dolls. And so do other people who send help. I only make sure folks know what people need. People are mostly good if you give them the chance. I just give them that chance."

She frowned. "People are worse and worse from what Papa says. You'd think I was in braids again from the way he and Mama watch me. I know it's just everything that has happened making them so cautious, but I can't bear it sometimes. There are as many wonderful things out here as there are bad. How is it I can feel so much life when they seem to be surrounded by fear?" She tightened her hand against his. "Honestly, I don't know how I shall ever manage to see you again soon enough."

He touched her cheek. "I am very clever, you know. And God's given me a very resourceful partner in our good reverend." The mission bells rung four, and he knew their time was close to over. "I suspect we'll find a way," he said, pulling her up to standing. They walked hand in hand to the back of the chapel.

"Reverend Bauers would say this is a time for God to be mighty."

He smiled. "He'd be right."

When they'd reached the small cross hung in a nook by the chapel's rear door, Nora took both his hands and held them fast. When she bowed her head, the moment felt rich and deep. One of the few times in Quinn's life he felt the word "holy" truly applied.

"Father God, protect this man." Quinn closed his eyes, feeling the closeness of her prayer as if God's hand had indeed rested on his shoulders. *"Be gracious and mighty to us as we try and work our way through these times. Grant us wisdom and courage. Thank You so very much for how You've brought us together, for saving us from dangers. I'm glad You know my heart, Lord, for it's too full to find words. Be with us, go before us, keep*

us in Your mighty protection until we're together again. Amen."

A knock came on the chapel door, and Reverend Bauers leaned into the room. "It's time to fetch you back, my dear. I do hope you've given him the encouragement he needs."

Quinn nodded, sure he must look beyond smitten. No doubt it'd be a week before he could wipe the grin from his face.

"If there are two happier people on God's green earth at the moment, I'm sure I couldn't find them."

Nora rushed up to the reverend and grabbed his arm. "You are the dearest man in the world, Reverend."

"Only just," Quinn added, who was at that moment counting Bauers as the finest friend a man could have. "You see her home safe, now."

"You've only enough time to make your appointment, Quinn. Off with you now before you're late."

Nora grasped his arm and kissed him on the cheek. "Be safe, Quinn."

"Always," he said. It felt like yanking his heart out of his chest to leave the room. "Watch for me, I'll find a way."

If there was ground under his feet as Quinn walked to his next training session with the major, he hardly knew it. Today, the Midnight Messenger walked on air.

Just as dawn was slipping strands of pink into the sky, Quinn leaned against the wall and sighed. "You're sure? You're absolutely sure?" Quinn had been dealing mostly with small-time grifters who'd started hinting that there were much bigger forces at work. When he'd relayed his suspicions, Simon promised to look into any large shipments that would be particularly attractive to the marketeers, and he'd identified one later that week.

"Gospel truth," Leo said. "He's only the front man. It's Sergeant Miller that's got the other half."

"Theft from the inside? Why would the army steal from the army?"

"When some things fetch so high a price, ain't too many men can resist. This kind of thing's been happening all along. It's just worse now. I know of three others besides."

"Three other army men?"

"Well." Leo cocked his head to one side. "One of 'em's navy."

Quinn let his head fall back against the wall. "Outstanding."

"What's the matter?" Leo flipped one of the coins and caught it midair. "Army own you or something?"

"No one owns me."

"So, take them down with the rest of the lot. It'd be nice to see some of the high-ups fall."

Quinn reconfirmed the address of the stockpile again with Leo. How this simple butcher got the information he had, he didn't know. And didn't want to know. Leo had friends in places Quinn hoped he'd never have to go. Even more than before the earthquake, there was a whole other city lurking under the one people saw. "You're sure?" he said once more.

"Dead certain."

"Let's hope I'm not dead if you're not certain."

Leo made a derisive sound deep in his throat. "No one'd shoot you. You're a legend."

"Read some history," Quinn said as he ducked back

around the corner. "Too many times it's the legends that go down first."

Quinn managed to get half the shipment redelivered to the official camp the following night. It took four trips—one of which entailed an entirely too close call with a nasty fellow bearing a nastier knife. The other half found its way to both Dolores Park and one of the other unofficial camps nearby. A few things were just too large for one man to carry, and Quinn decided it was worth letting those go. Truth be told, he wasn't quite sure how to tell Major Simon that it was one of his own army officers doing the stealing. On one hand, Quinn supposed Simon expected the ever-present corruption to work its way into army ranks eventually. On the other hand, Simon looked so pressed at their last meeting, Quinn feared the major might explode at such news. Is wasn't as if things weren't working. People in both the official and unofficial camps got help now. Quinn decided to bide his time, to look for another way than the Midnight Messenger to expose the grand-scale thieves. A way that didn't entail him meeting the business end of an army pistol.

Chapter Twenty-Three

Papa came to sit beside Nora in the bay window as she stared out into the street after breakfast. If you didn't peer too closely, things were beginning to look something close to normal. Streetcars went by, even if not nearly as often as they used to. Had it really been months since the earthquake? So much had changed, so many wounds were still fresh. Sam's foot had completely healed, banks and shops had reopened, but Aunt Julia still cried, people still lived in shacks and stood in line and Nora could still not look at the photograph of Annette on the piano without getting a lump in her throat.

"So quiet," Papa said, fingering one of Nora's curls. "Yet, you still think louder than anyone I know." Papa always said that he could hear her brain turning over a problem from across the room.

"The world is different," she said, thinking it a vague and cumbersome response. Still, how could she even begin to talk to her father about all that was swirling around in her thoughts?

"I'm glad you see that," he said, leaning back against

his side of the bay window seat. "It is a far more dangerous place out there these days. These are troublesome
times. I worry for you and your mother."

Funny, Nora had meant the *better* sort of different.
She had lived, she realized, in a glossed-over world. A
delicate, cultivated world where faith was more of an
intellectual, spiritual pursuit rather than a daily act of
trust. God as "daily bread," had become so much more
real to her. God was somehow nearer. Clearer. She saw
His hand in places she'd never even thought to look
before.

Nora turned to her father. "Do you believe Reverend
Mansfield when he says God sent the earthquake as
punishment?"

"Do I think God smote San Francisco for her sins?"
Papa sighed. "Most days, it's easy to say no. But I've
seen things that make me wonder. This seems to have
brought out the best and the worst of our city. People
have stolen from charity. But then people like Major
Simon have done so much good."

Nora decided to ask. "Do you think Major Simon is
the Midnight Messenger?"

Papa stroked his beard, smiling. "Well, now, I have
to say I haven't given the idea consideration. I've always
guessed he had something to do with all of it, but is he
the actual man? I couldn't say. He strikes me as a bit…"
Papa hesitated "…too mature for such exploits himself.
It'd be quite a story if he were, wouldn't it?"

Messenger or not, it was certainly hard to improve
on Papa's opinion of Simon.

"I do know," Papa continued, leaning in, "that he
greatly admires *you*. You should be very flattered, my
dear."

Nora didn't know what to say. Papa mistook her downturned eyes as modesty instead of bafflement, and perhaps that was for the best. How on earth could she ever tell her parents what she felt for Quinn? They'd never understand, nor would they ever approve. She did not yet know if she could be brave enough to defy her whole family. When Quinn looked at her, she felt strong enough to challenge the world. But here, alone, she faltered.

Papa tipped up her chin, much as he had done when she was a little girl. "What are your feelings on the matter of our renowned major, Nora? I'm of the mind he is seeking a match, and I'd like to know where you stand."

Nora had hoped it would not come to this. There seemed no way through this conversation without an outright lie to her father, and she didn't want that. "Where I stand? In regards to Major Simon?"

"Exactly. Should he come seeking a match, what would your answer be?"

"He is very well regarded."

She was stalling and Papa knew it. "That's true enough, but I am not asking what others think of him. I want to know what *you* think of the man."

"I think him well-bred, distinguished and very clever. He is certain to do great things." She didn't lie. Major Simon was those things. But he had not captured her heart. She could no more make herself love him than she could make herself stop loving Quinn.

She loved Quinn.

"Do you care for the man?" Papa asked it so tenderly, she couldn't lie to him. Most especially about this.

"No," she said softly. "He is an admirable man in

many respects, but he has not captured my affections, if that's what you're asking."

"That is exactly what I am asking. And yet, seeing you talk, I would not say that you find the man repulsive. I am wondering, Nora, if you read too many novels to see what constitutes a marriage in the real world. I did not sweep your mother off her feet when we first met. In fact, we mostly were afraid of each other. But I love her dearly now. We were a fine match then, and it grew into a fine marriage. I want the same for you. And so I ask you, if you do not care for the man yet, could you see coming to care for him as time went on?"

Perhaps before. But now her heart was no longer hers to give to someone else. She knew that if she married Major Simon, it would be turning from love forever. She knew so many women who took a sensible, lukewarm marriage on themselves without a moment's hesitation. A lifetime of mutual regard, of domestic partnership. Before the earthquake, before all that had happened to her, she suspected she could have done the same.

She could not now.

"I can't say." It was the closest she could come to the truth without rejecting Papa outright. Even the concerned disappointment in his eyes just now was painful to bear.

"You are old enough to know your own mind, Nora." Papa sat back. "But you have also been through a terrible ordeal. Let us simply say that more time is needed. It would be too soon and too cruel to move in such a direction in light of your Aunt Julia, anyway. But we will talk of this again soon, hmm?"

Nora could only nod. Nod and trust that Quinn had indeed found a way. *Be very, very mighty, God,* she prayed for what seemed like the hundredth time since leaving the Grace House chapel.

Nora was out in the tiny garden, tending to a forlorn patch of flowers she was trying to coax into bloom when a pebble fell at her feet. She thought nothing of it until a second fell a foot or two away toward the backyard fence. And then a third, closer to the edge of the fence. Someone was trying to get her attention from the other side of the fence. It didn't take much imagination to wonder who it was luring her to the secluded corner of the alley. Peering into the kitchen window to ensure no one watched, Nora nevertheless gathered up the weeds she'd just pulled and made it look as if she was meaning to toss them beyond the fence.

Quinn's face beamed as she turned the corner, and his smile melted her heart. She did love him. The world felt disjointed when they were apart and centered when they were together, no matter what the circumstances. She realized, as she slid her hand into his, that any efforts to build a future without him would never work. His future had been intertwined with hers. Her heart had moved from "if" to "how."

Quinn pulled her into his arms and kissed her forehead. "I can't seem to breathe without you." She felt his deep breath and knew what he meant. She'd become so acutely aware of his absence, so needful of his presence that it did feel as if she choked without him. He pulled her back to look at her. "Ma suspects."

"How?"

"Well, it might be closer to say she suspects something. She told me this morning I looked…oh, what was the word…besotted. And she had the oddest look when she said it. Something halfway between a scowl and a smile, or both together, maybe." He curled a lock of her hair around his finger. "I feel distracted all the time. You make it hard for a man to concentrate, did you know that?"

Nora melted against his chest. "How much longer? We don't have much time."

"We've time enough." When she shook her head, he pulled back to look at her again. "What's the matter?"

"Papa asked me to consider Major Simon. Wanted to know what would be my reply if the major...declared his intentions."

She felt Quinn stiffen. "Has he?"

"Not directly. But believe me, he's getting plenty of encouragement from Mama and Papa. I suppose I should be glad my father asked my opinion at all, from the way he talks."

"He'd better ask your opinion. You've the right to your own mind on this, surely."

Nora pulled out of his embrace to pace the alley. "He feels I'm too troubled by all that's happened to see clearly. I hesitated all I could, but he saw that hesitation only as confusion, not reluctance. I couldn't lie to him. I couldn't say yes just to please him, but I couldn't say no yet, either."

"You'll have to tell him outright, sooner or later."

"You know it's not that simple. My parents' anger aside, Major Simon isn't the kind of man to take such a rejection easily. I fear he would make things very difficult for my family, if not just you and I."

Quinn's features darkened. "If he knows your heart is elsewhere, why would he pursue you?"

Nora leaned back against the fence. "Papa says

matches of quality can't always be about love. He's going to ask me to trust him for what's best for me, I know it."

He looked at her, intensity sharpening his gaze. Quality had been exactly the wrong word to use. "And will you?"

"No," Nora said, turning to face him. "Even as I was talking to him I could see how impossible it was." She took a breath, realizing now was indeed the time to say it. "I love you. My life lies with you. I can't turn my back on that even if it made all the sense in the world." She put her hands on his chest. "You've got to find a way because I've got to be with you."

Quinn took her face in his hands, staring so deeply into her eyes she felt the ground drop out from underneath her feet. "I love you, Nora." His voice was deep and warm, yet very serious. "I'll not let another man take what I know God's given to me. We belong together. The how and the when, they're just details. You hang on to that. I love you." He kissed her—a declarative, powerful kiss that seemed to stake his claim to her heart and dare the world to do anything about it. They were so much stronger together than they were apart.

It seemed far too short a time before he sighed and said, "You'd best get back. I've loads to do and your ma will worry if she looks out the window and sees you gone." He kissed her hand, grinning as he had that first time back in Reverend Bauers's study; a cocky, dashing smile that melted her heart all over again. "I'll come again soon. Count on it. You hold fast and leave the rest to me."

Quinn pulled on his boots with a troubled heart. Simon was stepping up his pursuit of Nora. He was also

stepping up things all over the camp and the regiment—
the man was on the move. Toward what, he couldn't say.
He had the most foreboding sense of collision, however.
Of the impending crash of so many intentions—his,
Nora's, Simon's—that worked against each other. If
Simon succeeded, if he brought the relief efforts out
from under the corruption, it'd be partly through Quinn's
own hand as the Messenger. And Quinn would come
out as a man of position because of it. Her parents might
hold him in higher regard once they knew he was the
Messenger. Yet, there was the stark truth that even with
an army commission and the shot at a draftsman's training, he still couldn't compete with Simon's pedigree
and standing. Would it even matter if Nora expressed
her own mind on the subject? Simon's success meant
his own, but it still might not prevent his defeat where
Nora was concerned.

And then there was the small matter of army corruption. Could the Midnight Messenger really be selective
in exposing the grifters? Make trouble for the small-
time marketeers on the outside but leave those inside
the army alone? Or did he have to bite the hand that fed
him and trust God with the consequences? *I'll need so
much wisdom tonight, Lord, You'd better be watching
my every move.* Tonight he was tackling one of the larger
shipments rumored to have been diverted by Sergeant
Miller, right under Simon's nose. How it would all end,
Quinn had no idea.

The shipment that night involved a variety of things—
foodstuffs, building materials, medical supplies, dry
goods. The selection wasn't that unusual, but the quality
was the sort that would bring a particularly high price
to the right set of deep pockets. He'd managed one trip

to fetch the wayward goods without incident and was doubling back for a second when he spotted the sergeant himself standing guard. Someone had evidently realized things were going missing. By the time he'd managed to fill his duffel a second time, he'd been spotted. Shouts turned to drawn pistols, and Quinn found himself dodging bullets as he made his escape. It was far too close a call to chance a third trip—the rest of the goods would have to fall into the wrong hands. Not only that, but the shouts he heard as he fled made one thing crystal clear: the army grifters knew the Midnight Messenger had discovered them. How Simon would handle it from here, Quinn could only guess. There was no hope of keeping it quiet any longer.

Simon was curt with Quinn the next morning, but said nothing at all about the night's developments. It seemed odd—foolish, even—not to deal with the problem at hand, but the major's tension was all too obvious. Perhaps he had some reason for not discussing it. He was, after all, a very clever man who knew the army's intricacies far better than Quinn did. When he handed Quinn a relatively minor list of supplies for the Messenger this evening—hidden at a location off Fort Mason property this time—Quinn assumed Simon was backing off until a strategy could be developed. Minor was good. The location was also appealingly close to Nora's house. If he were quick about it, he might find a way to see her or at least leave some kind of gift. That proved too enticing an opportunity to miss. Quinn hadn't had a night he would classify as "minor" in two weeks.

The evening proved far from minor. Rather than an easy delivery, Quinn found himself escaping down the alleyway at full speed. The small stockpile of fabric and beans in no way merited the four men with very large pistols who were guarding it. Quinn ducked left as shots whizzed by him to the right, hearing a tin in his duffel hiss as it took an entirely too-close bullet. Where had all these armed thugs come from in this neighborhood? Why now, when tonight should have been easy pickings? Panting, Quinn tucked and rolled behind a barrel as another handful of bullets peppered the wall to his left.

Like a bolt of lightning, it hit him; this was no ordinary defense. These men were after him, and they weren't treading softly. After a quick glance at his surroundings—which offered painfully few options— Quinn shed his duffel and ducked into a cellar doorway. If there was any chance at all the pursuers were only out to retrieve their goods, the abandoned duffel should take care of that.

Peering around whatever cellar he'd entered, he saw only rubble at first, and then a small window on the far side of the building. Small enough, he hoped, to allow his exit while being too tight for the band of husky thugs at his back. As he made his way across the pitch black, he prayed the duffel had been prize enough for them. A storm of yelling and footsteps behind him told him otherwise. Quinn began leaping over boxes and beams, heading for the window with all the speed in him. If he had to dive through the glass to make his escape, a few cuts and bruises would certainly be better than whatever waited for him in that crowd.

Quinn pulled his mask off his face, wrapped the cloth around his hand and punched through the window at a run. Already earthquake-damaged, it gave way easily, and Quinn felt a flurry of scrapes on his knees and arms as he began scrambling out the broken window.

"Don't kill him, ya fools!" A voice came from behind him as Quinn worked to get the rest of his body out the window and on to the glass-strewn street. "The army only pays if he's alive."

"Nah, kill 'im. I heard a couple of fellers on the police force will pay more for him dead!"

In the split second Quinn paused to realize the army had put a bounty on his head, the bullet hit him. It was as if a cannon had gone off in his thigh, a burning, explosive sensation that shook the breath from his body. *Lord, save me, I'm shot.* It shocked him that his leg still worked, although every movement sent shards of pain throughout his leg. He grabbed at it, not daring to look down, and rolled away from the window as a second shot rang out. He fell more than ran around the corner, out of sight of the heads now surely poking out the window. He didn't stop to find out if they fit through the opening to follow him. Quinn ran until the edges of his sight began to swim, stopping only to take the bandanna and tie it around his throbbing thigh.

He was nowhere near Grace House, nowhere near Dolores Park, nowhere near help of any kind. *Father God, I'm done for. Help me!* He couldn't go home—this crew would think nothing of shooting mindlessly in the camp aisles, and too many people could get hurt in those close quarters. He couldn't go to Grace House— he didn't think he could make it that far. He certainly couldn't go to Simon at Fort Mason. He was injured, losing blood fast, and in very real danger of passing out.

He had to get help, and he had to get it without

revealing who he was. Which meant he had to get his mask, shirt and guns out of sight. With another prayer and a deep breath, Quinn looked around. There was a postbox at the end of the street. Ironic, but useful. It was the slimmest of chances that the Midnight Messenger's costume, if discovered in a postbox, would wind up in Mr. Longstreet's possession. And it was as good a place as any to shed his "identity." Wincing as he pulled the mask cloth from his leg, he shed the dark shirt, hat and boots, dumping them into the postbox with a sour thought: I'm going to die half-naked and alone. It was the furthest thing from the new future he'd thought to grasp.

Assessing where he was, there was only one place close enough. While it pained him to even think about bringing this to her doorstep, his only real hope of survival was the Longstreets. At least I'll see her again before I die, he thought, as he limped off toward her street, praying he stayed conscious long enough to die in her arms.

Nora was startled awake by the commotion. She panicked instantly, her body going back to the horrible earthquake morning before she was completely awake. There were voices, shouting, but nothing shook or rumbled. She heard her father call for something, heard Aunt Julia yelp as if something had frightened her. She found her wrap as quickly as she could, tucked her feet into slippers, and headed out the bedroom door without even bothering with a light.

Mama, Papa, Uncle Lawrence and the cook were huddled around the front door. Papa was calling for water, the cook was grabbing bandages from the basket that was supposed to go to Grace House this morning and unrolling them. Had someone been hurt?

She'd just made it down the stairs when Aunt Julia grabbed her arm, pulling her into the front room. "Stay away, Nora!" Julia said, her eyes wide with alarm. "Who knows what that ruffian's brought into my house!"

"Nora." A voice moaned from the center of the commotion.

The room went still. Mama turned to look at her, her face a silent shocked question as to why the person on the floor knew Nora's name.

Papa moved his arm, and Nora realized why her heart filled with fear.

It was Quinn.

Chapter Twenty-Four

Quinn Freeman lay bleeding on the foyer floor, his naked chest covered in bloody smudges and smears of dirt. His leg was soaked in blood, and every spark she'd seen in his eyes was gone when he turned to look at her. "Quinn?" she said before she had the chance to think better of using his given name.

Papa stared. Mama's hand went to her chest in shock. "You know this man?" Papa said, his voice dark with alarm.

"Papa," Nora said, pulling out of Aunt Julia's arm to kneel down. "This is Quinn Freeman. The man who brought me Annette's locket." For a minute she was astounded Papa didn't recognize him, then she realized Quinn didn't look at all like himself in his condition.

"Good Heavens!" Aunt Julia gasped from behind them, as if the thought of this bloodied thug touching her daughter's belongings made her ill.

"He's been shot," Papa said. "He's lost a lot of blood, from the looks of it. Call the police."

"No!" Quinn gasped.

"Why ever not?" Nora asked, brushing back the hair

from his eyes. He just stared at her, hard, then squeezed his eyes shut as cook tied off the bandage tight over his wound. The bleeding seemed to have been stemmed, but it still looked ghastly.

"He needs a doctor," Papa said, more calmly this time. "Call Major Simon—Fort Mason has the closest."

"No!" Quinn said through clenched teeth, pulling himself to sit upright against the wall this time. "Not Simon. I need Bauers."

"But Simon knows you, that makes no sense. We really should call the major," Nora said, looking at her father.

"No," Quinn insisted. "Get Bauers."

"Reverend Bauers?" Papa furrowed his eyebrows. "You're talking nonsense, man, you need a doctor, not the reverend."

"Bauers only, please," Quinn pleaded. He shifted his gaze to Papa. "There's a reason."

"There had better be a very good reason you're skirting the authorities, Mr. Freeman, and you'd better have out with it right now. I'll not have you bringing any danger to this household." As if the improbability of him falling on to their doorstep in the middle of the night had just hit him, Papa suddenly leaned in. "Why *are* you at our door, Mr. Freeman?"

For a moment Nora thought Quinn was rattled enough by his wound to simply state the truth. She caught his gaze and tried to hold it, fearing there was no way she could discreetly tell him now was not the time to declare affections.

"I was close by. I recognized the house. From when I came to get the pillar."

"Does it hurt?" Nora asked, before she realized what a foolish question that was.

Quinn actually managed a wink. "Only just." Nora noticed a sickeningly red spot now blooming on the white bandage cook had just tied. Something had to be done, and quickly. There wasn't time to stand here and argue whom to call.

"Papa, he's been nothing but kind to our family. He must have some reason, and Reverend Bauers is surely more used to these kinds of emergencies than we are. I think he even has basic medical skills. Please, Papa, can we send word to Grace House?"

Mama looked as though that were a thoroughly dreadful idea. Actually, she looked ready to thrust Quinn back out into the street to fend for himself. Aunt Julia looked like she could barely stand one more minute of this ruffian staining her front foyer carpet. Papa, however, seemed to actually consider her request. "Lawrence," Papa said to Nora's uncle, "help me get him onto the back porch." As Uncle Lawrence and Papa helped a swaying Quinn to his feet, Papa gave orders for cook to send her son off with the mail cart to Grace House, returning with the reverend at all possible speed. Much to Nora's dismay, he also told the boy that once he brought back the reverend, he was to turn right around and deliver a second message to Major Simon.

At least Bauers would get here first. At least Quinn wasn't tossed back into the alley. At least Quinn was still alive, although she had no idea what had happened. Whatever it was, it was more than some stray bullet or scuffle, for Quinn looked as if whoever shot him might burst through the door at any minute.

Heaping trouble upon trouble, Mama had seen too

much. She'd stared at Nora with suspicious eyes, cataloging every look she gave Quinn or instance where she touched him. Papa hadn't guessed it yet, but Mama knew. In truth, her face looked as pained and wounded as Quinn's. It was difficult to guess which set of wounds to tend first.

Mama made the decision for her, snatching her elbow as she went to follow Papa and Uncle Lawrence. "What have you done, Nora?" Her voice was low, her words clipped.

"Nothing, Mama." It was such a useless reply. Nothing but fall in love, actually, but she couldn't put words to that just yet. Not with the look in Mama's eyes. "I know him."

"How well do you know this man?" It was an accusation, not a question.

"Well." It said everything and nothing at all. Nora cast about for a better answer but found none.

Aunt Julia called Quinn a slurry of names Nora was glad he could not hear. "He's hurt, Mama," she said, pulling herself up with a strength she hadn't realized was in her. "He needs help. Now." Before Mama could reach out and stop her, Nora turned and walked down the hallway toward the back porch.

Quinn blacked out twice before Reverend Bauers came rushing out the door on to Nora's back porch. He went to work immediately, motioning for Papa and Uncle Lawrence to put Quinn up on a nearby table. "We'll need a candle if not a lamp." Suddenly, the gentle pastor she'd known was replaced by a fiercely calm commander, moving with military precision. She'd heard Quinn say once that Bauers hadn't been in the clergy all his life, and for an odd moment she wondered what kind of adventures he'd had before joining the church. Papa acquiesced and lit a lamp, bringing it over to where the reverend began peeling back the bloody bandage. Nora felt the room sway and backed up a bit to cling to the porch pillar. "I'd feared something like this would happen," Bauers said, fishing into a bag of medical supplies he'd put on the table. "No good deed goes unrewarded these days." He poked around in the wound, which snapped Quinn out of his faint to hiss through his teeth. "You're blessed. The bullet went clean through from the looks of it. That means you'll heal fine if you don't bleed to death first."

Quinn only moaned. And then did a bit more than that when Bauers began poking around some more. Nora wanted to rush up and hold Quinn's hand, to put a cloth to his forehead and let him know she was here, but Bauers managed to catch her eye and give her a barely perceptible "no" shake to his head. The point seemed moot when Quinn blacked out again once the reverend poured a generous dose of iodine into his wound.

"It's not ready to stitch yet. We'll have to pack it to stem the bleeding, then stitch it later. Until then, he can't be moved."

Papa did not look pleased. Nora was secretly glad to know Quinn wasn't going anywhere. At least she had a chance to find out what on earth had happened, and why Reverend Bauers didn't seem terribly surprised to find his friend shot.

The reverend looked at Uncle Lawrence. "I wonder if you wouldn't mind sitting with the man while I have a conversation with Miss Longstreet and her father. I doubt he'll come to anytime soon, but I wouldn't be surprised if he tried something reckless if he did."

That didn't do wonders for Uncle Lawrence's confidence, but he agreed to stay out on the porch with Quinn while Reverend Bauers asked if Nora and Papa wouldn't sit down with him and hear what he had to say. Nora had no idea what to expect and settled herself into a chair in the front room with the two men. *Lord, what is happening here? Stay close to Quinn. Stay close to me. I have no idea what's unfolding.*

Reverend Bauers eased himself into a chair and chose his words carefully. "There's more to this man than appears, especially tonight. I've no doubt he came here only out of desperation, for he's been taking pains for quite some time now to keep this from you." Nora could only guess what dark secret Bauers seemed to be alluding to, and it grew even worse when the reverend looked right at her. "He's sought only to protect you from any harm, Miss Longstreet."

Papa looked as though he was bracing for the worst. Nora wasn't far behind, as a long list of horrible secrets ran through Nora's imagination, chopping her breaths into short, anxious gulps.

"The man on your back porch is the Midnight Messenger." Bauers folded his hands and waited for the fact to sink in.

"Quinn?" she nearly gasped.

"Him?" Papa pointed in the general direction of the back porch. "That man is the Midnight Messenger? You can't be serious."

"It's precisely Quinn's…shall we say…'colorful' background that gave him knowledge and access to a certain side of the city the Midnight Messenger needed.

In a city as large as this, one clever man can make himself rather invisible."

Nora thought she ought to shake her head to clear it. On the one hand, it seemed utterly impossible. On the other hand, it made all the sense in the world. He had access to all the requests from the posts. He always looked tired. Her gifts in the garden always arrived at night. And he was infinitely clever as well as caring to a fault. He was as strong as he was impulsive. Why couldn't he be the Midnight Messenger?

"All those times he said he knew someone who could help, all my questions he dismissed, they were all…"

"To keep you from any danger your knowing might bring," Bauers cut in. "As you can see, the Midnight Messenger has made enemies. He's taken many great risks to help the refugees in the unofficial camps, exposed a great many evils, but he'd never bring that risk to your doorstep."

"Which is *exactly* what he's done." Papa was trying not to shout for Mama's sake.

"And I'm guessing there must be a very good reason for that, but we might not get the chance to learn it tonight."

There was a scuffle in the back hallway. Nora heard Uncle Lawrence shout something and was just rising from her chair when Quinn stumbled into the room.

Quinn's gaze flashed from her to Papa to the reverend. "You told them," he growled at Bauers. Quinn's eyes held the same barely checked temper she'd seen when he confronted Ollie.

Nora rushed up to steady him as he leaned against the wall. "Nora!" Papa said, his disapproval radiating out of the single word.

She ignored her father, locking her gaze on Quinn instead. "Is it true? Are you the Messenger?" He only nodded, and she didn't even need to see that. It was clear in his eyes.

"Impossible," Papa argued, although Nora could hardly guess why. He'd just as much admitted it and Bauers had little reason to lie about such a thing.

"I shouldn't have come here." Quinn pulled away, but only succeeded in making it one or two steps down the hall before he fell against the wall again.

Bauers had found a wooden chair from the hallway and essentially shoved it under Quinn. "If you won't lie down, at least *sit* down. You're too big for me to haul off the floor alone."

Papa stood up to pace the floor, and Nora could see his thoughts churning. Her thoughts should be in a tumble, too, but somehow she saw how the puzzle pieces fit together almost instantly. It seemed impossible that she hadn't put the facts together before, now that she knew them.

She put her hand on Quinn's shoulder, ignoring the dark look it produced from Papa. "Seems to me this business is best sorted out by Simon or the police," her father said wearily. "He'll settle it soon enough when he arrives."

That made Quinn nearly bolt out of his chair, almost sending Nora tumbling. "Simon's coming?"

"He's on his way now."

"Simon's the reason I'm shot!" Quinn exploded, and Reverend Bauers's hand thrust on to Quinn's chest with a power and speed she'd never have attributed to a clergyman in his eighties. "The army's put a price on the

Messenger's head, and the police seem to have upped the offer. I'm as good as dead now."

"Why?" Nora nearly shouted, planting herself in the middle of this trio of angry men. "What's Major Simon to do with this?"

"He's been getting me the supplies," Quinn said. "He's been part of it from the beginning. Only things went a bit deeper than that, and he began giving me gold to buy information on where stolen goods were being kept."

"So Major Simon *has* been in on this?" Papa asked, wiping his hands down his face.

"He trained Quinn and served as a supply source," Reverend Bauers explained. "It served the army's purposes to see that goods got where they ought to have gone. Major Simon is clever enough to see that one renegade could spur a thousand stories of good deeds, and do any number of things an army couldn't. Or shouldn't."

"Oh," said Quinn with a dark laugh. "You'd be amazed what the army can do. I proved too smart for my own good when I figured out half the trouble was coming from within the army itself." He glared at Bauers, who looked as if that was news to him. "Don't you see? Marketeers weren't just finding their way to the army, it was a couple of rats on the inside selling freely to the marketeers. And I knew. I've become an embarrassment because I can expose the corruption *inside* the army. Under Simon's own nose. And only he knows I'm the Messenger. If he didn't *start* the manhunt, he did nothing to *stop* it, and I'm sure there were dozens of volunteers. I haven't exactly made friends with this."

No one knew quite what to say. It seemed so impossible.

Quinn sunk into the chair and looked up at Nora. "He said he was going to tell the whole city what I'd done when it was time. Give me a commission in the Army Corps of Engineers. An apprenticeship as a draftsman. I'd be someone you could…" His words fell off. Nora held his eyes, perhaps more in love with him at that moment than she had ever been.

"He told you this?" Bauers obviously knew nothing of this new bargain.

"And I believed him," Quinn replied bitterly. "I took all those risks on his word, fool that I am."

"Major Simon is an honorable man who's given me no reason to think he'd do something so outrageous," Papa said.

A knock came on the door, bringing everyone in the room to a standstill. Papa looked at Bauers, then at Quinn.

"That has to be Major Simon," Nora said, coming over to her father. "Papa, don't let him in."

"Of course I'm going to let him in. It's the only way we can get to the bottom of this."

"He'll deny it. It'll be his word against mine." Quinn called after Papa to no effect. Despite his injuries, Quinn looked as if he might bolt for the back door at any minute. In his condition, he'd get all of two blocks before Simon or who knows how many other members of the army would be at his heels. Panic burrowed under Nora's ribs, stealing her breath and making her heart gallop.

Simon strode into the room as if he ruled the world. "Quinn, are you all right?"

How he managed to appear so concerned was beyond

Quinn's reckoning. "Only just," Quinn ground out through clenched teeth. He found himself using every ounce of the major's lessons on focusing anger—all trained on not thrusting a knife into the man's ribs this very minute.

"He's been shot," Nora said curtly. "As I assume you know."

"Nora!" Mr. Longstreet didn't much care for his daughter's tone. That was fine with Quinn; he didn't much care for his so-called ally's betrayal, either.

The major only raised an eyebrow. "So your man told me. I'd actually heard from one of my regiments that there was talk of the Messenger being shot." Simon looked straight at him. "I was out looking for you…"

"Or sending thugs out after me?" Quinn cut in.

"…when one of my lieutenants came to find me, saying someone had come to the fort pleading for me to come here. Here, Quinn? However did you end up here?"

"A man can only go so far with a bullet in his leg," Quinn replied darkly, "But then again you knew that. I suppose I should be thankful not all your trainees are as good a shot as I am, Major?"

"Gentlemen!" Reverend Bauers stood between them. "Can we please remember where we are?"

"So you admit, Major, that Freeman is the Midnight Messenger?"

"He was working for me as that, yes."

"I do not work for *you!*" Quinn shot back. He'd always known Simon thought of him merely as another gun in his arsenal.

"It was actually me who put these two together, Mr. Longstreet." Bauers put his hands up between Quinn and the major. "I knew of Quinn's desire to help in this…unusual fashion, and I felt the major's skills and resources would make for an excellent partnership."

Some partnership. Quinn could barely keep from voicing the thought.

Bauers looked at Simon with narrowed eyes. "Did I misjudge, Albert?"

"It was a brilliant idea, Reverend." Simon leveled his glare at Quinn. "At the time. I fear it's gone too far for all concerned."

"Do you, now?" Quinn's knuckles itched to knock a dent into that dignified jaw. The searing pain in his thigh was making it harder and harder to keep a lid on his temper. He felt Nora's hand settle on his arm, cool and steady, and he willed those qualities into his thundering nerves. Major Simon saw her gesture, and raised an eyebrow again. Quinn didn't care one bit for the look of disdain that settled in his eyes.

"I wasn't aware," Major Simon said as he took very particular notice of Nora's gesture. "How unfortunate a complication. Quinn, you exceed my expectations at every turn."

"I expect I do," Quinn said. He felt his body begin to break out in a sweat and wondered how much longer he'd be able to stand.

"Mr. Freeman claims he was fired upon by your orders." Mr. Longstreet sounded entirely too much like he'd already made up his mind on the subject. Quinn wondered why he was surprised. What good was the word of someone like him against the upstanding Major Simon?

Simon looked from Nora's father to Quinn. Could no one else see the supreme annoyance, the carefully veiled anger in Simon's eyes? Quinn realized with a sinking sensation that the major could lie through his teeth this very moment and everyone in the room would believe it. His future was lost; any chance at the education or commission—if he lived long enough to even consider it—was long gone now.

"I believe," Simon said smoothly, "that the Messenger has made enemies. Enemies that might go to great lengths to make him suspect his own had betrayed him. As such, I have no doubt that Mr. Freemen believes I sent those thugs after his life."

"I never *said* anything about a group." Quinn pointed a finger at Simon.

Simon didn't skip a beat. "It's always a group. Cowards travel in packs." Simon turned to Nora's father. "I'm so sorry this business has ended up on your doorstep. Why don't you let me see to Freeman's wounds at the fort infirmary. We can protect him there, too, from whomever it is that's done this. And I insist we post a guard outside this house for the next twenty-four hours. I've no intention of your kindness bringing you further trouble."

"Papa, don't you dare let him take Quinn!" Nora burst out. Quinn's heart both swelled at the thought of her championing him and broke knowing that her efforts would come to no use. Defying her father only made it worse. The strongest-standing wall in San Francisco—the mile-high societal wall—had defeated him in the end. The only thing he could do now was save Nora from her own sweet loyalty to him. He tried to slide her hand from his shoulder, but she only clasped him harder, puzzlement in her eyes.

"Nora, I think you should go upstairs and join your

mother and aunt." Mr. Longstreet was dismissing his daughter with the same patronizing tone Simon used with Quinn.

"Absolutely not. I will not stand here and allow you to send Quinn off with someone who means to do him harm. Not after all he's done for this family. For me."

Simon looked at Nora. "Do you really believe me capable of such evil, Miss Longstreet? I'm disappointed. I'd rather thought I'd made quite an impression on you." He actually smiled, and Quinn realized he'd underestimated Simon's cleverness. "Let's have this business over with, Longstreet. I'll protect the man until we can get to the bottom of this."

Quinn shot a panicked look to Bauers, knowing all too well what fate awaited him if he went to Fort Mason tonight.

"Perhaps it would be best for all concerned if I took Quinn with me," Bauers offered. "Grace House is as safe a place for him as any, and I'm sure I can tend to his wounds. There's no need to trouble the major further."

"Oh, I hardly think that's wise," countered Major Simon.

"No, I think that's by far the best choice," Nora declared, coming round to stand in front of her father. "Until we can sort this out."

Quinn had had just about enough of people thinking for him. "It's clear I'm not dying," he said, looking at the reverend, "so I'll make my own choice, thanks. Reverend, if you'll drop me off, I'll tend to *myself. At home.*" He didn't care one whit that no one in the room seemed to think this a good idea. With a wave for Bauers to follow him, Quinn pushed himself down the hallway toward the front door.

And watched it fade into a yawning cave of blackness.

Chapter Twenty-Five

Nora thought she would never survive the night. It was getting on toward dawn, and she hadn't slept one wink. It was bad enough that she'd barely convinced them to let Reverend Bauers take Quinn back to Dolores Park on the shared but unspoken idea that Quinn would probably only make it as far as Grace House. Bauers pushed hard for this, despite Major Simon's objections. When Quinn slumped to the ground a second time as they argued, Nora burst out crying. Papa was so shocked—and Simon so disgusted—that the whole lot of them left in such a commotion that Nora realized she never did learn where Quinn would spend the night.

She was angry enough with herself for that bit of foolishness, but the scolding Mama gave her after everyone left was worse. She looked so disappointed in her, so incapable of understanding why Nora would ever do something so irrational as take up with "his kind." As if Nora had betrayed her entire family and everyone's hope for happiness. The only reason Mama stopped short of likening her to Annette and her terrible fate was that Aunt Julia had come downstairs.

No one seemed to care that her own happiness was in more ruins than the city. Perhaps that was what made it so easy to throw all caution to the wind, get dressed and go find Quinn. The soldier Major Simon had posted in front of their house evidently didn't take his charge too seriously, for she found him fast asleep on the house's front stoop. The sun was just coming up as, with a calm that certainly didn't fit her reckless circumstances, Nora set out.

The only reasonable place to start seemed to be Grace House. Still, it wasn't as if she could simply waltz out her front door and amble down the dark street before dawn alone.

Or could she?

The clang of a streetcar bell confirmed that the cars did run this early…after all, the docks never really shut down and people had to get to work. It struck her that she'd never thought about anyone having to get to work at such a terrible hour, but certainly it happened to people every day. There was so much she never saw before this. So much she never considered.

It was colder than she expected, and by all rights she ought to be tired, but the exhilaration of her mission made the blocks fly by. It seemed only a matter of minutes before she was reaching into the pocket of her coat and handing coins to a very surprised man aboard the streetcar. She was glad that while his expression said "Out and about at this hour?" he never actually voiced it.

She'd never seen Grace House—or any of this part of the city, for that matter—at dawn. Despite the signs of destruction that still lingered everywhere, the neighborhood had a delicate calm, tinted rose and gold by the sunrise and peppered with tiny clusters of people coming and going. There was something poetic and uncluttered in the simplicity of the people going about their daily business. Quinn had once used the word fussy to describe things in Lafayette Park. He'd meant it as a jest, a good-natured teasing when she'd turned her nose up at something, but looking around, the word fit. She realized, as she turned the corner into the back kitchen door of the friendly, tattered mission building, that perhaps its unfussiness is exactly what attracted her to Grace House. Why the simple chapel felt more holy to her than the starched formal sanctuary of their church up the hill in the "better" part of town.

Quinn *had* to be here. She couldn't fathom that Reverend Bauers would agree to let him be carted off to some horrible fate at Fort Mason. And he couldn't go home, not in that state, although she didn't think Quinn had many other choices. The cook looked surprised— and rather annoyed—at being roused hours before breakfast.

"What are the likes of you doing here? At this hour?" He yawned.

"I'm looking for Reverend Bauers…and Quinn Freeman." When the hefty man stared blankly at her, she added, "It's terribly important."

"I imagine it is," he said, motioning her into the cold kitchen. The fires hadn't even been lit for the day's meals yet. "You sit here and I'll go fetch him."

"Thank you." It suddenly struck her, as she sat down on one of the benches that lined the worktable, how cold and tired she really was. Everything seemed so out of joint and jumbled. What must Quinn be feeling? Thinking? Was he in much pain? He was so very dark and angry—a side of him she'd only seen even a glimpse of the time he'd rescued her. *Oh, Lord, watch over him. I don't know what to say to him, what to do.*

"Odd," the cook remarked, yawning again as he came back into the kitchen. "He ain't here. Looks like he left in a hurry, though. One of the boys says he ain't been back for hours now."

So he *hadn't* been successful in keeping Quinn from the major. The thought turned Nora's blood to ice. *No.* She wouldn't consider that possibility. The reverend must have found some way to get him all the way to Dolores Park. Or elsewhere. Maybe the resourceful Reverend Bauers had many secret hiding places. There really was only one place to go next: Quinn's mother in Dolores Park.

Twenty minutes later with her pulse pounding in her ears, Nora took a deep breath and knocked on the entrance to Quinn's shelter in Dolores Park. "Quinn?" she called, even as she knew the folly of thinking he'd actually made it here, "Mrs. Freeman?"

After a moment of rustling from inside, Mrs. Freeman poked a half-asleep face out of the doorway. "Miss Longstreet?"

"Is...is Quinn here?"

She frowned even as her eyes widened. "What's happened to Quinn?" she asked, alarm cutting sharp edges on her words.

There was nothing for it. Nora lost her battle with her composure and began to cry. "Something's happened, Mrs. Freeman, something terrible."

Mrs. Freeman pulled Nora into the shelter and sat her down. A quick version of the entire story was nearly impossible, but Nora did the best she could as Mrs.

Freeman sat astounded. "Quinn? The Midnight Messenger? Of course—how could I not see it? All that time gone, those nights, the things that arrived. God save him, he's been the Messenger from the beginning."

"But now it's all come crashing down," Nora said, clutching Mrs. Freeman's hand as she relayed the story of the shooting, the confrontation in her parlor and how certain she was that if Quinn was not here, then he was surely in the clutches of Major Simon, and no good could come of that, even if Reverend Bauers was still up and about and trying to save him. "They fought terribly. Quinn is sure Simon put the price on his head, but I don't think my father believed him. Major Simon will do something to him, I know it."

Mrs. Freeman, who now fought back tears of her own, stared at Nora for a long moment. Sighing, she reached out and touched Nora's cheek. "You care deeply for him, don't you?"

"I love your son," Nora said, feeling the declaration of it settle her, drawing a surprising strength from the ability to say it out loud. "And I believe he loves me."

Mrs. Freeman's eyes fell shut for a brief moment, then opened with such a tender expression in them. "I know he does, child. I'd suspected he'd finally lost his heart to someone, he just wouldn't tell me who. Now, perhaps I know why. Oh, darlin', I wouldn't wish such trouble on any lass."

"It's Quinn who's in such trouble. I've got to help him. There *has* to be a way." Quinn was so clever. What would he have done? Could she be as clever as he, now that his life might depend upon it? She tried to look for connections in all the various pieces of this mess. People. People loved the Messenger; they might rise up to save him if they knew he was endangered. Or at least keep Simon from doing anything that might be poorly misconstrued. Simon was on the lookout for his good prospects—maybe there was a way to leverage that. A plan—one might even say a scheme—began to form in her head. There wasn't time to think it all the way through—she'd just have to make it up as they went along. "Mrs. Freeman, how many people know Quinn?"

"Nearly everyone. Quinn's always had many friends—at home and here. And I'd guess the Midnight Messenger has even more."

"What if...Mrs. Freeman, can you pull together an army of your own? Major Simon would never do anything to the Midnight Messenger in public, so I think we'll simply have to bring the public to the Messenger."

"Fill the fort with people? Wouldn't the army shoot at a mob like that?"

"Not if reporters were there. And if it was clear the people were looking for the Messenger, the army couldn't do anything that might get in the papers. Simon will have to bring Quinn out. He's got to be in there, Mrs. Freeman, I can't see where else he'd be. It's the only thing I can think of to do."

"Well now, I don't see how I've got much choice. Got my son, does he?" Mrs. Freeman stood up. "I'd say it's high time Major Simon had more visitors that he'll know what to do with."

Nora felt her strength mount as she walked back to Grace House. The sun was up, she'd fashioned a plan even Quinn would admire and her determination to see it through was galvanizing with each step. She prayed as she walked, beseeching God to bless her efforts and to keep Quinn safe—even though the panicked thought occurred that it might already be too late if Major Simon was as dark as she suspected. *"No,"* she prayed aloud, *"Lord, You can't have brought him through the earthquake only to meet that end. I won't believe it."* I can't, she added in a tight, frightened corner of her heart.

Grace House held good and bad news. Reverend Bauers was there—looking exhausted and worried. Still, he confirmed that Quinn was still alive although in bad shape. He was being kept at Fort Mason for his own protection, the reverend reported with an expression that told Nora he shared the same doubts as to Quinn's prospects under the major's watch. The challenge came when Papa stormed through the front door in search of his daughter.

"Come back home," he ordered. Nora thought being in a house of God was the only thing currently keeping a lid on Papa's temper. She'd never seen him like this, and it should have frightened her into submission. It didn't. Instead, it steeled her determination to do what she knew was right. Papa could not see that now, and that couldn't be helped. She'd spend all her efforts to convince him later, but for now defiance was the only route open to her.

"I'm sorry, Papa," she said in a voice so steady it surprised even her. "I must do this."

"Do what?" Papa said, exasperated. Reverend Bauers stood between them, cautious but willing to let her have her say.

"Try to save Quinn."

Nora expected Papa to ask "from what?" thinking his

high regard for Major Simon wouldn't allow for the possibility of Quinn's current danger. Instead, Papa asked the most dangerous question of all: "Why?"

It should have been difficult. Frightening, even, to declare it to Papa after all his lectures. Instead, it came out with the ease of truth, necessary as breath. "Because I love him."

Papa stared. For all Mama's suspicions, evidently Papa was genuinely stunned by her admission.

Reverend Bauers chose that moment to step in. "There's a good deal to sort out, no doubt, but I do agree with Nora that desperate measures are in order. Let me accompany her to Fort Mason and you have my word she will talk with you further about this. For the moment, time is very much of the essence."

Before Papa could even gather his wits to respond, Reverend Bauers had Nora by the arm and they were heading out the back door to climb aboard the minister's rickety cart and head to Fort Mason. Nora prayed for Mama and Papa the whole way, for in some very real sense they'd lost the daughter they once had. She hoped the new, transformed daughter they now gained would still be welcomed when today's dust settled.

Annette would have been proud. For all her adventures, Nora's bold cousin had never spent a day such as this. As she stared out the window of Major Simon's office at Fort Mason, Nora could scarcely believe the size of the crowd Mrs. Freeman had gathered outside. Or that her plan had worked. Then again, perhaps Major Simon never stood a chance; once Mrs. Freeman discovered someone had placed her son in harm's way for his own gain, Nora was sure God's ears burned with the justice she called down upon the major's head.

He'd never looked so unnerved. "Are you quite sure, Miss Longstreet, that your father's only the postmaster?" His words were smooth, but his knuckles were white as he put down his pen. "It seems to me you've a politician's blood running through your veins."

"I'd think twice about that phrase 'only the postmaster,' Major," Reverend Bauers advised. "This entire plan was Nora's doing. I fear she could easily devise another one nowhere near as favorable to you. And I am quite astounded at how enamored with her those two reporters are at present."

When Major Simon had refused an earlier meeting, Nora wasn't surprised. She hadn't ever expected the major to cooperate. Instead, Nora asked Reverend Bauers to take her to the offices of the city newspaper. It had been far easier than she imagined to get the reporter to follow her back to Fort Mason. The exclusive revelation of the Midnight Messenger's true identity was far too good a story to miss. And evidently, when one reporter rushes out of his office, others hear about it soon enough; now no less than four photographers were currently waiting outside with the crowd of refugees from Dolores Park.

Bauers had been busy as well. As Nora met with the reporter, he'd used the newspaper wire service to arrange for a hefty reward for the names of the army officers who'd been given the instructions to let word out about the price on the Messenger's head. The size of the reward wired from one Sir Matthew Covington— a friend of Quinn's from England, who, thanks be to God, happened to be in New York on business—ensured quick success. In addition to that, Nora could now ensure that the men's corroboration of Quinn's story reached her parents' ears.

"You have the papers?" Nora extended her hand to receive what she had just watched Simon write: Quinn's commission into the Corps of Engineers, his subsequent draftsmanship education and even a decoration for outstanding citizenship. "I'll find it difficult to be cooperative outside without this in my pocket."

"He'll come to no harm. I had no intentions of having him shot," Simon asserted.

"I cannot believe you," Nora said calmly. And she couldn't. She slipped the folded paper carefully into the pocket of her skirt, feeling jaded.

Major Simon eyed her. "If I'd have wanted him dead, Miss Longstreet, he'd have been shot hours ago. I have enough authority to control someone like Freeman without having to shoot him, you know."

"No, I don't know that." And she'd done her best to make sure he couldn't shoot Quinn now. Not with the crowd outside his window. She was glad for that, seeing the unnerving darkness in the major's eyes.

The strength of the midday sun was broiling the crowd into impatience. They could either learn enough to cheer Simon for his accomplishments, or learn more and jeer him for what he would have done to the Midnight Messenger. Nora would be lying if she said the thought of publicly humiliating Simon didn't appeal to her at the moment. The simple truth was that Simon was currently the lesser of all available evils, and he was still very good at what he did. To remove him from the relief efforts entirely would do little more than heap chaos upon chaos.

She didn't need revenge or glory; she needed Quinn. Unharmed and with the commissions Simon had originally promised him. All she was really doing, Reverend Bauers reminded her, was using the leverage they had—namely the press and the mayor's keen need of good news to tell the world on behalf of their damaged city—to ensure the major kept his original word.

A knock came on the door, and the reporter poked his nervous head inside. "It's a powder keg out there. If you're going to make an announcement, you'd best get to it." As if on cue, a wave of cries for the Messenger could be heard outside. They'd been told they'd find out who he was today, and they didn't seem much in the mood to be patient about it.

"Remember, my good major," Bauers said as he walked over to stand beside Simon. "I'll be listening to every word. I'm anticipating a lovely speech. It'll be a grand day for San Francisco. And you get the rarest of all opportunities—a second chance to do the right thing."

Someone splashed water on his face. Quinn moaned, knocking the hand away without even opening his eyes. He knew he'd ended up in some kind of cell, but not much more. During several waking moments over the course of the night, he'd managed to surmise that his attempts to go home had failed. The last thing he remembered was making for Nora's front door, then it all went black until he woke up here.

He had a pretty good idea where "here" was. And who held the keys.

"Freeman, up with you," a gruff voice said.

Quinn's head pounded, his ribs ached, he still had

cuts on his hands and arms from climbing out the broken window, and his leg felt as if it would burn right off any second. He definitely was in no mood to stand up and be neighborly. Why they hadn't simply shot him yet, he didn't know. Actually, he didn't want to be shot again, ever. Last night had put him off guns for life, even if life only lasted a few more hours.

It had all come unraveled. All the help he'd been was of no use. In his arrogance, his craving to be a man of importance, he'd misread God's calls to him in ways that hurt everyone he loved.

Nora worst of all. The one detail he did remember last night was the scorching look in her mother's eyes when Nora'd touched him. As if she'd committed some unforgivable sin by loving him. He'd tainted her future by trying to graft it on to his own. She deserved far more than he could give her now. The physical pain couldn't hold a candle to the gnawing ache in his chest. It felt like his very soul had been yanked out of his body.

"Wash up, you've got company and an appointment to keep."

An appointment with the business end of an army rifle, no doubt. Why on earth did they think it a good idea to wake him up to shoot him? Or dress him? Somebody threw a damp towel and some clothes at him. An army uniform. Quinn was really starting to hate Simon's sense of humor.

"I don't care what he looks like," someone said outside his cell door. "I insist you let me in right now!"

He must be delirious—the voice sounded like Nora's. Well, God had answered his prayer—he'd at least gotten to kiss her. He rolled his body away from the light, sinking back into the pain that pulsed with every heartbeat. "I hope Heaven hurts a whole lot less," he muttered.

"I hope you don't see it for a very long time," the tender voice said, and he felt a cool, smooth hand on his brow.

He rolled back over and forced his eyes open. Nora's sweet face stared down at him like God's gift from Heaven. "Am I alive?" he whispered, reaching out, expecting his hand to slide through the mirage.

The mirage smiled. "Only just." She grabbed his outstretched hand and kissed it.

It was her. He pulled her hand toward his face, pressing it to his cheek. Glory, it really *was* her, here with him. His pain-fogged brain couldn't make sense of it.

"You've got to get up and put these on, Quinn. I haven't time to explain more."

Something had happened. People were rushing about, there were shouts and yells outside. He pushed himself upright, hurting everywhere. Nora took the towel beside him and began wiping his hands. "What's going on?" he asked, shaking his head in an attempt to clear it.

"You're going to need to stand in a few minutes. Can you do it?"

He took the towel from her and wiped his own face. The cool cloth brought him a shred of clarity, and he looked at the vision of beauty in front of him. Without a moment's thought, he took that face in his hands and kissed it. Soundly. Bliss. She tasted like sheer, sweet bliss.

"Time's a wastin', Romeo," the gruff voice said from behind him. "There'll be time enough for that later."

Later? There'd be a later?

"You're to be announced as the heroic Midnight

Messenger in a few minutes," Nora said, blushing. "We need to get you cleaned up and dressed."

"I don't understand..."

"I've found a way. Don't worry about that right now, just trust me and put these on."

"They're army clothes!"

"Indeed they are."

"Am I going to be shot?"

"No, Quinn, I think they said you're going to be a corporal."

The sunlight stung his eyes. Reverend Bauers had a hand on his shoulder, helping him stay upright. The bandage on his leg was too tight, a throbbing distraction, and sweat was pouring down his back. He didn't care.

He did care that Nora was yards away from him, standing next to a fellow with a camera and notebook instead of by his side. She had yet to explain why Major Simon was making a speech about the Midnight Messenger, saying all kinds of wonderful things about the "hero who slipped through the night to help those in need." Reverend Bauers had only barely stopped him from lunging at Simon when they finally met up just inside the doorway. *"Touché,"* was all Simon had said, tipping his hat in what could only be called a simmering resignation. He held Quinn's gaze with a nasty glare that evaporated instantaneously the moment the major stepped on to the podium placed on Fort Mason's front steps.

And then he heard his name.

Bauers led him forward as the crowd cheered so loud Quinn thought his head would split open.

People cried out his name and the mayor came to

shake his hand. He'd been revealed as the man behind the Midnight Messenger, as a hero. He saw Ma, standing down off to his left, her face a mixture of joy aimed at him and an anger he guessed was aimed at Major Simon. She knew. Still, Quinn couldn't figure out how they'd gone from last night's chaos to this morning's glory.

And glory it was. Simon continued his speech, describing the commission he'd originally promised, eliciting more cheers from the crowd. Quinn would begin serving as a draftsman's apprentice the moment he was well enough to do so. He'd been made a corporal in the United States Army Corps of Engineers. An officer. More men shook his hand. Amazing as it all was, the edges of Quinn's vision begin to blur and turn colors. "I can't stand up any longer," he whispered to Bauers. "Get me out of here." How funny that a moment he'd been dreaming of for weeks was not nearly as pleasant as he'd imagined. He was grateful—deeply grateful— but all he wanted right now was Nora and sleep, in that order. Glory, it turns out, hurt a lot.

Ma came rushing through the door a few moments later, bouncing back and forth between fussy praises for his deeds and teary-eyed scoldings for keeping such secrets from your own Ma.

"Where is she?" he asked Bauers and his mother, hoping at least one of them would fill in the host of missing details.

"Your Nora?" Ma said, smiling. "She'll be along. Don't you worry about that."

"I worry about that," he said trying to peer around Ma and Bauers to the door that still opened on the activities outside. "Where *is* she?"

Bauers's hand came down on his shoulder. "I imagine she's with her mother and father by now. I asked them to come. I doubt it will be a short conversation, so you'd best find some patience."

At that moment, Major Simon came in through the door, surrounded by a quartet of very official-looking men. Quinn stood up, wobbling a little when he did. He held Simon's eyes until the major said, "Excuse me for a moment," to his companions and walked over. Bauers and Ma both tensed.

"They were only supposed to bring you in. I'd no plans to do you harm," Simon said, nearly under his breath.

"I don't believe you," Quinn returned, equally quietly.

"I suppose you wouldn't." The major extended his hand. Shake his hand? Now? After all he suspected happened?

Quinn took that hand and gripped hard enough to hurt Simon. It may have looked like a handshake, but it wasn't. It was a warning. "I ought to run you through right here, in front of all these people," he murmured loud enough for the major to hear. "But someone once taught me to do the unexpected to my opponents."

Simon pulled his hand away.

"I don't know what all happened," Quinn continued, "but I will. I won't stop watching you, Simon."

"You got caught in the cross fire, Freeman, nothing more."

"I don't see it that way."

"And now is not the time to have this conversation," Reverend Bauers cut in between them. "Let the matter rest for the moment, gentlemen, too many eyes are watching."

"You're *blessed* I'm in no shape to do anything more," Quinn growled.

Major Simon paused for a second before replying, "Perhaps I am."

Chapter Twenty-Six

Quinn was tired of sitting. Funny, he could remember the days he'd give anything to sit for hours on end, but now the inactivity was driving him crazy. "Where is she, Ma?"

Ma looked at him as if he were no older than Sam. "It's not yet two o'clock, Quinn. The sun doesn't hurry across the sky just because you're in love." She looked at the pile of goods filling their shack. "Someone brought more sugar. Why people think the Midnight Messenger needs sweets is beyond me. Where do they think we can bake out here?" She pointed at him. "Bring me a real oven and a real kitchen to put it in, then I'll sing and dance."

"I'll dance with you now, Ma."

"Ye will not at that." She scowled at him playfully. "You're supposed to be off that leg for another three days."

"Three days…I'll go mad," Quinn moaned.

"Keep looking at those books the army sent over. I can't imagine how much you've got to learn."

"Sam!" Quinn yelled. "Sam, come here!" Ma gave

out an exasperated sigh. Sam poked his head into the shack a moment later. "Go see if Miss Nora's come yet, would you please?"

Sam was no fool. He looked straight at Ma, who pulled a watch out of her apron pocket and shook her head. "It ain't two," Sam said with an annoying amount of authority for someone who came up to Quinn's waist.

"I'm outnumbered." Quinn let his head fall back against the cot where he was propped up.

"Even heroes have to do as they're told," Ma said teasingly. "On occasion."

Quinn sighed, picked up one of the dry texts he was trying to make his way through before he started studies next month and thought patience was highly overrated for heroes. Even ex-heroes.

He'd lasted no more than ten minutes, when he heard Nora's voice call out from beyond the shack door. "Hello, Mrs. Freeman, hello Quinn!"

He went for the door, but Ma thrust a hand to his shoulder. "Back down with you. She can take the six steps it takes to get inside, son, there's no worries there."

Quinn sat up and ran his hands through his hair just as Nora ducked inside. Followed by a sight he never expected to see: Mr. and Mrs. Longstreet. "I've brought someone with me," Nora said, smiling.

It was an awkward moment, to be sure. Mr. Longstreet looked uncomfortable, Mrs. Longstreet looked downright panicked. Nora wore a cautiously hopeful expression, and Ma looked flustered. A bristling silence filled the crowded shelter until Ma flung up her hands and said, "I think I'll make tea. We've got real sugar, we might as well enjoy it."

Nora reached out her hand to Ma, smiling. "That'd be lovely, I think. Mama, why don't you sit here?" She motioned to the shack's only chair and motioned for her father to take a seat on the large trunk nearby. When her parents were seated, Nora perched on the edge of the cot by Quinn. He wanted to reach out and touch her, but the moment seemed too delicate.

"Thank you for coming," he managed, sure his face was flushed. He knew what it cost them to make this trip, the grace they'd somehow found a way to extend to him. And their daughter.

"How are you healing?" Mr. Longstreet said stiffly.

"I expect I'll limp for a while, but good as new eventually." He looked at Nora. "Maybe better."

"Oh," said Nora, giving Quinn a package he hadn't even noticed she was holding. "Reverend Bauers sent this over for you. It came all the way from New York."

"Who'd be sending me something from New York?" Quinn asked, looking at the package. He grinned when the return address read "Sir Matthew Covington," care of some fancy-sounding hotel with a New York address. He pulled open the package to reveal a handsome set of drafting tools. A thick card with elegant handwriting read,

I hear you've put my last gift to good use. I pray you'll do as well with these. Best, Matthew Covington.

"Glory," said Quinn, running his hands over the unfamiliar tools. "They're something, aren't they?"

"Lord Covington seems to think rather highly of you," Mr. Longstreet offered.

"He's been a good friend." Quinn looked up into the older man's face and offered a smile. "We got off to a very bad start, he and I, but things managed to improve after a bit."

"You have many good friends," Nora said. "And much to look forward to."

"Perhaps," Mr. Longstreet said, planting his hands on his knees and looking at his wife, "this is one of those times where it was darkest before dawn. Perhaps a better day is coming for all of us, hmm?"

It wasn't much of a speech, but it said everything Quinn had been hoping to hear. "I hope you're right, sir. I sure hope you're right."

Mrs. Longstreet actually managed a nod. He nodded back, knowing how big a step that was for her. Over the course of the many hours he had to sit and think it over, he'd come to feel compassion for Mr. and Mrs. Longstreet. How wrong was it for them to want the best for their daughter, to cling to their familiar standards when everything else was collapsing around them? They loved Nora as much as he did. Surely there had to be a way to find some common ground in all that. God was a mighty God, after all, and He'd shown Himself in ways mightier than even Quinn could have dreamed.

He'd decided long ago that there'd be no stealing Nora away in the middle of the night. He'd wait until they came around. By the looks of today, just maybe they'd begun.

Mr. Longstreet checked his watch and stood up. "Well, it's nearly two o'clock, there's mail to tend to across the street. Nora dear, why don't you stay here for a bit. I think I can manage a little while without you."

He reached for his wife's hand, and while she hesitated, she took it and they ducked out of the shack together.

Quinn managed to count to five before he grabbed Nora's hand and pulled her to him. She was a wonder. The finest thing God had ever sent to him. Her kiss could convince a man the world was a wondrous, hopeful place. "You're mine, love, and I'm yours." He kissed her, feeling its warmth fill up the room and spread all the way to Heaven. "It's only a matter of time now. And you know how impatient I am."

"I do, indeed." Nora nestled her head on to his shoulder.

He kissed the top of her head and closed his eyes, oblivious to the world—until Ma's voice pulled him from bliss.

"Well, I see you've run off our guests already, before anyone's had tea. Do you think you two lovebirds could manage to tear yourselves away long enough to suffer a cup with your own mother?"

"Only just," they said at the same time, catching each other's eyes.

Epilogue

Surely my heart will explode, Nora thought as she stood trying to breathe in Reverend Bauers's study. I won't survive the day, much less the ceremony.

Papa caught her hand, the tenderest of looks in his eyes. "My brave Nora? Trembling? Surely it can't be the prospect of marrying Quinn to put such fear into you." He was teasing her, dispersing the tension, but the edge in his voice gave away his own frail composure. "My baby girl, no longer a baby girl." He sighed. "And hasn't been for some time."

"Oh, Papa…" Nora couldn't hope to finish the sentence. A featherlight kiss on her cheek was his only reply, and Nora thought the combined lumps in their throats might render them speechless for the rest of the year.

The mission bell chimed the hour, signaling it was time for the ceremony to begin. Papa swallowed hard as he opened the study door and offered his elbow. "Best not to keep Corporal Freeman waiting. I imagine Quinn's current state would rival yours, impatient as he is."

Nora's steps down the hallway felt heavy and ill-placed. She feared her grip on Papa's elbow was so tight he'd cry out any second. Not one part of her considered this wedding a mistake, and every fiber of her being yearned to be Mrs. Quinn Freeman, but the sheer enormity of the moment seemed to pound down upon her. In a split second's musing, she wondered if Reverend Bauers was having any luck keeping Quinn from pacing the altar.

A cascade of lovely notes wafted down the hallway. Mama's friend was certainly working wonders with Grace House's old, cranky organ. Despite all the— what was the word Mama had used?—"rustic" charm of Grace House's chapel, to marry Quinn anywhere else would simply seem wrong. Grace House, and all it stood for, was too much a part of her life and Quinn's to join them elsewhere.

Turning the corner to start down the aisle, Nora thought she'd simply cease breathing and fall on the spot. Until her eyes met Quinn's. His gaze erased the distance between them in a heartbeat, calming her with the warmth she saw there. She watched him go still, saw his shoulders settle from their panicked breaths, felt them find their home in each other's eyes as they would for the rest of their lives. She would always draw her strength from this man God had sent her. Just as she would always pull from within him the man God intended Quinn to be. They were, truly, God's gift to each other. The phrase seemed timeless now, instead of trite.

The ceremony unfolded around them and still she spent it transfixed in Quinn's eyes. Both mothers cried and kissed their children, vows were spoken, blessings asked, rings exchanged. All of these things made them "married." But it was the time-stopping kiss, the tender-sweet seal of their union surrounded by raised army swords and the enthusiastic pealing of the church bell, that made it real.

She was his and he hers. Today was full of joy and celebration. When tomorrow dawned, Corporal and Mrs. Quinn Freeman would deliver a new message to the world: all the hope their hearts could hold.

* * * * *

HISTORICAL NOTE

There really was a heroic postmaster during the San Francisco 1906 disaster. I chose not to use Arthur Fisk's real name or his personal details, but to base my story around his generous declaration to deliver mail regardless of postage. He says it best himself: "The Postal Service as a means of communication among hundreds of thousands of distressed people was, I believe, an untold blessing." His awareness of how the littlest of things can hold back despair became the seed from which this novel grew. It is, of course, fiction. There was no Black Bandit (save a cheeky stagecoach robber in the 1880s), nor a Midnight Messenger. The U.S. Army, presented with the gigantic task of holding the city together in its darkest hours, did an outstanding job. While there was plenty of corruption to go around, the army marketeering in the novel is more my invention than any real historical suspicion. Careful researchers will note I've played a bit with the geography, and I trust they will forgive my liberties in service of the story. One important and amusing fact to relate is that, in fact, a record number of marriages and romances are attributed to the disaster. A good reminder that love does, indeed, conquer all.

Dear Reader,

You don't have to look far to find disasters these days. Personal, professional, regional, national and even global calamities threaten our hope on a daily basis. It is how we choose to respond, however, that makes us who we are. And lets God be who He is. Even the darkest of trials can hold great treasures if we are willing to unearth them. And nothing, ever, in the history of the world, has overcome the power of love. I hope this story helps you see the messengers of hope in your own life. I hope it inspires you to be a message of light into the darkness you can see around you. God never fails to equip us for that task, even when we feel least able. As always, I love to hear from you at alliepleiter.com or P.O. Box 4026, Villa Park, IL 60181.

With hope,

QUESTIONS FOR DISCUSSION

1. Nora gets her life "upended" in a way most of us may never see. When has your life been shaken to its core? What did you take away from the experience?

2. Reverend Bauers says, "God does not deal in luck or happenstance." Do you agree or disagree? Where has your life given you evidence for your view?

3. What do you think of Quinn's teeter-totter contraption? Are such distractions valuable or frivolous under such dire circumstances? Can you think of any similar situations in your own life?

4. What would you have done if you were Quinn and found the Bandit's possessions after so many years?

5. "Why am I here?" or in Quinn's case, "Why am I still here?" is one of life's most basic questions. What answer would you give today?

6. Do you think Major Simon's "painful lesson" was vivid teaching or just cruel? Could he have made the same point a different way?

7. Nora feels such a strong calling to help the people of Dolores Park. Have you felt such a calling? How did you respond?

8. Is Nora brave or foolish when she delivers Edwina's doll? Where do you draw the line between those two? When is it worthwhile to cross it?

9. Have you had a token such as Nora's locket that meant so very much to you? What's useful about having such a touchstone? What's dangerous?

10. Quinn says, "Everybody needs a partner." Do you agree? Why?

11. Major Simon admits, "Hope is a very powerful weapon." When has hope sustained you? Is there ever a time when hope isn't enough?

12. Where is the line between secrecy and deceit? How does God deal with each in terms of Nora and Quinn?

13. Do the "walls" Quinn and Nora face still exist? What other walls have kept people apart in your life? How does God go about removing them?

14. Was Nora right or wrong to withhold what she knew about Annette? What would you have done in her circumstance?

15. Nora gets "the fight knocked out of her." Has that happened to you? What role did God play in healing you? How did friends and family help?

Love Inspired.
HISTORICAL

TITLES AVAILABLE NEXT MONTH

Available September 14, 2010

THE OUTLAW'S BRIDE
Catherine Palmer

DANGEROUS ALLIES
Renee Ryan

REQUEST YOUR FREE BOOKS!

2 FREE INSPIRATIONAL NOVELS
PLUS 2
FREE
MYSTERY GIFTS

Love Inspired.
HISTORICAL
INSPIRATIONAL HISTORICAL ROMANCE

YES! Please send me 2 FREE Love Inspired® Historical novels and my 2 FREE mystery gifts (gifts are worth about $10). After receiving them, if I don't wish to receive any more books, I can return the shipping statement marked "cancel". If I don't cancel, I will receive 4 brand-new novels every other month and be billed just $4.24 per book in the U.S. or $4.74 per book in Canada. That's a saving of over 20% off the cover price. It's quite a bargain! Shipping and handling is just 50¢ per book.* I understand that accepting the 2 free books and gifts places me under no obligation to buy anything. I can always return a shipment and cancel at any time. Even if I never buy another book, the two free books and gifts are mine to keep forever.

102/302 IDN E7QD

Name	(PLEASE PRINT)	
Address		Apt. #
City	State/Prov.	Zip/Postal Code

Signature (if under 18, a parent or guardian must sign)

Mail to Steeple Hill Reader Service:
IN U.S.A.: P.O. Box 1867, Buffalo, NY 14240-1867
IN CANADA: P.O. Box 609, Fort Erie, Ontario L2A 5X3
Not valid for current subscribers to Love Inspired Historical books.

Want to try two free books from another series?
Call 1-800-873-8635 or visit www.morefreebooks.com.

* Terms and prices subject to change without notice. Prices do not include applicable taxes. Sales tax applicable in N.Y. Canadian residents will be charged applicable provincial taxes and GST. Offer not valid in Quebec. This offer is limited to one order per household. All orders subject to approval. Credit or debit balances in a customer's account(s) may be offset by any other outstanding balance owed by or to the customer. Please allow 4 to 6 weeks for delivery. Offer available while quantities last.

Your Privacy: Steeple Hill Books is committed to protecting your privacy. Our Privacy Policy is available online at www.SteepleHill.com or upon request from the Reader Service. From time to time we make our lists of customers available to reputable third parties who may have a product or service of interest to you. If you would prefer we not share your name and address, please check here. ☐

Help us get it right—We strive for accurate, respectful and relevant communications. To clarify or modify your communication preferences, visit us at www.ReaderService.com/consumerchoice.

LIH10R

MARGARET WAY

introduces

**The lives & loves of
Australia's most powerful family**

Growing up in the spotlight hasn't been easy, but the two
Rylance heirs, Corin and his sister, Zara, have come of age
and are ready to claim their inheritance. Though they are
privileged, proud and powerful, they are about to discover
that there are some things money can't buy....

Look for:

Australia's Most Eligible Bachelor
Available September

Cattle Baron Needs a Bride
Available October

www.eHarlequin.com